ONE TOUCH

LENA HENDRIX

Developmental Editing by Becca Mysoor, Fairy Plot Mother

Copy editing by James Gallagher, Evident Ink

Proofreading by Julia Griffis, The Romance Bibliophile

Cover by Echo Grayce, WildHeart Graphics

Photography by Wander Aguiar

Cover Model: Robbin Kooiman

For every woman who thought his grumpy older brother was hotter—you were right.

LET'S CONNECT!

When you sign up for my newsletter, you'll stay up to date with new releases, book news, giveaways, and new book recommendations! I promise not to spam you and only email when I have something fun & exciting to share!

Also, When you sign up, you'll also get a FREE copy of Choosing You (a very steamy Chikalu Falls novella)!

Sign up at my website at www.lenahendrix.com

AUTHOR'S NOTE

This book contains explicit sex scenes (you're welcome).

It also contains the death of a parent (off page/not detailed, but referenced) and a parent with early onset dementia.

ABOUT THIS BOOK

Falling hard for my ex-boyfriend's rugged older brother was *never* in the plan.

Beckett Miller may be my brother's best friend, but he's also the last person on earth I want to ask for help. He's stubborn, demanding, and doesn't care at all what people think of him—everything his little brother wasn't, and definitely **everything I should *not* want.**

Thanks to my own stubbornness and my three infuriating siblings, he is the only one who can help me renovate my beloved aunt's farmhouse.

Beckett thinks I'm a doormat, and I *know* he's an arrogant prick, but toss in one late-night game of tipsy strip poker, and before long, endless summer days turn into scorching nights.

Every stolen touch—every kiss—is wrong in the best ways.

I can fix everything around me: my friends' problems, my brothers' love lives, maybe even the decades-old rivalry that divides our cozy coastal town. So Beckett's snarl and heavy sighs are no match for me.

The only thing I can't seem to fix is the way my body reacts when he swings a hammer. I built walls to protect my heart after what his brother did to me, but I'm finding it could all come crumbling down with just ***one touch***.

ONE
KATE

"IF YOU GET ME ARRESTED, I swear I will tell everyone about the time you snuck into Dorothy King's house and replaced all of the photos of Jesus with a picture of Ewan McGregor dressed as Obi-Wan Kenobi."

My older brother Lee looked at me, and a laugh sputtered out of him. He schooled his face and shot me a stern look as he pressed a finger to his lips.

I crouched lower and huddled next to him against the brick wall in the darkened alley. "I'm not kidding. I'll sing like a canary."

His stare widened as he mouthed *SHUT. UP.*

I rolled my eyes at him, and nerves skittered through me.

I have only been home a day. How the hell had he roped me into this?

It was because Lee was too charming for his own good, that was how. It seemed it was Lee's life's mission to orchestrate ridiculous pranks against our rivals, the Kings. This one was payback for plastic-wrapping our oldest brother Duke's car to a light post last week. The rivalry between the

Sullivans and Kings went back generations, but the pranking itself had been something Lee had championed since his time overseas.

Usually harmless, always ridiculous.

"Okay, he's coming. Stay low until I say go."

I peered around Lee's broad shoulders to see JP King walking down the sidewalk toward his car. Typically JP was expertly dressed with Tom Ford suits and silk ties, and he was usually clean shaven, not a hair out of place. But tonight? Tonight he looked like total shit.

"What happened to him?"

Lee's eyebrows perked up. He tapped his temple. "Psychological warfare."

JP was disheveled. His suit was rumpled, his dress shirt was half-untucked, and his hair was a mess—like he'd dragged a hand through it a thousand times. To any red-blooded female, JP was model gorgeous—all sharp edges, strong shoulders, and tailored suits. Not that I'd ever admit that aloud. He was a King, and I was a Sullivan. The mere thought of finding him remotely attractive made my ancestors roll in their graves, of that I was sure.

Still, a girl could see the appeal in a well-dressed, strait-laced businessman, and I had a type.

"Ready?" Lee nudged my shoulder, and I shook out any thoughts of JP King. "When you bump into him, make sure this ends up in the car." Lee held up a small device, only about one inch long, that looked like the inside of a computer. He tucked it into my hand. "Try going for the floorboard or under a seat or something. It's got to be hidden."

We waited a second longer; then he gently pushed me forward. "Go!"

I shot up from my hiding place beside Lee and, dressed

in running tights and a sports bra, jogged off in JP's direction. Once he'd opened the door to his Tesla, I made my move.

"Oh shit!" I slammed into his shoulder and plopped onto my butt. "I am so sorry!"

JP scowled at me once it registered who I was, but then he immediately reached down to pull me up. I yanked my earbuds out of my ears and feigned confusion. My eyes slanted to Lee, who was still crouched behind the nearby building, grinning with unrestrained enthusiasm.

"I think I dropped my phone." I bent down and moved my hands around, looking for my not-really-missing phone. JP also glanced around for it.

While he was distracted, I pulled the plastic tab from the tiny computer thing, like Lee had shown me, and tossed it under the driver's seat.

Within seconds, a soft cricket noise emitted from the device, and I stifled a laugh.

JP stood ramrod straight. "Did you hear that? Tell me you heard that."

I stood with a grunt and inelegantly dusted off my butt. I shook my head. "I didn't hear anything."

JP's hands tore through his hair and patted at the jacket of his suit. "The cricket. It's following me. First at the office. Now here." He was definitely frazzled. "I . . . I have to go."

Without trying to help me any further, JP folded himself into the car and swung the door closed so quickly I had to take two steps back.

He revved the engine and pulled out onto the street before disappearing. Lee's laughter came up behind me as he swung an arm over my shoulder.

"That was perfect! Catfish Kate strikes again!"

I shrugged his arm from my shoulders and pinned him

with a glare. "Don't call me that."

He laughed and pulled me into a hug. "Aww, poor Katie."

Poor Katie my ass.

He wasn't the one with the ridiculous childhood nickname that had followed him into adulthood.

"Come on," he continued. "Let's get you home before there are any more witnesses."

When we pulled up to Aunt Tootie's farmhouse, I couldn't help but sigh.

Home.

I was twenty-five and back in my hometown, living with my elderly aunt.

Awesome.

Though I had a college degree, I still hadn't found my calling—whatever it was that lit my soul on fire. It sucked, but I felt totally *stuck*.

I had always loved my hometown of Outtatowner, Michigan—a coastal tourist town in Western Michigan. Its Instagram-worthy beaches, massive sand dunes, and cozy small town meant growing up as a townie was a dream. Our family blueberry farm had thrived with wholesale business combined with tourists flocking to our town to experience a beach vacation with a side of small-town U-pick berry farms.

And then Dad had gotten sick.

My oldest brother, Duke, had taken over the family farm and buried himself in work. By then Wyatt was a famous quarterback in the NFL, traveling the country. Once Lee signed up for the Army, it had felt like I was the only Sullivan left.

Stranded in a sea of people.

I had clung to my relationship with my ex, Declan, and,

like an idiot, believed him when he said we'd be together forever. I even believed him when he'd convinced me a scholarship opportunity at a college five states away would be a good thing.

I'd lived in, and loved, Tipp, Montana, but Outtatowner would always be home. A place for forgetting all the ways his deception and lies had screwed me over.

Looking up at the timeworn house, I saw a painful reflection of myself. A tattered heart clinging to some semblance of normalcy. I had no idea the house had gotten this bad until my brothers had called and said they needed me. I couldn't say no, so there I was, on the battered porch of my old family home.

Ready or not.

Lee walked up the porch steps and paused. "When the hell did that happen?"

I moved around a Duke-size hole in the front porch, which had since been covered by a sheet of plywood haphazardly screwed down. "Yesterday."

Lee frowned at it. "That's a big hole."

I shrugged. "Duke's got a big foot."

The thought of our grumpy oldest brother falling through the porch and being thoroughly pissed about it was enough to send Lee into a fresh round of laughter. The string of curses that had flown from Duke's normally very serious mouth *was* pretty funny.

We walked into the house, and the interior wasn't much better. Though Tootie tried to repair or hide what she could, it was a disaster.

"Kate, this is . . ." Lee's hands fell to his sides.

I nodded and forced a smile. "I know. I can fix it."

It was what I had learned to do. What I discovered I *loved* to do. Fix things. People, problems, hundred-year-old farmhouses that were crumbling around me. I could do it. I planted my hands on my hips.

God, I hope I can do this.

"I don't know. It seems like a lot. Maybe you should stay at Highfield House with Wyatt and Penny."

Stay with my older brother and his seven-year-old daughter while he's pretending to not be crying over his girlfriend in California? Hard pass.

I scrunched my nose at him. "I'm good here. Tootie and I are going to meet with the new contractor tomorrow morning. I'll get everything sorted out, and hopefully we can start work right away. Bit by bit we'll get it done." I nodded, satisfied with my resolve to fix the house and my little broken family.

Lee swallowed hard, and I narrowed my eyes at him when he stayed quiet. Something was up, and it was more than my brothers' chronic underestimation of me.

"What?"

He dragged a hand across the back of his neck but didn't say anything more.

"What?" I asked again.

"Nothing. I have to run. Early shift at the fire station tomorrow." He smiled, but I wouldn't be fooled again by his boyish charms.

Something weird was going on, and Lee wasn't telling me.

～

I HUFFED a breath and looked at my watch. "He's late."

My aunt patted my arm and clucked at me. "Five minutes. It's fine, dear."

The strange way Lee had bolted the night before had

me on edge. My brothers were hiding something from me, and I didn't like it. Not at all.

Tootie looked out onto the yard. Summer was waning, but the morning sun was warm and welcoming. The picturesque way the yard sprawled out toward a gently rolling blueberry field almost offset the peeling paint and sagging wood.

Almost.

When a work truck pulled down the long driveway, I perked up and dusted my palms down the front of my summer dress. I flipped my long brown hair over my shoulder, straightened my back, and painted on a bright, welcoming smile.

If this contractor was as good as Duke had promised, he'd have his work cut out for him, and we'd be spending a lot of time together planning and executing the renovations. I wanted it to be perfect for Aunt Tootie. She deserved as much.

The truck parked, and a large work boot, followed by one long, denim-clad leg, emerged from the vehicle. I squinted against the morning sun but didn't miss the way the man filled out his jeans.

Holy shit.

He unfolded his tall frame from the cab of the truck.

"Oh my . . ." Tootie's breathless voice snapped my eyes away from the man as he walked toward us, and Tootie's hand went to her chest.

I elbowed her gently, but I couldn't help but stare too. His T-shirt was a tight navy blue against a muscular chest, and his biceps strained the fabric. His waist tapered, and my belly did a somersault. Apparently long days of construction work did many, *many* wonderful things to a man's body.

My stare moved upward. His face was partially hidden by a baseball cap and dark sunglasses. His mouth was in a firm line as he walked up to greet us.

Tootie fussed and smiled. She waved her arm. "Good morning!"

The man stood in front of us. He was nearly the same height as me despite the fact I was on the steps of the porch.

His frame blocked the harsh rays of the sun, letting me focus on him.

My smile melted away.

Beckett fucking Miller.

My heart rate immediately skyrocketed. Standing before me was my horrible, no-good, heartbreaking, can-rot-in-hell ex-boyfriend's moody older brother.

He reached out a hand. "Ms. Tootie."

"Oh!" She fussed and gripped his hand with both of hers and shook them up and down. "Welcome. Come in, please."

My teeth ground together. Memories of my ex Declan and what he had done burned through my mind.

Six years.

Beckett and I had a shared history of the odd holiday and an occasional family dinner, and it was not a pleasant history. Beckett was cold and unfriendly, and he was related to the scum of the earth. If I had to rate him, he'd be up there among my *least favorite people on the planet.* Definitely in the top five.

Despite the number of times I had attempted to be friendly and accommodating, he had always looked at me with something akin to indifference, or maybe even pity.

Had he known all along?

I took a steadying breath. *This is so not happening.*

"I think there's been a mistake." I infused my voice with

as much friendliness as I could muster, but it still came out a little strangled. I cleared my throat and sucked in a deep breath.

"What do you mean, dear?" Tootie smiled and blinked at me.

Hot rage simmered below the surface as awareness bloomed.

They knew.

They all knew, and I had been set up by my own family.

"Aunt Tootie, can I have a moment?" I gently guided her to the left, careful to avoid the patch on the floorboards. My voice lowered as soon as we were out of earshot. "Are you kidding me with this?"

Tootie patted my hand. "Oh, honey. It'll be fine."

"Fine? That is *Declan's* brother!" I shot a glance toward him, and Beckett stood, washed in sunlight and looking completely unfazed. My nostrils flared.

"He is Duke's best friend and promised to do honest work to renovate the house. He's a real pro."

"No, he's a real jerk! I thought loyalty was the foundation of this family. Apparently not!" I hissed.

My aunt only shrugged. "If this is too much, I completely understand. We don't have to do anything. We'll get by without him."

Relief washed over me. "Thank you." I straightened my dress, stood tall, and stomped back to where Beckett was standing.

I couldn't read his expression behind the dark sunglasses.

"Sorry for the misunderstanding, but we're all good here." I clapped my hands together, rocking back on my heels. I swallowed down the bubble of nausea as I tried to place something like a smile on my face.

Beckett stared at me, and his intensity set my nerves on fire. He leaned slightly, taking in the run-down house over my shoulder. I closed my eyes, knowing exactly how bad it looked.

"I'll start with fixing that hole." He pointed to the shoddy repair Duke had made after he fell through the rotted porch boards. "But really the whole wraparound porch will get replaced. First, I'll get the inside renovations complete and then worry about the exterior."

I scoffed. *What a condescending asshole.* "We do not need your help."

He glanced at my aunt and completely ignored my dismissal. "Plans to sell?"

She shook her head. "Not till I'm in the ground, at least. Then I suppose it'll be up to the kids."

He nodded once, as though everything had already been decided. "When we get to it, I'll have you weigh in on landscaping, but for now my focus is on the interior repairs. Getting everything up to code." He flicked an arm in my direction when I stayed rooted to my spot. "Let's go inside, Princess."

Princess? Untethered anger, the kind that had been simmering below the surface in the six months since Declan crushed my heart, coursed through me. "No."

I crossed my arms and lifted my chin before swiveling on my heels and stomping toward the front door.

But, of course, in my rage-fueled exit, I forgot to dodge the remaining weak boards, and I stumbled, my foot wedging itself in the wood. Over my shoulder, Beckett had the balls to *laugh* as I tried to free my kitten heel from the soft boards.

He shook his head, climbed the stairs, and walked past me and straight into my house.

TWO
BECKETT

I HAD COUNTED on Kate being pissed when I showed up at her aunt's house, but what I hadn't expected was for her to throw me out on my ass after a quick walkthrough of the house. That show of backbone was altogether surprising.

Even her aunt seemed momentarily stunned.

Tootie Sullivan had tried to smooth things over, but I'd assured her there was no need. In the few moments before Kate insisted that she could handle the reno, I'd gotten an eyeful of what needed to be done to the home.

A lot of fucking work.

After talking with Duke, we planned to keep as much history in the home as we could, but it was going to take a full crew and a hell of a lot of time to get it done.

I didn't need his pissy little sister being a thorn in my side the entire time.

It had been the better part of a year since I'd seen Kate at my family's Christmas. A few months ago, my little brother had mentioned in passing that they'd broken up, and the way he talked about it, it seemed like maybe it was a mutual parting.

But there was fire in her eyes. She was going for blood in a way that had heartbreak written all over it.

"Can I get you another Coke?" The server smiled down at me.

"Sure. Duke?" I snagged my best friend's attention, but he shook his head. The server smiled and wandered away.

From the small outdoor patio of Outtatowner's local café, we were enjoying lunch in the late-summer sun, as we often did when I paid him a visit every few months. Tourists from all around were walking down the sidewalk, some toward the beach and others popping in and out of the little shops that lined the main thoroughfare through Outta-towner, Michigan.

My family had been vacationing in the quirky coastal Western Michigan town for as long as I could remember—a reprieve from city life. It was how I'd ended up becoming unlikely friends with Duke in the first place.

"What?" he asked when I stared at him.

"Remember when you broke my nose?"

He shook his head and stifled a grin. "You deserved it."

I laughed and shook my head. "You took a cheap shot."

Duke pointed a french fry in my direction. "You wouldn't stop flirting with my girlfriend."

I smiled. He wasn't wrong. Duke was a townie and broke my nose after I flirted with his girlfriend one too many times at a beach bonfire. Their relationship hadn't lasted longer than that summer, but our friendship had. Despite my rigorous work schedule in Chicago, I made it a point to disconnect and make the two-hour drive. My easy friendship with Duke had helped me escape the demands of my life.

I touched my fingers to my nose. "It's still a little crooked."

Duke grinned. "That'll remind you to keep your hands to yourself."

Friendship with Duke was simple. The most real relationship I had in my life, and he was more like a brother than my own.

"I appreciate you coming out. I know it's been busy for you."

"Yeah. Busy is good, though." I tossed my napkin down and took in the small town. Nothing ever felt busy in Outta-towner. Just the slow, easy pace of people enjoying their beach vacations.

"It is, but I'm sure you could use some time off."

I smirked at my friend. If anyone called me a worka-holic, he was a close second. We both deeply understood the benefits of burying yourself in work to avoid the hassle of dealing with other people.

"What the hell is she doing . . . ?" Duke's voice trailed off, and I followed his gaze across the street.

I spotted his little sister. She had a cap pulled low over her eyes, and her long brown hair flowed out of the back in a ponytail. She was trying to go unnoticed, but it was her all right. There was no mistaking those long, muscular legs and the way they flared out to the most perfect ass I'd seen in a very long time.

Not that I ever noticed that.

Kate was ducking into the hardware store, looking around as though she was afraid to get caught. Rightly so. The hardware store on the corner was owned by the Kings, and it wasn't above a Sullivan to drive out of their way to the next town over to avoid giving a King their business. The fact that Katie was willingly going inside was not only uncommon, but it was downright curious.

Duke stared hard across the street.

Only minutes later Katie came out with a tool belt in hand and a power drill box with a bright-red Milwaukee logo across it.

At least she has good taste in tools.

Duke sighed. "Jesus Christ."

I stifled a laugh. "She's welcome to try to do the reno herself."

I'd never known Kate to have a backbone—quite the opposite, really. Pretty eyes and a great ass? Sure. But a spine? Never. Surely she'd realize that modernizing a dilapidated farmhouse by herself was completely out of the question.

Duke eyed me before tracking his sister as she loaded the items into her white Jeep. "She sure must be pissed at you if she thinks this is a better option."

"Pissed at me? What did I do?"

The corner of Duke's mouth lifted. "Unfortunately for all of us, it's what your brother did."

I nodded. I had always known Declan was an asshole. A smooth talker. The life of the party, when really it was all bullshit. He steamrolled anyone in his path with a flashy smile and false promises. The fact that Kate would ever be with someone like that was pathetic.

The topic of my family was typically off limits with Duke and me. Our friendship was rooted in his acceptance that I was the black sheep of my family—more like a Sullivan than I'd ever been like the prestigious Millers.

Initially I'd been pissed when Declan had set his sights on the littlest Sullivan. Anyone could have predicted that it would end with him breaking Kate's heart. But she'd had years to walk away, and she never did. That was on her.

"Are you going to stop her?" Duke looked at me like I

should storm over there and put an end to her YouTube renovation dreams.

"Nope."

"She's going to screw something up."

I smirked. "Probably."

Duke shook his head and sighed as the server brought my refill. "I don't know what happened in Montana. She's not normally so hardheaded."

I took a sip and let the bubbles burn down my throat. "Just call me before she breaks something expensive. You know where to find me."

It took only three days to get the call from Duke.

"Are you still in town?" He was pissed and more than a little frustrated.

"At the house." I sat on the sprawling back porch of my family's vacation home, looking out over Lake Michigan. The house was rarely used anymore. Its cold, modern exterior was a travesty against the natural beauty of Michigan's dune-covered shoreline. My parents had built it as an investment property, and while we used it every summer growing up, or as a place for my father to go when Mom had uncovered yet another affair, it was largely unused.

I stood and walked through the door to the wide-open lofted living room. The wall of glass that looked out onto the lake could have been stunning, but the builder had focused only on sharp lines and cold, hard materials. It felt too open. Exposed.

"Beck, she really fucked up. Something with the water lines in the downstairs bathroom."

I bit back a shitty *of course she did* and slipped my feet into work boots. "I'll be there in ten minutes."

I pulled my work truck down the familiar winding driveway to Tootie Sullivan's farmhouse. Duke's truck was parked to the side, and his dog, Three-legged Ed, chased my truck tires until I came to a stop. When I climbed out, Ed gave me a throaty bark and then ran off in search of a new adventure.

In the yard, Wyatt was kicking a soccer ball with his little girl, and I offered a friendly wave but focused my attention on the run-down farmhouse.

From the porch, I could hear shouting, so I slammed the truck door shut and stomped my way up the porch steps, then let myself into the house. Inside was pure chaos. Down a long, narrow hallway, shouts erupted from the small bathroom, and I could make out Kate and Duke arguing. As I walked in, Tootie was sitting, and laughing, at the kitchen table, sipping tea. I nodded a greeting and followed the raised voices.

"I don't know what to do!" Kate yelled over the sound of spraying water.

"To the *left*!"

"I *am* turning it left. It's not moving."

I stepped into the doorway. Kate's body was half sticking out of the small bathroom vanity, her ass sticking up in the air. Duke was grabbing towels from a hook and tossing them over the sink as water sprayed everywhere.

"I don't know what the hell she did!"

I crouched down to where Kate was unsuccessfully trying to turn off the water. "Move."

She glared at me and scooted backward out of the tight space. Her jaw flexed as I waited for her to get out of the way. Once she was gone, I reached in and found the water shutoff. It was broken—that much was clear—but with a few hard turns, I was able to get the water from a deluge to a trickle.

I unfolded myself from under the vanity and stood. Katie was still in the bathroom, her tight white—and very wet—T-shirt plastered to her trim little body. Her hands were planted on her hips, and she glared at me like I had been the one to fuck up. I held her hard stare and tried not to notice how the outline of her lace bra only enhanced the fact that her nipples were hard little points through her wet shirt.

"Jesus, Katie." Duke wiped his hands down his own wet clothing.

"The valve is broken," I offered.

"We don't need your help." Kate crossed her arms in an unsuccessful attempt to cover herself.

"Is that all?" I ground out, annoyed at how the sight of her sent heat spreading through me.

She was about to argue again when a knock at the front door had us all turning. We filed into the hallway, Duke throwing his sister a dry-ish towel to cover up.

Tootie answered the door, revealing a man who was short, round, and not at all friendly looking. He held a clipboard in one hand and adjusted his striped tie with the other.

"Josiah. What brings you here?"

"Tootie." The man nodded at her and narrowed his eyes at the three of us piled in the hallway. "Now I hate to do this, but I got wind that you're planning some renovations without the proper permits. You know this home is registered with the Remington County Historical Association."

I shot a glare at Kate, who only pulled the edges of the towel tighter around her shoulders and lifted her chin.

Tootie stepped aside to let the man in. "Permits? Why, I'm sure I don't know what you're talking about. We're planning some simple updates. That's all."

The portly man shook his head and tapped his clipboard. "Don't you go playing innocent. Any renovations require a building and zoning permit application for all building-related projects on a historical homesite. If not a permit, then the association has to approve the design at the very least. To ensure you're maintaining the integrity of the house!"

He shook his head again. "Lots of folks saw Kate here at the hardware store, loading up on supplies. When I heard that, I went ahead to check on the permits, and lo and behold . . . not a one was filed."

"So someone saw Kate and snitched is what you're saying?" Duke crossed his arms.

"Now, I didn't say that. I heard rumors is all."

"Yeah." Duke knew as well as I did that it was a King who'd sold her the supplies in the first place and had taken the first opportunity they could find to get her into trouble.

The man looked down at his clipboard again. "Now I have to issue a fine, because without the proper permits, a reputable builder who—"

"I'm the builder." I stepped forward, and the man's head snapped up. He raked his eyes up and down, knowing full well I wasn't a townie.

"Have *you* filed the application for permits, then?"

I smiled the friendliest, most business-appropriate smile I could manage and tipped my head toward a fuming Kate. "Overeager homeowner. Had plans to file the applications in person myself on Monday. I can assure you that no other work will be started before we line everything up with your office. I take the considerations of the historical society very seriously."

The building inspector raised his nose in the air, clearly disappointed he had lost his footing on reprimanding the Sullivans. "Hmm. Very well." His hand dropped. "Consider this your one and only warning. Any renovations will be done by going through the proper channels. I'm going to make sure of it."

"We understand," Duke assured him.

"Well, now that it's settled, I'm sure you have a lot of very important work at your office, Josiah." Tootie's voice dripped with saccharine as she placed a hand on his shoulder and guided him back out the door.

Duke turned to me. "Thanks for coming."

Kate let out a huff.

I let my eyes wander over the fuming Kate. I'd never seen her with a flush of anger in her cheeks. Pure, unfiltered annoyance danced in her eyes. It suited her. My mother would hate it, of course. She always spoke of how she adored how accommodating and pleasant sweet little Katie was.

I scoffed at the irony.

Amid the commotion, Wyatt and his little girl walked into the house. "I can see your boobs."

"Pickle," Wyatt said, issuing a soft warning, and his daughter only shrugged.

Kate pulled the towel tighter around her shoulders, and color flooded her cheeks.

Shaking off the image of Kate and the way she looked with the wet fabric of her shirt plastered to her chest, I turned to Duke. "Let's take a look around. I've already made calls for a local crew, but I need a plan of attack before we get underway."

"I have to get back to the farm. Wyatt can walk you around."

"No can do." Wyatt shook his head. "Penny's got a play-date, and I have a meeting. I was just dropping her off with Tootie."

Duke turned toward his sister. "Can you take care of it? *Without* the side of attitude?"

Clearly annoyed, Kate offered her brother a tight smile, but stayed quiet.

I shook Duke's hand as he said his goodbyes, then made a sweeping gesture toward Kate. "After you, Princess."

THREE
KATE

If Beckett Miller wanted to stick his nose in our business and take on this renovation, then I was determined to make his life a living hell.

Yes, I knew he was a talented hotshot builder in Chicago. I'd heard Duke moon over him plenty of times, and the Millers never forgot to mention whenever he won some prestigious award. His parents *loved* the accolades and attention their sons brought the family name.

But I knew the truth.

Declan had told me all about how *he* had been the favorite son. Star athlete, top of his class, following in his father's footsteps since birth. The brothers weren't close, and Declan didn't talk about him often, but when he did, it wasn't very kind. Over the years I'd had only a handful of interactions with Beckett, but despite my efforts to be kind, he was always surly and dismissive.

Dealing with him face-to-face for god knows how long was going to test the limits of my resolve. But I was determined to prove to my family that I was different. Strong and capable. I wasn't little Katie who needed saving. My best friend in Montana was the strongest woman I knew, and I was digging deep to channel my inner Gemma.

I took a breath and walked down the small hallway and tried not to notice how good Beckett smelled—like he'd freshly showered and used some kind of macho tobacco-and-leather-scented aftershave that should not have smelled so good on someone so frustrating.

Beckett looked at me with equal parts annoyance and indifference. I knew he wanted to help his best friend, but the smug smile that pulled at his lips was infuriating.

Of all the builders in the state of Michigan, why him?

Because I am living in hell, that's why.

I walked toward the front living room, relieved when Beckett followed me.

"The floors in this hallway are original. I'd love to keep those as long as you and your crew don't destroy them."

Beckett stopped and tested the boards with his weight, bouncing a few times. "Seems solid. That shouldn't be a problem."

"The kitchen is the heart of this place. Tootie loves to cook and have people over. I want to give her a space where she can do that. A space she can be proud of."

Beckett took in my words and only nodded.

"You should probably write that down."

The look he gave me was pure disdain.

Prick.

I sighed and looked out the living room window to see Tootie fussing with her beloved chickens. "The house is too big, really, but she'll never leave. I think it was built around the early nineteen hundreds, maybe? She and my father grew up here, and she moved back when Dad got sick. It's got a lot of Sullivan memories tucked into its walls. The bathrooms are a disaster, and nothing has been updated since the eighties. I can handle things like paint and taking down that hideous swan wallpaper in the hallway."

Beckett stepped toward me, and I instinctively mirrored a step backward. "I'm hired to do a job, and I'll do it. Just stay out of my way."

Declan always claimed his brother was an insufferable asshole. *Guess he wasn't wrong about that.*

"Correct. You were hired, which means you work for *me*, Miller."

Something sparked in his eyes when I pointed my pink-manicured finger in his direction. I was bone-tired of being the accommodating, sweet-natured Katie who let a smooth talker like his brother trample all over me. If Declan wasn't around to feel my fury, then his surly pain-in-the-ass arrogant older brother would be a perfect substitute.

"You're paying the bills, then?" He raised one dark eyebrow, unafraid and unwilling to back down.

"My family will take care of it . . . assuming you don't jack up the prices just to take advantage."

Beckett rolled his eyes and crossed his ridiculously muscled arms. I knew his friendship with Duke would mean we'd get a fair price on his work, but it was an easy shot, and I was just petty enough to take it.

"When can I expect your crew to show up?"

Beckett considered. "I'll have a cleanup crew ready in the morning to start hauling out any trash and furniture. We'll start with the living room. Then it'll be a few days before the demo starts. I need a little time to, you know, get the proper permits and all."

I ignored his petty little dig. His stupid handsome face was distracting, and I had to remind myself that despite the fact he was doing us all a *huge* favor by taking on the job, he was still the same jerk who'd ignored my attempts to be friendly every Miller family holiday.

"Is that all?" he asked.

"Just try not to be late again tomorrow."

The smirk melted from his face when I dropped the towel and strode past him, not caring in the least that my see-through T-shirt was putting my breasts on full display.

BECKETT MILLER WAS NOT LATE the next morning when he pounded on the front door at 5:00 a.m. sharp.

I rolled out of bed, rubbed furiously at the dried drool at the corner of my mouth, and tried to pat down my tangle of hair. I listened at the top of the staircase as Tootie answered the door. While I couldn't make out their words, the deep rumble of Beckett's voice was unmistakable. Within moments, the door closed, and the house was quiet again, except for the soft hum of Tootie's singing.

I carefully padded down the stairs, looking for any signs of Beckett.

"Morning, dear," Tootie singsonged as she swirled a spoon in her freshly brewed coffee.

I sighed in relief at finding us alone.

"Morning." I walked straight for the coffee maker and poured myself a large cup and doctored it with lots of cream and sugar.

"You just missed Beckett. He and his crew will be back around seven to haul out junk and get to work." I didn't miss the wistfulness in her voice.

I put an arm around her shoulder and pulled her in close. "None of it's junk."

Tootie laughed. "Oh, I'm sure enough of it is."

"We won't get rid of anything you don't want to, and I'll make sure everything is perfect. I promise."

Tootie rested her head on my shoulder. Deep, warm affection ran through me. After my mom died, Tootie had stepped in. She and my dad were close, and when he couldn't quite navigate the waters of raising four kids by himself, she'd filled in the gaps.

When Dad got sick and his memories started to falter, she became our only parent figure, and she did what she could to save us all from ourselves. Somehow we'd all scattered to the wind despite her efforts. Duke buried himself in responsibility, Wyatt grabbed onto a successful football career, and, when he was finally of age, Lee signed up for the Army.

I had been stupid enough to believe a boy when he'd said he had my best interests at heart.

"Should we stay with Wyatt and Penny at Highfield House while Beckett and his men work? This is shaping up to be a bigger project than I expected."

I scrunched up my nose. "No way. This is *our* home. A little dust and noise should be fine. They can work around us." Plus, being close would allow me to make sure Beckett didn't screw anything up.

By 7:00 a.m. on the dot, Beckett rolled up in his truck. Others pulled in behind him, and I watched from the front porch as he instructed his crew. Some were sent around to the side of the house to clear brush and the tangle of weeds that had started to overtake the wraparound porch. Tootie followed to be sure that she could point out what plants she hoped were salvageable.

Beckett touched his fingers to the bill of his hat. "Ms. Tootie." My traitorous aunt only blushed as he strode away toward the side of the house.

Other workers marched toward us and headed for the house itself. Each politely passed me with a nod and a small smile. Not a woman to be seen on Beckett Miller's crew.

Figures.

Didn't matter. I tightened the tool belt around my waist and waited for him to come to me. From the porch, I watched him. Beckett stepped back to survey the farmhouse, grumbling under his breath. He took in the surrounding landscape and made a few notes on a large metal clipboard. He exuded confidence and respect as he discussed something with a few crew members, pointing to the side of the house and out into the yard. It was clear he was in charge, directing his team with a series of gruff orders.

How did he manage to be both handsome and infuriating at the same time?

I stifled a smile as Bartleby Beakface stalked behind him. Bartleby was an Old English Game rooster that Tootie had rescued. He was huge, with a pale blond head, rust-colored wings, a black body, and gorgeous tail feathers that shone hunter green in the sun.

He was also a major asshole.

Bartleby darted out from the bushes and aggressively pecked at his boots. "Hey." Beckett lifted a foot and moved his leg to try to shoo him away, but Bartleby wasn't deterred.

Beckett tried to ignore the rooster and continued to bark orders at his crew, but the rooster persisted.

Big mistake.

There was one thing Bartleby Beakface couldn't stand, and that was to be ignored.

With a flap of his wings, the rooster jumped onto Beckett's back, flapping his wings and crowing loudly. The hens in the yard scattered. The man next to Beckett yelled, "Oh shit!" and jumped a few feet back.

Beckett spun, trying to shake off the rooster, but it was no use. The bird was a master of chaos. Bartleby squawked and flapped as a string of curses flew out of Beckett's mouth.

"Get this fucking thing off me!" Beckett's arms flailed.

A laugh burst from my chest. The rest of the crew was trying to stifle their own laughter as they watched their boss wage war with poultry.

Satisfied that he'd proven his point, Bartleby released Beckett and went flying into the bushes.

Beckett turned to glare at me. "Is something funny?"

The crew's laughter died as they got back to work, and Beckett stomped toward me. A ripple of heat moved through me at the intensity of his scowl.

His stormy gray eyes flicked from the empty tool belt to my smug smile. "What the hell is that?"

I planted my hands on my hips. "Never seen a woman in construction before, Miller?"

Declan had once pointed out that Beckett hated when anyone called him by their last name, so I made sure to slip it in, just to goad him.

"Seen plenty. Though I'm not sure an empty tool belt is going to help rip out old carpeting." He dusted himself off before pointing at my legs. "Probably going to tear up those legs, too, if you don't put something on other than whatever the hell you call that scrap of denim."

I tugged at the hem of my short shorts. It was already warm in the summer sun, and the day was forecasted to be nearly ninety. Jeans would be insufferable, and if cutoff shorts meant I could annoy Beckett, I was keeping them.

I snorted. "Worry about yourself."

He moved past me on the stairs. "I intend to."

When I walked inside, Beckett was already instructing his crew to clear the living room furniture. Whatever we were keeping would be stored in the unused barn at Highfield House until the room was complete and could be reassembled.

When I stepped up next to Beckett, he released a sigh. "We're starting here. New carpeting, fresh paint. New windows. I want to tackle it before gutting the kitchen. Just leave me to it and—"

I ignored his words and strode straight into the living room to pick up an end table and haul it outside.

Oh no. There would be no *just leaving him to it*. I was going to be a thorn in his side whether he liked it or not.

FOUR
BECKETT

KATE WAS STUBBORN, I'd give her that.

I watched in amusement and mild horror as she grunted and ripped up old carpeting with my crew. She didn't hesitate but jumped right in. When I dropped a pair of work gloves at her feet and strode away, I could feel the daggers she threw at my back. It didn't matter that I had the smug satisfaction of seeing her wearing them the rest of the afternoon.

In an effort to smooth things over with his sister, Duke had invited me to dinner with the Sullivans at the farmhouse. His brother Wyatt brought his woman, Lark, who was back from an acting job in LA. Wyatt's daughter, Penny, was a cute distraction from the daggers Kate shot at me and from the not-so-under-her-breath grumblings, but more than one awkward silence filled the air. After the main course, I'd excused myself, and it felt as though the entirety of the Sullivans breathed a sigh of relief.

After the long day, I lowered myself into the tub of the primary bathroom and exhaled a deep sigh.

I still wasn't sure why I'd agreed to the job in the first

place. Sure, I was loyal to Duke, and we'd always had a no-questions-asked type of friendship, but the truth was, I really didn't have time for such an extensive renovation. While the bones of the old farmhouse were strong, everything else was turning out to be a nightmare.

Especially that fucking devil rooster.

My phone dinged on the floor beside me. I shifted to turn it over. Seventy-two emails. Instead of cracking it open and tackling them, I turned the phone on silent and lowered myself deeper into the hot water.

The enormous pedestal-style freestanding tub was one of the only redeeming features of the cold and empty house, and after a long day hauling furniture and the first stage of demo, my muscles ached. I raised a glass of bourbon to my lips and let the warm burn spread through my chest as I looked out of the wall of windows that faced Lake Michigan.

What a waste of a house in such a perfect location.

Had it been up to me, I would have made sure the house that sat on this bluff worked with the natural landscape around it. It wouldn't be an eyesore, but rather a tribute to the trees and sand and water surrounding it.

I hated the house and everything it stood for, but if I was in Outtatowner until the Sullivan house was completed, then it would be impractical to leave it empty.

My phone buzzed from the marble floor. Two rapid-fire texts:

MOTHER

My son was on the cover of American Builders Quarterly!

DUKE

Headed to the Grudge. You in?

Ignoring my mother—her praise came only on the heels of public recognition, and I'd learned a long time ago that waiting for any kind of meaningful validation was too little too late—I typed up a reply to Duke that I'd meet him out. Then I downed the last of the bourbon and dipped my head below the hot water to drown out the world.

～

"This round's on me." Duke clinked his bottle to mine before I swiped it from the bar. "You deserve it after the hell Katie put you through tonight."

I nodded in salute and took a deep pull.

For a weeknight, the Grudge Holder was crowded, but that wasn't uncommon in the tourist town. Often it seemed like every night was an opportunity for visitors to grab dinner and a few drinks before heading down for a late-night walk or a bonfire on the beach.

What tourists didn't realize was that, for townies, the Grudge was distinctly separated. The Sullivans and those aligned with them, like myself, on one side. The Kings and theirs on the other. Ever since that first summer when Duke and I became unlikely friends, I'd never strayed to the east side of the bar.

A few of Duke's cousins were in a band and just starting their set. We sat in comfortable silence, listening to the live band play classic rock covers and watching the tourists slowly getting drunk and filling the dance floor. Duke's eyes scanned the bar and stopped suddenly on the Kings' side. I stiffened, ready for trouble.

When I tracked his gaze, I was surprised to see whom it had snagged on.

"That's a King girl, right?"

Duke's eyes darted to mine, and a scowl passed over his face. "Hell if I know."

I scoffed. "She's the one who works at the Sugar Bowl. What's her name?" He knew every person in this town better than anyone.

He shrugged. "They all run together."

"Who runs together?" Lee, the middle Sullivan, walked up with a big smile and a slap to Duke's back, which earned him a dirty look.

I gestured subtly with my beer. "That one. She's the King girl. What's her name again?"

Lee looked over. "Sylvie. She works for Huck at the bakery." Lee turned to his brother. "You know that."

Duke shrugged and shifted his body away from the King side of the bar. His elbow leaned against the worn oak bar top as he assessed his little brother.

Unbothered by Duke's permanent scowl, Lee signaled to a bartender and planted his hands on his hips. "It looked like you got a decent start at Tootie's today."

"The crew cleared the place out so we can see what we're working with. It'll take a lot of work, but you'll be happy when it's done."

Lee accepted the beer from the server with a smile that made her blush. "Katie still giving you trouble?"

I bit back the *of course she is* retort that nearly fell from my mouth. He'd seen for himself how she'd acted at dinner. "It's been fine."

"I'm happy to jump in on my off days. I have a shift at the fire station tomorrow, but then I'll be free to help when I can."

"One night off means you gotta tie one on?" Duke shook his head in disapproval.

Lee grinned. "That's the plan. Where is Katie? When I texted her, she said she'd probably be up here tonight."

My back stiffened. After being chided by Tootie, Kate and I had successfully ignored each other all evening, and I didn't need Lee dragging her over and ruining my buzz.

Duke pointed with his bottle. "She and Annie are already tearing up the dance floor."

Mischief played in the younger Sullivan's eyes.

"Lee. Do not embarrass her," Duke warned, but Lee only wiggled his brows before snagging his beer from the bar top and walking toward the dance floor. I turned to watch him.

"Catfish Kate!" Lee shouted above the music and shot both arms in the air. Kate rolled her eyes and pushed at his chest, but she was grinning at her older brother.

Lee had always been the life of the party and liked to mess with his little sister. As a kid I hadn't really noticed her. Duke and I would go off and find whatever trouble we could, and we'd left the younger Sullivans to find their own fun.

The unfortunate nickname her brothers had given her was stupid to me even then. Sure, her emerald eyes were a little too big for her delicate features, but it didn't make her look like a catfish.

Some doe-eyed femme fatale, more like.

Annoyed at the very thought, I downed the last of my beer. "Want another?"

Duke looked at the contents of his own, finished it off, and nodded. "Yeah, what the hell."

Happy to remain at the outskirts of the bar, Duke and I caught up on life. Duke was running himself ragged managing operations at his family farm. The tourist season also meant

U-pick was going strong. The Sullivans supplied a few local businesses, like the Sugar Bowl, with fresh, local blueberries, and the rest were shipped to one of the many packing facilities in the area, to be distributed throughout the country.

On the flip side, I shared with him a few recent builds I'd completed. The multimillion-dollar homes were a far cry from rural farm life, and the slow, easy pace of Outtatowner made it easy to forget that the demands of Chicago were waiting for me two hours away. The rapidly growing unread emails were a relentless reminder of that.

"I'm proud of you, ya know."

I eyed my best friend and scoffed. "Shut the fuck up."

"I'm serious. You did it. Went against the grain and followed the path you wanted to take."

Our closeness meant Duke knew how poorly my parents had reacted to my choice of careers. They were horrified to learn they'd raised a *laborer*. After a lifetime of feeling disposable, they came around only after I made sure my successes were too big to ignore.

Duke, on the other hand, had his own dreams. Dreams that had taken a back seat when his dad got sick.

Rare emotion was thick in my throat. I swallowed it down with a swig of beer and a nod.

As the evening wore on, one beer turned into three, which turned into a round of playing quarters, and I then lost count. My brain was fuzzy, and my body buzzed with an unfamiliar energy.

"All right." Duke dropped a heavy hand on the table and wobbled on his feet. "I'm calling it."

I laughed and clamped a hand on his shoulder, but together we weren't much more stable. "Are you going to be okay?"

Duke's lips formed a thin line. "Yep. I'm getting a ride home. You?"

"Walking."

The Miller vacation home was only a few blocks out of town and up a massive hill. The neighborhood was packed with vacationers, and while the trek home was a steep climb, I'd manage.

Duke squeezed my shoulder and pulled me in for a quick, awkward hug and a pat on the back. "Thanks, man. For all of it. Don't fall off a cliff."

I scoffed and downed the last of my beer. "I'll do my best."

Duke raised a hand toward the dance floor. He'd caught Kate's attention, and she beamed at him and raised a hand in the air to say goodbye. "Keep an eye on her, okay?"

My tongue was thick and slow. I offered an unsteady nod, but he took it as an agreement and left me.

Alone at the bar, I didn't have to hide my assessment of the youngest Sullivan. Kate was in the middle of the dance floor, moving and singing to the cover songs. Her friend Annie, a redhead with wild curly hair, danced next to her as they both shout-sang the lyrics. From where I was, it looked like Kate was about as half in the bag as I was.

A surge of protectiveness poked beneath my ribs.

Lee was off to the side, flirting with some random woman, and Kate seemed to be completely oblivious to the eager eyes of the man dancing behind her. My nostrils flared as his eyes dipped lower to her bare, toned legs.

Those goddamn legs had been on display all day.

I stood from my seat. I didn't like the way the guy moved in closer and let his hand drag over her hip. Kate laughed but shifted, her body language clearly communicating that she wasn't interested. The man leaned closer to shout over the music and signal toward the bar.

When he left, the girls leaned in to talk to one another. I stared at the man as he walked right up to the empty space next to me to signal the bartender.

"Two beers and a vodka soda with lime. Make that one extra strong."

My shoulders bunched. I turned toward the cocky bastard, fury radiating through me. I tipped my chin at the mixed drink. "What's that about?"

The man looked between me and the bartender and laughed. "Ah, sometimes you gotta loosen her up for a good time."

You've got to be fucking kidding me.

The satisfying thought of grabbing him by the back of the head and slamming his face down on the bar coursed through me.

With his cocky, pretty-boy smile he gathered up the drinks and headed back toward the dance floor before I could act.

I stood and immediately caught eyes with Lee. With a grim face, I shook my head and tipped my chin toward Kate. His eyes whipped to his little sister.

Leaving behind the woman he was talking to, Lee made a beeline for Kate. As the douchebag went to hand Kate her overly strong drink, Lee snagged it and chugged it with a playful laugh. Kate laughed with him and swatted at his arm. Then Lee wound his arms around Kate and Annie to guide them off the dance floor, leaving the other guy stranded in the middle of the room.

Relief flooded my system. Kate was a pain in my ass, but the thought of someone trying to get her drunk and *loosened up* just didn't sit right.

I tossed some bills on the bar and tucked my wallet back into my pocket. I didn't need to sit around and babysit her. Lee was here and could make sure she got home.

Not my job.

I was headed for the door when Kate's breathless voice stopped me. "Had enough sulking for the night?"

I looked over at her. Her cheeks were flushed from dancing, and a strand of her silky brown hair had slipped from her ponytail. I fought the ridiculous urge to sweep it back behind her ear. Instead I stared at her, schooling my features into an impassive glare.

"I saw you watching me."

My teeth ground together. "No, you didn't."

"Yeah. You were." Kate laughed, and it floated up above the noise of the bar. "But that's okay. I won't tell your secrets."

I leveled her with a stare and lowered my voice. "If anything, I was surprised to see the always demure and pleasant Kate Sullivan getting wrecked in public."

"I was just dancing." She lifted a shoulder. "Besides . . . maybe I'm not the girl you thought I was."

Trouble was, I knew exactly who she was. My silver-tongued little brother's ex-girlfriend, who'd allowed someone to make decisions for her for years. Never a hair out of place or a disagreeable word to be spoken.

"Well, try not to let your Stepford wife image get too tarnished in one night."

I knew I had hit a nerve because she turned on her heels, sending her floral perfume flying and hitting me square in the chest. I also didn't miss the mumbled *fuck you* she shot over her shoulder before she stormed away.

Pissed at myself for the shitty comment, I finally headed home. The warm lake air hit me as soon as I pushed my way out of the Grudge. The summer evening was busy with people meandering down the sidewalks of Outtatowner. A soft glow from the lampposts illuminated the main roadway, which led down to the large public beach. The lighthouse at the end of the pier loomed and blinked in the distance. People walked, laughing and eating ice cream or sitting on outdoor patios.

As it always was, the vibe in Outtatowner was relaxed and happy. As I stomped down the road, I took a left to walk up the neighborhood sidewalks toward the house. Mentally I ticked off the list of things I planned to accomplish at the Sullivan place tomorrow.

My thighs burned and my blood pumped as I climbed the steep hill toward my house on the bluff. I swung the front door open and peered into the cold, empty house. The dark, cavernous room felt like a prison, but its solitude was the only thing keeping me from the overwhelming urge to turn around and apologize to Kate.

FIVE
KATE

I῎ᴛ ᴄᴇʀᴛᴀɪɴʟʏ ᴡᴏᴜʟᴅ ʙᴇ ᴇᴀsɪᴇʀ to be annoyed at Beckett if he didn't look so damn delicious. Hauling out the remaining matted-down carpeting from the living room was dirty, sweaty work. At some point Beckett grabbed the hem of his T-shirt to swipe sweat from his face, and the thick garbage bag I was hauling slipped from my grip when I spotted the cut lines of his abs.

Beckett was unlike any man I was used to. Certainly the opposite of his little brother, who wouldn't be caught dead in faded, worn-in blue jeans. During my time in Montana, I'd learned to appreciate the snug fit of a good pair of Wranglers, but the way Beckett's jeans hugged his ass was downright unfair.

After the living room was completely cleared and swept, I stepped up to the threshold of the room beside him. I mirrored his stance with wide legs and crossed arms. Without any furniture, the space felt massive. Under the old carpet was a glorious surprise—the same hardwood floors that ran down the main hallway continued into the large, square living room.

I sighed. "Well, we can't cover these up."

Beckett scowled beside me. "Obviously."

I huffed a breath and turned toward him. "Are you always this rude to your clients?"

He shrugged but didn't give me the satisfaction of another verbal sparring match. In fact, he'd been quietly moody and sullen all morning.

"I'm documenting the whole renovation on Instagram, you know." He stayed quiet beside me, so I continued: "I thought it would be a fun way to see the progress. Keep in touch with my Montana friends. I'm already getting a few followers, which is fun. *Home Again.*" I moved my hands in a rainbow to emphasize the cuteness of the IG handle. "You know, because we're making the house a home again. Get it?"

He harrumphed beside me.

Annoyed, I planted my hands on my hips. "Okay, well, *Fixer Upper* was already taken."

Beckett's piss-poor attitude today and last night's crappy comment about being a wannabe Stepford wife still stung. I don't know what the heck I had done to make him so hostile when all I was trying to do was have a fun night out with my friends.

Without another word, Beckett moved into the empty living room space. He circled the bare floor before stopping in front of one of the windows. Without the usual floor lamps, his frame was silhouetted by the large windows overlooking the wraparound porch. Impulsively, I slipped my phone from my back pocket, checked that it was on silent, and quietly snapped a photo.

The Brutish Builder.

The quick caption was the only text I put on the picture before I hit post.

"We could open this all up." Beckett's voice startled me, and I slipped the phone back into my pocket. "Add a few more windows for natural light to come through."

I hummed in agreement and considered how beautiful it would look with more sunlight streaming in. The living room itself was large and open but held no visual interest with its plain, bare walls.

While we had a blank slate, and he was already annoyed with me, what better time to poke the bear?

"I want a bookshelf." I pointed across the room to a tall, straight wall. "Over there. A big one with one of those dreamy rolling ladders."

Beckett turned to see where I was pointing and shook his head. "No."

I scoffed. "Whatever. I'll just build it myself."

He stifled a groan and mumbled under his breath. "You're incompetent."

I snorted. "Watch me."

I turned to leave before we got into another pissing match. Sure, I had no idea how I was going to build a bookshelf, but there had to be at least a hundred YouTube channels to show me how. Besides, I could document the whole thing on my new Instagram page.

It would be fun.

"A bookshelf like that wouldn't work in this room." I turned at the sound of his voice. "You'd need somewhere specifically designed for a library. A cozy spot that balances natural light with warm wood tones. A nook for a deep, cushy couch or even a bay window where you could sit and read or look out into nature."

His eyes were unfocused, as if he could perfectly see the

design in his head. The dreamy picture he wove was enticing and romantic and not at all like the insufferable man who stood before me.

"Then let's build it!"

Beckett shook his head again. He gestured toward the living room. "With the new windows and redoing the floors, it's not in the budget."

It took everything inside me not to stomp my foot like a child. "You know, for someone who can pull such a romantic design out of his ass, you are fundamentally lacking a heart."

My words did nothing to move him.

I lifted my palms. "This isn't just a *house*, Beckett. It's a home."

The muscles in his jaw worked. "I know that."

I scoffed. "Really? You know that?" I gestured through the kitchen. "The back mudroom was Wyatt's favorite hide-and-go-seek spot. Did you know that? In high school, Duke made a ladder to sneak girls up to his room and pretended it was a rose trellis. Did you know that?"

I pointed to the large staircase at the center of the house. "I hid under those stairs with Lee the night Mom died, and we cried our eyes out until Dad found us the next morning. Did you know *that*?" My voice wobbled on the last word, and I took a deep breath. "This is my family. My home. Don't act like you have the slightest idea of what this house means to us!"

As the tears threatened to spill over my lashes, I stormed outside. Narrowly missing a few rotted boards, I stumbled down the porch steps and didn't stop walking until I rounded the large chicken coop in the backyard.

The free-range birds clucked and gathered at my feet,

assuming I was bringing them kitchen scraps or treats. The screen door of the house banged, and I sneaked a glance around the coop. Beckett stood at the edge of the porch, looking out into the yard. His body was tall and imposing, but he fit perfectly with the varying stages of construction around him.

I slunk back and pressed myself against the coop. I hadn't meant to unleash our family trauma on Beckett, and I was damn sure not going to give him the satisfaction of seeing me cry. I closed my eyes and focused on steadying my breathing.

A low grumble sounded behind me, and I turned to see Bartleby Beakface cocking his head at me.

"Shh . . . ," I soothed with my palms up. "It's okay. Don't rat me out, okay?"

Unimpressed with me, Bartleby scratched at the ground and strutted past me. I sighed in relief and, after counting to thirty, peeked out from behind the coop.

Beckett was no longer on the porch but was instead hauling the last of the day's trash into the dumpster at the side of the house. He pointed at another pile, and his team got to work clearing the debris and keeping Tootie's yard as clean as possible during active construction.

This house and the memories it held meant everything to us. To Beckett it was little more than a paycheck, but if I found a way to put a little more pressure on him, then I was going to do just that.

THE SUMMER SUN beat down on me as I lifted my face to the sky. "Mmm. I did miss this."

Annie chuckled as she stretched out on the towel beside

me. "Hot beach, cold drinks, not a care in the world? What's not to miss?"

I clinked my cup to hers. "Amen, sister. Montana was beautiful, but there's something about a beach that just feels like home."

"It's the air. Something about it that sticks with you."

"Probably the fish smell," I teased.

We dissolved into a fit of laughter. The Lake Michigan air was clean and crisp. The hot day meant the stretch of public beach was filled with families and vacationers, but we had settled for our quieter spot down the shoreline. While it was still walking distance to a few beachside cafés, it provided a little more seclusion than the crowded main beach area.

While we sunbathed, couples gathering sea glass or children running along the water passed. A few kids raced down the massive dunes behind us. Coastal Michigan was a lakeside paradise that felt more and more like a hidden gem.

"That's the Miller place, right?" Annie squinted against the sun as she pointed to a looming beach house in the distance.

"Yep." The multimillion-dollar home was a hideous eyesore jutting out from the bluff. Its sharp lines and harsh features warred with the soft sand and tall trees that had yet to succumb to erosion and time. I hated that house and everything that had happened inside. Shame burned my cheeks.

"Are you worried that Declan will come around now that Beckett will be staying a while?"

My stomach pitched. "I would prefer it if you referred to him by the name Epic Douchebag."

That earned me a laugh from Annie as I tried to focus

on the rolling waves and not the nausea that simmered in my belly.

How had I been so stupid?

I shrugged. "Declan always hated it here."

"Is that why you never really spent holidays here?"

I nodded. "The Millers only see that house as an investment property. Once the boys got older, they stopped coming."

"Is it weird for you? For his brother to be working on the house?"

I rolled to my stomach to rest my head on my arms and looked at Annie. Her copper curls were piled on her head, and a scarf tied it all up in an effortlessly chic updo. My wild messy bun was moving in the breeze.

"Beckett is exactly like I remember—cold, quiet, and detached." I gestured to their vacation home in the distance. "That house is perfect for him. Plus, Bartleby hates him, and he's an excellent judge of character."

Annie let out a deep sigh. "That's too bad." She peeked out of one eye. "Because that man is a *snack*."

I swatted Annie's arm. "Stop! That's so wrong."

Annie laughed. "Oh come on. Don't tell me you never noticed that Beckett Miller is *fine*."

I rolled my eyes. "Well, of course I *noticed*. But he was my boyfriend's brother, and Declan never had a kind word to say about him." I lifted a finger. "Things, I might add, that are proving to actually be true."

Annie tipped an eyebrow. "You know he's not your boyfriend's brother anymore . . ."

I shook my head. "Yeah, he's my *ex*-boyfriend's brother. That's even worse. It doesn't matter if he's hot, he's still an asshole."

Annie fiddled with her phone before tipping it toward

me. "Well, that's not what the internet thinks. They think his hotness matters *a lot*."

I shielded the screen from the sunlight and willed my eyes to focus. Apparently my Brutish Builder post was gaining momentum. The photo of him, strong and silhouetted by the window, had already gotten hundreds of likes and had garnered a slew of new followers demanding updates on the old farmhouse *and* the mysterious man by the window.

"Oh my god, he would hate this." A giggle threatened to bubble up from my chest. "This is perfect."

"Maddy494 thinks you should bang him. So do the other fifty-two people who liked her comment."

I scrunched my nose, but a tingle bunched in my belly at the thought of Beckett and me naked. *Having sex.* I shook my head. "No way. Besides, Duke would lose his mind. Do you remember how he went apeshit after he found out his friend Billy Dunley kissed me in the seventh grade?"

Annie and I laughed, remembering how Duke still scowled at poor Billy Dunley when he saw him around town.

"But . . . if the internet wants more Brutish Builder, they're gonna get it."

Annie clicked off her phone and plopped it on the towel next to her. "Just make sure you get some shots of him all sweaty and dirty. You know . . . for the fans."

I laughed and winked at my friend. "I'll see what I can do."

SIX

BECKETT

"WHAT THE HELL ARE YOU DOING?" I looked over my shoulder to find Kate leaned in close with her phone. Her perfume was driving me insane and we had a shit ton of work to do before the inspector arrived.

I stared down at the spot where Kate's hand balanced on my forearm as she centered her shot. Her delicate fingers wrapped around the muscle of my forearm, and hot sparks shot up to my shoulder and chest.

"Snapping a picture. For the fans." Kate smiled up at me, and I forced myself to look away, but I didn't move.

For the past three weeks Kate had done more *documenting* and less helping the actual renovation, unless you counted providing her unsolicited opinions on every minute detail. Apparently her little Instagram page had started to take off—people were actually interested in seeing the process of transforming a hundred-year-old farmhouse into the modern age.

Initially I'd complained that she was in the way, but when email inquiries into my business tripled seemingly overnight, I shut my mouth. Her page was drumming up

more work for myself and struggling Outtatowner businesses, and it was free advertising. But it did mean that I
had to endure her bending over to get a close-up shot or
leaning in for a reluctant selfie and assaulting me with her
intoxicating perfume.

Kate started typing on her phone. "What are these
again?"

"Casement windows."

"And why did you choose that style?" She held the
phone up to me and mouthed *it's recording* as she nodded
and circled one finger in the air.

I clenched my jaw and crossed my arms. "Casement
windows offer versatility in both form and function." I
gestured toward the freshly hung living room windows.
"Lined up like this and you have an unobstructed view of
the landscape. The windows swing outward to allow
airflow, and there's plenty of opportunity for sunlight to
brighten an otherwise dark room."

I dropped my arms. "Happy?"

Kate's bright-white smile grew as she lowered the
phone. "That was perfect! People are going to love it!" She
went back to typing something.

"If you say so." I swallowed back the lump that her
bright smile and enthusiasm drummed up inside me as I
turned to walk away.

Truth was, the more time I spent in Outtatowner, the
more time I spent with *her*, the more out of sorts I started to
feel. For six years I'd known Kate to be the kind of woman
to stay quiet, appease everyone, and not make a scene. That
woman was *not* the effervescent Kate Sullivan with the
arresting smile behind a rapidly growing Instagram page.

Granted, my previous interactions were limited to
uncomfortable holidays or the odd family obligation I was

guilted into, but this new version of her was at war with the woman Declan had strung along or the sweet little sister Duke talked about.

I couldn't think about it too long or a headache would inevitably throb at the base of my skull. For the moment I would tuck that information away and ignore the nagging feeling that I may not know Kate Sullivan as well as I had assumed.

I stepped out into the afternoon sunlight and spotted Ms. Tootie spreading scratch grains on the ground for her beloved chickens. She clucked her tongue, and they happily clucked back as she meandered through the yard.

"Ma'am." I nodded at her when I caught her attention.

She grinned. "Oh, stop with that. How can I help, dear?"

"Just an update. The windows are in and look great. Paint will be up this afternoon, and the trim guy is already at work with measurements. Once that's done, the crew will be free to move on to phase two."

"Oh"—she feigned interest—"phase two. Sounds exciting."

The corner of my mouth lifted. Of all the Sullivans, Tootie seemed the least concerned about things like phases and progress. "That's the kitchen demo. It'll mean a lot of noise and a whole lot of mess, but we'll do our best to keep it to a minimum."

She nodded. Living in construction was difficult, and after the dressing down Kate had given me about the house, I had done my best to demand the crew treated their home with the respect it deserved. "It won't bother me any. I plan to move back in once everything is all done."

"I didn't realize you and Kate were moving out. That actually makes things a bit easier since—"

"Not Kate. Just me."

I frowned at her.

Ms. Tootie smiled. "Kate's got a stubborn streak she's currently leaning into. The poor girl's been through a lot, and she's still finding her footing. She's planning to stay through the renovation, but I just can't deal with the dust. It gets into my hair, dries it out. I don't prefer that at all."

The thought of Kate being alone in the old farmhouse didn't sit right with me, but I'd learned the woman's stubborn streak was a mile long. If she'd decided to stay, it wasn't my responsibility to talk her out of it.

I nodded at the sweet old woman. "I'll do what I can to get you home as soon as possible."

She reached out and patted my forearm. "I know you will, dear. Thank you." It was a sweet, maternal gesture that made my throat feel dry.

When Tootie turned her attention back toward the chickens in the yard, I eyeballed the rooster, whose head popped up to stare me down. I jerked my shoulders toward him, and he squawked and stepped back.

That's right, fucker.

I rubbed my eyes, sighing at myself for engaging in a pissing match with a rooster.

Only in Outtatowner.

I stood like an idiot, watching Tootie fuss with her birds and trying to understand the pull this town was having on me. Not once had I felt the familiar tug toward Chicago and the mounting work I'd left there, and that was a problem.

∾

"Okay, boss, the living room floors are sealed. Plastic is hung to limit dust, and I taped off the entry so no one accidentally steps in there and fucks it all up."

I nodded at Bob Klein. He owned a flooring company a few towns over and had several men on the local crew I'd hired. The hardwood floors we'd unearthed from years of being covered by carpet needed a lot of love, and Bob and his men had worked magic to sand, buff, and stain them. I made a note on my clipboard to have Kate mention Bob's company again when she posted the reveal on her Instagram page.

I turned to him. "And the kitchen?"

He turned toward the cramped space. "That wall is going?" he asked, pointing to a center wall that cut off the kitchen from the main space. It was load bearing, so we'd planned a new support header, and while it was expensive, it would make all the difference in giving Ms. Tootie the kitchen of her dreams.

"Yep. Demo starts as soon as the cabinets get here."

Bob looked around at the flooring and considered. "Once it's all out, we'll cover the existing floors to protect them. Then we will join the original flooring with whatever new pieces we'll need to lay down. Should be seamless."

I held out my hand. "That's what I like to hear. I'll keep you updated on when it will be ready for you."

Bob looked into the kitchen area. Boxes of plates and cups were stacked. Hardly any had been marked for donation or trash, and I'd have to find a way to keep the crew from breaking anything that was meant to be kept. It significantly slowed down our progress.

As if Bob could read my mind, he said, "Kind of hard to work efficiently when the homeowner is around."

I let out a grunt in agreement. "Tell me about it."

"Hello!" Kate's singsong greeting floated from the front door to the kitchen, where we were standing.

In the late morning sun, she was radiant. Her brown hair was swept up, leaving the long line of her neck exposed. The late-summer rays were already beating down, so she was in a tight white tank top, but she'd swapped her denim cutoffs for a pair of tight jeans and work boots.

Should have kept my mouth shut.

"Hi!" She beamed at Bob and me. "Whoa, looks like a crime scene in here."

Bob smiled back. "The plastic will keep dust and debris off your gorgeous new flooring. I want to make sure it's perfect for you and your aunt."

I narrowed my eyes at him.

Traitor.

"Well, aren't you thorough." Kate batted her lashes.

Bob practically floated out the door when Kate said her goodbyes and gave him the full power of her smile.

"Can you not?"

She blinked at me. "What?"

"Flirt with my guys."

Kate rolled her mossy-green eyes at me. "I was not flirting. If I was, you'd know it."

A strange surge of jealousy bubbled in my gut. Bob was easily twenty years her senior, but the idea of Kate flirting with him awakened some feral, Neanderthal part of my brain.

Instead of dealing with it, I decided to push her buttons instead.

"You need to clear out all this shit so we can get started."

Kate's jaw worked before she turned her back on me to

close the flaps on a box, giving me an unobstructed view of her pert little ass. "Always the charmer."

"Work starts tomorrow. Get it done."

Annoyed—at myself or her, I wasn't sure—I stomped toward the front door, letting the screen slam behind me.

SEVEN
BECKETT

I PULLED into the garage of the beach house and sat in the dark, gathering the courage to go inside. It felt like everything in that house was a constant reminder of the life I hated. I let out a deep sigh as I got out of my truck and trudged up the steps to the door.

As I entered the house, the emptiness hit me hard in the center of my chest. It was a feeling I had become all too familiar with. I tossed my keys on the kitchen counter and collapsed on the couch, staring blankly at the wall in front of me.

My phone rang, and I groaned after seeing it was Mom calling. She had been trying to set me up on *mutually beneficial* blind dates for weeks now, and I had absolutely no interest in playing her games. She had little interest in my happiness but was highly invested in what a relationship of mine could do for her social standing. I let the call go to voice mail and leaned my head back against the couch, feeling like trash.

More than anything, I was pissed at myself. I had snapped at a crew member, only to find out he was late because his little daughter was sick. The way he apologized to *me* and assured me it wouldn't happen again only made me feel like a bigger asshole.

It also didn't help my mood that I'd spent all day having to watch Kate strut around in her tiny shorts, smiling at my guys, moving plants, hauling away debris. I had no right thinking about my best friend's little sister at all, let alone the things that came to mind every time she bent over.

I got up and headed to the bathroom, needing to cool off. As I stood under the hot spray of the shower, I tried to push all thoughts of Kate out of my head. I tried to think of anything else, but flashes of her lips, her long hair curled around my fist, her soft skin under my rough palms, wouldn't stop.

Closing my eyes, I let my hand slip over my abs. Then lower still until my rock-hard cock was waiting for me. Aching for her.

"Goddamn it."

I ground my teeth together as I gave myself one long, hard tug. Fuck, it felt good to stroke my cock with her face in my head. Warm water moved over me as I let the images of Kate consume me.

I imagined the tiny little smirk that flashed when I really pissed her off. I wanted to get her riled up and then keep her quiet by putting her on her knees and slipping my dick between those plush lips of hers.

Stroking harder, I braced my other hand on the cool tile across from me. Alone and with no one to hear me, I let her name slip past my lips on a groan, and it felt good.

Too good.

My hips bucked forward as I stroked myself to the mental image of Kate sprawled in front of me. I had a feeling she'd be the kind of woman who'd take it and beg for more. I had always known her to be quiet and demure, but the sharper edges she'd been showing me lately were what really lit my fire. I had a sinking feeling that I could go toe to toe with her and she'd refuse to back down.

Until I got my hands on her.

"Fuck, Princess."

I stroked myself, over and over, to the image of her until I was spent. I rested my head against the tile and let the rapidly cooling water beat down my back.

As I stepped out of the shower and wrapped a towel around my waist, I sighed. In the span of a few minutes, I had stooped lower than I thought possible, even for me.

I needed to get my shit together. I couldn't keep living like this, feeling sorry for myself and secretly lusting after Kate. Sure, the idea of fucking Declan's ex—the ultimate slap in the face—held a certain appeal, but I couldn't go there with Duke.

I wouldn't. He was a good man and an even better friend.

I needed to forget all about the curve of Kate's neck or all the ways I could drag out a satiated, heavy sigh from her. I needed to find a way to get this reno done and forget all about sexy little sisters with fierce eyes and pouty lips.

"WHAT THE HELL are you doing up there?" I glared up at Kate as she wobbled on a rickety ladder, leaning far to the left with a paintbrush in her hand. I had turned a corner to find her on the side of the house, ten feet in the air and not a safety precaution in sight.

"Painting samples. Tootie couldn't decide which shade she liked best, so I'm going to have our followers vote on the exterior paint color. It's great for engagement. Did you know that we've already hit ten thousand followers? I still can't believe it!"

I stared up at her, feet planted wide and arms crossed. Kate looked down and bit the paintbrush between her teeth before slipping her phone from the back pocket of her jeans. She snapped a picture of me frowning up at her before I could protest.

"I'm posting that one."

I dropped my hands. "I'm sure you are. Now get down."

Kate didn't listen. She never did.

Instead, she surveyed her work and, with a satisfied little nod, held the brush and small jar of paint as she navigated down the unsteady ladder. That damn ladder wasn't even one of mine, so who knew where she got it from.

I held the sides of the ladder still as she took tentative steps down. Within moments, her ass was inches from my face. An ass I'd spent an embarrassing amount of time focusing on as I jerked off in the shower.

What a scumbag.

Kate stopped and pulled me from my self-loathing. "What are you doing?"

"Making sure you don't kill yourself."

"I don't need your help."

"That may be true, but if you die or break a leg, I'm sure I'll hear about it from your brothers." I inelegantly grabbed her by the hips and lifted her off the ladder before she stepped on the rung that was nearly cracked in half.

"Hey!" she fussed when I plopped her on her feet.

My hands burned from where they'd sunk into her plush hips. I took a step back and wiped them together.

Kate pointed up at the six squares of paint she'd put up on the side of the house. "What do you think?"

I glanced up. "None of them."

She shook her head. "You have shitty taste."

I snorted. *Look at who you spent six years in a relationship with.*

I pointed up at the paint samples to make my point. "None of those colors are reflective of the traditional coastal palette." I stared down at her as I jabbed a finger toward each color. "That one is too yellow. That one has gray undertones that will lean purple in the wintertime. That one is too cool for the landscape. The middle two are close but not quite the right saturation."

Kate looked between me and the swatches she had painted with a frown.

Satisfied that I had won that little round of sparring, and since Kate was safely planted on the ground, I stomped back toward the front of the house.

Kate followed me, paintbrush still in hand. "Well, are you going to help me pick one?"

I shook my head. "Nope. Let your little internet friends decide."

She shot me a glare before stomping up the porch steps like a child. Before I could call out and tell her I'd found another weak board, she stumbled. Her paintbrush clattered, splattering paint on the graying wood, and I snagged her upper arm to catch her from falling.

Her soft skin was warm under my palm, and my other arm wrapped around her rib cage as I righted her. Two inches higher and I'd have a handful of my best friend's little sister's tits.

I pulled my hands away. "Watch where you're walking," I growled.

Her cheeks were flushed.

Fuck, she'd felt it too.

"Fix this stupid porch!" The fire in Kate's eyes was enough to have my dick springing to life.

I fought a smirk. "Is that all?"

With a huff, Kate slammed the door behind her, and I lost the fight against that grin.

EIGHT
KATE

It took me a second to realize that the pounding in my brain was not from an afternoon of too much sun and physical labor. I blinked away the sleep and confusion as I sat up in bed. I glanced at the clock as the rhythmic pounding continued.

Five. Freaking. A.M.?!

I pulled myself from bed and stomped down the stairs and through the hallway. I yanked open the front door and stopped dead in my tracks. In the early morning light, Beckett was dressed in work boots, jeans, and a hunter-green T-shirt that stretched over his massive chest. Sweat already formed in a V down his back and clung to his muscles.

I swallowed hard. My nipples went rigid, and I sucked in a breath. "What are you doing? It's five in the morning."

Beckett didn't even give me the satisfaction of a glance in my direction. "What's it look like I'm doing?"

I planted my hands on my hips. It *looked* like Beckett was already underway, tearing apart the dilapidated porch despite the fact that it was supposed to be one of the last construction projects completed on the house.

I would know. I had a list.

"I thought the kitchen was next."

Beckett glanced up at me, his eyes snagging for a fraction of a second too long on the front of my shirt. I crossed my arms to try to hide the fact that I hadn't bothered with a bra yet.

"Plans change." Beckett took the long handle of the tool, slipped it under a porch board, and pulled with a grunt. The wood split and released from the frame below it. He bent down and, with one hand, picked up the loosened board and tossed it onto a growing pile.

"Did this have anything to do with me tripping yesterday?"

His eyes flicked over me. "No. You bitched at me to get it fixed. I'm just following orders, Princess." He pried free another board. "Besides, I can't have my workers getting hurt on the job. The porch needed to be replaced."

I looked down at the open floor joists, another term I'd learned since my Instagram page had gained in popularity and I'd scrambled to soak up as much as I could about home renovations.

"It's five in the morning."

"You mentioned that." He let out a heavy, annoyed sigh. "I'm just getting it started so we aren't behind on the rest of the projects."

Another grunt. Another board pried free, and Beckett's muscles worked as he tossed it aside.

I cannot sit around watching him grunt and sweat all day. But god, what would it be like for him to put those rough hands on me? To bicker only to have him shut me up with his kiss?

Still, I stood in the doorway, unable to look away. In a swift move, Beckett reached behind his collar and pulled off his shirt, leaving him in nothing but snug-fitting jeans, work boots, and a backward ball cap.

That's it. I'm out.

Without another word, I turned and slammed the front door behind me. I absolutely could *not* allow those thoughts to run away from me.

After a few deep breaths in the safety of my room, I quickly got dressed for the day and checked my latest Instagram post. A happy little zip of excitement danced through me as I typed back as many replies to comments as I could.

Before bed, I had posted about the exterior paint color, asking the slew of new followers to weigh in and give their opinions. I'd also slipped in a line asking if we should get the Brutish Builder's opinion—that choice was currently winning, obviously.

Insert heavy sigh and eye roll.

The actual truth was that as soon as Beckett had pointed out why the colors Tootie and I had originally chosen wouldn't work, I'd hated them all. I hated the fact he was spot-on in his assessment even more.

Though he was short tempered, grumpy, and moody, Beckett Miller was frustratingly good at his job.

I dragged a brush through my hair and secured my loose waves with a fluffy silk hair tie. The summer sun had begun to deepen my natural olive coloring, so with a simple swipe of black mascara and some sunscreen, I was ready for the day.

I typed out a quick message to my friends Gemma and Sophie.

ME

It's wrong to objectify a man, correct?

SOPHIE

Probably.

GEMMA

Not if it's the guy you posted on your Insta last night.

SOPHIE

Hold please. Holy crap—I just checked IG, and my feminism just flew out the window.

ME

It's Declan's brother. He's also a prick.

GEMMA

All's fair in love and war, baby. Give him hell.

SOPHIE

Can I request a butt pic? Those jeans are really snug.

ME

I forgot you're a hoe for a tight pair of jeans. I'll see what I can do.

Laughing, I flipped through my recent photos on my phone to determine what else I could post about. Certainly the surprise porch deconstruction would be a fun topic of conversation—especially if I could get a few shots of Beckett half-naked and sweaty while he worked.

For Sophie, of course.

Just outside the kitchen window, he was still working at prying off old porch boards and readying the project for his crew. I dug a ceramic cup out of one of the boxes I'd packed and walked over to the small coffee maker I had set up in the hallway. Though we would be without a kitchen for a while, there was no reason the crew and I had to suffer through Beckett's shit attitude without caffeine.

I ignored the low, not-at-all-like-sex grunts coming from outside as I waited on my coffee. After doctoring it up with cream and sugar, I hastily made a second cup.

Dressed this time, I opened the front door again to find Beckett had made steady progress removing the porch boards. I eyed the open slats in front of me.

I gently cleared my throat, and his stormy gray eyes moved to mine. "If you're redoing the porch, instead of just wrapping around the front, I think it should wrap all the way around the north side too."

Beckett wiped the back of his hand across his sweaty brow. "Is that all?"

My pulse danced as a tingle slid dangerously low down my belly. I placed the spare mug of coffee on a row of boards that had yet to be removed and lifted my chin.

Steadying my balance, I tiptoed across the joists and hopped into the soft grass.

The heady weight of his gaze was on me the entire time. I lifted a shoulder without looking back as I strode toward my Jeep. "Open concept with no railings would be nice too."

Without waiting for his response, I climbed inside and headed to town.

"KATIE'S TAKING care of everything. It's a heavy burden off my shoulders." Aunt Tootie beamed at me as she sung my praises in the small book shop that held a weekly book club for the women of Outtatowner.

It was surreal sitting in the small book shop, the women

of Outtatowner—King and Sullivan women, no less—chatting together, talking over each other, and laughing. Growing up, the Bluebird Book Club was always an elusive, secret society of women from every family in town. I had always hoped to be a part of the inner circle. Something about it was mysterious and bold and *just for us*. My mother was a Bluebird, and I had wanted to be one too.

I glanced over at the wall of framed black-and-white photos behind the cash register. My eyes immediately found the photo I was looking for—Mom. She was frozen in time, exactly how I remembered her. Dressed in an airy skirt and blouse, laughing at something someone was saying off camera. There was no denying I'd grown to look more and more like her as time wore on.

The whoosh of coastal air and the tinkling of the bell at the door pulled my attention from painful, unfaded memories.

"Sorry I'm late!" Annie burst through the door, several bottles of wine tucked under her arms and her wild copper hair lifting in the breeze. She blew it out of her face and grinned widely. "I brought booze to make up for it!"

I laughed as Annie was welcomed in with smiles and raised plastic cups. She made her way around the small shop, saying hello and depositing bottles of wine around the room like a flittering little woodland sprite.

When she got to me, she plopped down on the chair beside me with a grunt. "Ooof. This day."

"Long one?" I asked, handing her the bottle opener to my right.

"Slow, which is so much worse." Annie was a local artist —pottery, painting, glass blowing, mosaics. She was deeply talented but sometimes lamented that it was difficult to stand out and sell pricey custom art in a tourist town littered with stores selling steeply discounted trinkets. Still, she refused to discount her art, and I applauded her for standing her ground.

"I had plenty of time to flip through social media." She bumped her shoulder with mine. "Look at you going viral."

Heat crept up my cheeks. In the time since I'd randomly started documenting the farmhouse renovation, the followers to my page just kept flooding in. Every post or reel I put up got hundreds, even *thousands*, of views, likes, and comments. I was even getting sponsorship requests almost daily. It was hard to wrap my head around.

"It's strange, but fun and exciting. I love documenting the whole thing, but I think mostly people just like the fact that I objectify Beckett."

Annie laughed. "Oh, and you don't enjoy it?"

"I like to push his buttons, and posting half-naked pictures of him does the trick. Besides, he hasn't objected to the people who are now vying for the Brutish Builder to do a little custom handiwork."

"Bet you wouldn't mind a little *custom handiwork*." She wiggled her eyebrows and stifled a grin as she sipped her wine.

My face twisted. "Ew. Annie, no. Besides, he's my ex's *brother*. And an asshole, remember?" I lifted a finger to emphasize my point.

"Whatever, Declan was a spineless dog. He missed out on what an absolute treasure you are. Doesn't mean Beckett is that dumb."

I shook my head. The whole conversation was absolutely absurd. "Can you imagine—showing up at a Miller family party as Beckett's date?" I scoffed and ignored the warm tingle that the image drummed up.

"Serves the bastard right for what he did to you."

I swallowed a large gulp of water, emptying my cup. "This conversation is over. The only thing between Beckett and me is a house renovation and mutual, petty annoyance."

Annie clicked her tongue. "If you say so . . ."

"Hey, gals." MJ King leaned over from the conversation she was having with her older sister, Sylvie.

I offered the youngest King girl a small, polite smile. She was a nurse at Haven Pines, where my dad lived due to his worsening illness. Shame flooded me, as I couldn't remember the last time I'd visited him. I was sure she had noticed, but seeing Dad was just . . . hard.

While the King women and their relatives were mostly tolerable, there was no denying that the King *men* were not. Broody, heartless businessmen. More than once they'd tried to sweep in on our farm like vultures during the lean years. Duke would never have it. Neither would the rest of us, but if Sullivan Farms ever landed in the hands of a King, it would truly break my oldest brother.

Generations of Sullivans and Kings goading and one-upping each other meant even the women weren't ever truly friends. Despite being tucked inside the walls of Blue-bird Books, tensions sometimes simmered.

Poor, sweet MJ often acted as the go-between.

"Is JP okay?" Fine, I felt a *little* bad about the whole mystery cricket thing.

MJ laughed. "He's fine. But I doubt he'll be camping anytime soon. Even real cricket sounds are freaking him out right now."

I gave her a smile that was a bit more like a grimace. "I swear . . . I was an unwilling accomplice."

Sylvie lifted a shoulder in dismissal as she overheard our conversation. She was the coldest of the King women, often scurrying off to the back kitchen at the Sugar Bowl, where she worked, whenever we came in for baked goods or coffee. Why she worked there despite the owner Huck making it a point to not take sides in the town feud was beyond me.

We all knew how the back-and-forth of pranks between the Sullivans and Kings played out. It was only a matter of time before the Kings found a way to get us back. Mostly it was playful and harmless. Sometimes a prank would bruise an ego, and it would come to blows outside the Grudge. The small scar above Lee's left eye was a testament to that—it had also prompted a strict no-hits-to-the-face policy.

We all knew the stories—the Kings had wronged the Sullivans all those years ago, but Amos King made it monumentally worse.

Annie whispered and pulled me out of my wandering thoughts.

"Hey, speaking of Lee . . . he was asking what book we were talking about tonight, so if he mentions it, just say *Interview with the Vampire*."

"*Interview with the Vampire*?"

Annie waved her hands in the air. "I don't know. I panicked. It was on Netflix and the first thing that came to mind. Besides, sexy vampire Brad Pitt? Yes, please."

"You realize that book-version Louis wasn't all that good looking, right?"

"Doesn't matter." Annie shrugged. "I'd bang sexy vampire Brad Pitt."

"But he was so *pale* in that movie. You're deranged."

"Obviously." She raised a bottle of cool white wine. "Drink up."

The laughter that trickled out of me was a comfort. At ease, I allowed her to fill my plastic cup and took a sip. The wine was crisp and buttery and so smooth. Complex flavors I couldn't quite identify danced over my tongue.

"Mmm," I hummed and raised an eyebrow at her. "Another Charles Attwater recommendation?"

Annie blushed. Charles was new in town and owned a wine shop. Business was booming, and Annie seemed to be smitten with the handsome newcomer. "He's very knowledgeable."

"I can't believe he hasn't asked you out yet." Truly, Annie was a knockout with her amazing red curls, a light dusting of freckles across her nose, and a killer body. She'd been best friends with Lee since they were kids, which was why he probably didn't even notice that his bestie was super hot.

Men are so clueless.

"You could always ask *him* out," MJ offered. "Maybe invite him to the Fireside Flannel Festival. That's always a good time."

"No, that's still a few weeks away," Sylvie spoke up from a few seats down. "Just get naked. See if he's interested."

Annie sputtered on her wine at Sylvie's suggestion. "What?"

Huh. Maybe Sylvie wasn't such a stick-in-the-mud after all.

Sylvie's smile stretched across her face, and her sharp features softened. "Okay, maybe not *walk into his shop naked*, but let him see what he's missing." Sylvie shimmied her shoulders and gestured to all of Annie. "Invite him to the beach and wear a tiny bikini. Then . . . *oops*"—Sylvie leaned forward as if her top was falling open—"wardrobe malfunction."

We howled in delight at her absurd suggestion. Somehow, in the time I'd been away, Sylvie had gotten *funny*.

Annie looked down at her curves. "Oh yeah, just flash him my tits and see how it goes? You're insane."

I topped off Annie's cup with more wine. "Go on, take her suggestion. Show him your boobs."

"I'm telling you"—Sylvie pointed in our direction—"a man gets an eyeful and his expression will tell you right then and there whether or not he's interested."

"You are all ridiculous." Annie stood. "I'm going over there to chat about *books*."

I laughed again at the mere idea anyone would be talking about actual books at book club. "Oh, sure. Just make sure you cover all the high points of Louis and Lestat in case there's a quiz later."

Annie playfully stuck her tongue out at us as she walked away, and we dissolved into a fresh round of giggles.

His expression will tell you right then and there whether or not he's interested.

Sylvie's words bounced around my head as I remembered Beckett's expression the day my shirt had been soaked through.

Oh, shit . . .

NINE
BECKETT

WHAT A LONG-ASS DAY.

I stretched and twisted my back, hoping the aches and tired muscles would last me another hour or two. I checked my watch and frowned as the sun sank lower over the trees at the edge of the yard. Splashes of ruby and indigo warred in the sky over the blueberry field in the distance. Crickets and cicadas sang out into the evening, and the clouds in the distance were growing thick. We'd lucked out with the weather, but the forecast called for rain, and my crew had worked all afternoon to get to a spot where the wet weather wouldn't delay us further.

It would take a few weeks to fully complete the porch project, but the crew had made good headway in ensuring the underlying structures were safe. The smell of rain was already clinging to the thick summer air. I stared down the driveway.

Where the hell was she?

After Kate came outside this morning in nothing but thin pajamas, my focus was shot. When she'd left me a warm cup of coffee despite my surly attitude, guilt rode my ass all day. I'd pushed the crew harder and made certain they could accommodate her request for an open concept, wraparound porch.

The crew would put in the labor, but I'd make sure it was perfect.

As the minutes ticked by, I grew impatient. Pulling my phone from my pocket, I pulled up Duke's number.

ME

Seen your sister around?

DUKE

Book club most likely. Want to come over and watch the game?

I checked the time again and considered a low-key night with Duke versus another solitary one in my temporary home. I glanced down the driveway again.

ME

No, thanks. I'm beat.

I huffed another impatient breath as I tapped my middle finger against my thigh.

I should go. No reason to wait around.

I dug my keys from the pocket of my jeans, but paused when my phone rang.

"Hello, Mother."

"Hi, dear. It's your mother. Not sure if you remember me."

Tension bunched in my shoulders. Speaking with my mother always came with an extra serving of guilt. "How are you?"

"Oh, you know. Busy as always. Your father and I have been looking at places in Malta."

"Another vacation?"

She laughed. "No. For winters."

Ah, yes. Of course. Another overpriced vacation home that will remain largely unlived in but make for perfect social media pictures.

"Anyway," she continued. "Have you spoken to your brother? I think he's having a midlife crisis."

"He's twenty-five."

"Well, what else would you call it when he breaks up with the love of his life, galivants around the city with *trash*, and then when I politely ask him about it, doesn't call me for six weeks?"

Kate was the love of his life? Jesus.

Mother rattled on despite my silence. "I'm going to need you here on Saturday. The Feldman gala. I told the Johnsons you'd be available to talk about their ideas for their in-home au pair suite."

I stifled a groan. "I'm sorry, Mom, but I'm working."

"Working? Where are you?"

I dragged a hand over the back of my neck. "Outta-towner, actually."

"Hmm." I could imagine the line of irritation already thinning her lips. "I told your father to sell that house years ago."

"It's no Malta." *No, Outtatowner is unpretentious. Peaceful. Like a home should be.*

That pulled a chuckle from her. "You've got that right. Kate was the only good thing to come out of that town. Such a pity. Have you seen her?"

My eyes darted up the driveway. "Yeah. She's around."

My mother's voice went misty. "I miss her. She kept Declan in line, knew how to dress for a fundraiser—not like this new one he's got. She wore *red shoes* to the Lakeshore Social charity auction. Can you believe that?"

Disbelief and unbridled disdain dripped from my mother's words, as if the mere idea of colored shoes was ridiculous. Though, I guess to her and her elite social circle, it was. Mother laughed as though I was an insider to the joke.

I shook my head and sighed. I had nothing to offer her. No way to relate to my own mother. As I looked to find a way to end the call, Kate's white Jeep pulled down the driveway.

She parked and had stepped out from the driver's side when my eyes caught on her bright-red Converse.

I fought a smile and cleared my throat. "I have to go, Mother. My client just arrived."

"Okay, but when are you coming back to the city? Martha Kensington was also hoping to have lunch." Another one of my mother's rich friends with too much time on their hands, looking for a way to one-up each other or pair off their children for societal domination.

It was exhausting, but custom home building paid well. Really well. Enough to brush off the occasional blind date setup.

"Not for a while. Current job is a big one."

"Don't complain. It's unbecoming. And don't forget that you chose this profession. You could have been a lawyer, so I don't want to hear it."

I ground my teeth together. I wasn't complaining. "Good night, Mother."

I disconnected the call as Kate made her way toward me, glancing at the construction of the porch. My stomach flipped as a small, satisfied smile softened her face.

"It's late." I looked at the darkened sky behind her. Thick, heavy clouds covered the moon and stars.

"Oh," she teased. "Am I past curfew, Daddy?"

My mouth went dry and my dick twitched to life. "Don't call me that."

Kate laughed and stepped past me up the makeshift stairs.

"I dropped Annie off at home. She hit the wine a little hard at book club." I turned, and she wiggled an unopened bottle of wine in the air. "But I got her leftovers."

Kate frowned when I didn't react to her playfulness, and she looked me over. "Why are you still here?"

"I wanted to update you on the work and our timeline."

Kate sighed and rolled her eyes in a way that tugged a sly smile to my lips. "Fine. Come on." She tipped her head toward the door and left me staring after her.

"I think I can see it." Kate stood in the middle of the empty kitchen space with eyes closed.

I took the opportunity to let my eyes wander over the soft planes of her face, her straight nose, the long column of her delicate neck.

Speaking with my mother inevitably dragged to the surface things I tried not to think about—the distance I felt with my family, how Duke was more of a brother to me than Declan ever had been, how different I felt from the very people who were supposed to be my family.

Kate moved through the small kitchen, asking questions, talking with her hands, making suggestions. I listened, but my mind wandered to her and my little brother. Their relationship irritated me more now than it ever had in the six years he'd had her.

Though I made it a point to stay busy and not have to suffer through family functions, during the odd holiday or obligation, the picture I had formed of Kate was vastly different from the woman standing in front of me, waxing poetic about exposed brick.

"What's this?" Kate moved toward a corner of the interior wall, marked with a large black X for removal. While I was inspecting the wall to plan for the new header to support the upper floor of the house, the wallpaper had peeled away. Curiosity had gotten the best of me, and I'd peeled it further to reveal writing on the wall beneath it.

"Found it after the cabinets were removed."

She bent down, and her fingers moved over the horizontal lines. Dates, names, heights—covered up when the kitchen had been updated years ago. When I had found it, my finger had moved over her name—*Katie*.

"This is . . . I think it's my mom's handwriting." Emotion was thick in her voice as she bent down for a closer look.

"I thought it might be important."

She looked at me, hope swimming in her eyes. "This whole wall is going?"

I paused, but nodded once.

Kate cleared her throat and stepped back to snap a picture of the wall. She turned and pasted on a tight smile. "Pretty neat." Her dismissive shrug shot a pang beneath my ribs.

Well, that won't do.

"The storm is here." Clutching the bottle of wine, she gestured toward the window as fat raindrops started to fall. "Want to wait it out? Have a glass with me."

Kate set the bottle on a stack of boxes. She rifled through one marked *kitchen crap* and dug out two vintage glasses with cartoons on the front. With her teeth, Kate pulled the cork from the bottle of wine and poured it with a heavy hand.

"Here."

I turned the cup to see a blue teddy bear with a rain cloud on his belly and a scowl staring back at me.

I lifted my brows at her. "Care Bears?"

"Grumpy Bear. I thought it was perfect for you."

"Which one do you have? Pain in My Ass Bear?"

"Har har." She turned her glass to me. "Bedtime Bear, my second favorite."

I nodded and took a tentative sip. "Makes sense. Bedtime Bear doesn't like those five a.m. wakeup calls."

She shot me a bland look. "Bedtime Bear is strong and brave and stands guard to ward off bad dreams."

A ripple of sadness washed over me as I thought about young little Kate needing something like a Bedtime Bear when she was scared. The Sullivan kids had been dealt a shit hand.

"If he's your second favorite, then who was your favorite?"

Kate grinned and my heart pounded. She gestured toward me. "I always liked the grumpy one."

With a sly smile, Kate turned away from me. I sucked in a deep breath and tried to tame the wildly inappropriate thoughts that rattled through my skull.

Walking to the open space, Kate threw a thick moving blanket on the floor and plunked herself down. She patted beside her. "Sit with me. My feet hurt."

I looked over her red sneakers as she toed them off and shook my head.

"What?"

This time, I didn't hide my smirk. "Nothing."

Folding my legs, I lowered myself and sat across from

her. Kate leaned back and dug through another box, pulling out a rusty coffee can full of pennies and a deck of cards on top.

"Still raining." She wiggled her eyebrows at me. "Wanna play?"

I sipped the wine and dismissed the fifty reasons why it was a bad idea. Namely, Kate was borderline tipsy. "What's your game?"

Looking all too satisfied with herself, Kate smiled as she started shuffling. "Texas Hold'em."

Her green eyes held mine.

Fuck it.

I drained my cup. "Deal 'em up."

TEN
KATE

Four games later, I was kicking his ass and feeling pretty damn confident.

Beckett's long legs were folded beneath him as we sat across from each other on the floor, rain streaming down outside.

His gray eyes narrowed as he slapped his cards in front of him. "Son of a bitch. Duke taught you, didn't he?"

I grinned and scooped up the cards to shuffle after another winning round. "Sure did."

Beckett groaned as he unfolded himself from the floor and went in search of something. He flipped open a few boxes, then unstacked and restacked them against the wall as heavy rainfall continued outside.

"Can I help you find something, nosy?"

He moved another box. "I know there was a bottle of Blanton's in here somewhere."

I pointed to the stack of boxes tucked into the corner. "Try the one marked *For When Beckett Is Insufferable.*"

Amused confusion crinkled the lines around his eyes, and I tamped down the roll of desire that crept up.

I shrugged. "I got bored marking boxes, so Aunt Tootie and I had a little fun."

He shook his head and kept rummaging past another box labeled *Rubber Bands and Other Weird Crap*. "Here we go." Beckett pulled the bourbon from the correct box and studied the label.

I raised my glass with a smile. "Well, stop looking at it like you're gonna make out with it and serve it up."

Beckett smirked as he moved back to the blanket. That man had swagger. His long legs moved in a way that was graceful, but predatory. I was suddenly hot and nervous. Cocooned and alone in a dark house with Beckett, I listened to the rhythmic drumbeat of the rain, which seemed to shelter us from the outside world.

Intimate.

Sensual.

Wrong in all the best ways.

I had to remind myself that this was Beckett freaking Miller. Duke's best friend and the man in charge of renovating my aunt's house. Worse, he was my ex's older brother, who made no qualms about letting me know how annoying and useless he found me.

But there was no denying the look in his eyes was transmitting something entirely new, and it was definitely *not* annoyance.

I focused my attention on the cards as Beckett sat and poured us each a healthy portion of bourbon. "Another hand?" he asked.

"Sure, but let's up the stakes." I peeked from under my lashes to gauge his reaction.

Beckett held the bourbon in his mouth before swallowing it down. "What did you have in mind?"

I bit back a smile as I dealt. "I win, I get . . ." I looked him up and down, taking my time and appreciating the broad expanse of his chiseled shoulders. "Your shirt."

He leaned back on an arm. "Well, that doesn't seem very fair. What do I get if I win?"

A smile lifted the corner of my mouth as butterflies danced in my belly. "Well, you haven't won a single hand yet. What do you want?"

His eyes moved with an aching slowness from where my pulse hammered at the base of my neck, across my chest, and down the length of my legs.

Heat pooled between my thighs, dampening my underwear. I tried not to squirm under his lazy assessment as I shifted on the blanket.

He let out a soft, grunt-like chuckle, and it filled the space between us. "Those ridiculous socks."

I looked down and wiggled my toes. The brightly colored toucans against a teal background danced as I moved my feet. "These are adorable."

"Just deal."

I placed two cards, face down, in front of each of us. Beckett peeked at the cards but gave nothing away. His eyes flicked from me back to his cards. His middle finger tapped his outer thigh.

"Fold."

"Ha!" I raised a fist in the air. "Chicken," I teased.

He pinned me with an unamused glare.

"Hand it over . . . that shirt's mine." I moved my elbows outward. "Bawk, bawk."

Beckett huffed out a breath, then pushed his cards in my direction. He reached behind his head, grabbed the collar of his shirt, and pulled it off. In a swift movement, he tossed the shirt in my face, and I caught it with a peal of laughter. The warm, leathery scent of his aftershave surrounded me, and I fought the urge to press the shirt to my nose and inhale. Instead I feigned disgust, but tucked the shirt under my leg.

Up close, his body was even more impressive. Cut abs with a light smattering of chest hair. My fingers itched to see if it felt as soft as it looked. When I glanced up, Beckett was staring at me with a satisfied smirk, having caught me eye fucking him.

I pushed the cards toward him. "You deal."

He quickly grabbed them and started shuffling. "What's the bet?"

I clenched my jaw to keep from grinning. "Your boots." I wrinkled my nose. "Unless your feet stink."

He nodded and looked at me. "Your tank top'll do."

My eyebrows lifted. "Oh, feeling confident now, are we?"

Beckett didn't answer but dealt two cards to each of us. I swallowed hard and painted on a smile of cool indifference as I looked at them.

Hell yeah.

A pair of fives was a healthy start.

I schooled my face and watched for any tells Beckett might give away. Without breaking eye contact, he dealt out three more cards, face up, between us. *Nine. Queen. Nine.*

My heart raced.

"I'll see your T-shirt and raise you . . ." My eyes moved lower to his belt buckle. "Those jeans."

Beckett cleared his throat and checked his cards again. Anticipation hummed under my skin.

"I'll call." He dipped his chin in my direction as his gravelly voice lowered. "Your shorts."

My tongue moved to my cheek as I calmed my breathing. Beckett turned over the next community card between us.

Three.

I lifted my chin and tried to give nothing away. "I'll check."

"Nervous?"

I smiled primly at him. "Just hoping you'll fold."

He smirked, and nerves sent a tingle down my back. "I'll raise. Those socks are coming off."

"Fine. Yours too."

Beckett turned over the last community card.

Ten.

He lifted his eyebrow and waited.

"Check." I knew I was the one being a chickenshit, but he was impossible to read.

A low sound rattled in his throat. "All in."

"All in? As in . . ." I waved a hand in front of me. "Everything?"

"You're either in or you're out, Princess."

I checked my cards again. Two pairs were better than nothing, and I wouldn't have put it past him to bluff. "You're on. All in."

He wiggled his fingers in my direction. "Let's see them."

I flipped over my cards. "Ha! Two pair—fives and nines." I folded my arms over my chest to hide how tight my nipples were beneath my shirt.

His lips pressed together as he studied my cards with a frown. "Not bad."

My eyes grew wide. *I knew it! He* had *been bluffing.*

Beckett turned over his cards and lifted his eyes to my face. "Just not as good as mine."

My heartbeat thunked between my ears.

A fucking straight. No, no, no, no, no . . .

Beckett leaned back on the blanket, and his eyes made a lazy pass over me. "Well, let's go."

I lifted my chin and swallowed hard.

A bet was a bet . . . right?

My hand slid over my knee and down my leg. Beckett's gaze was hot on my skin as I made a show of moving down my thigh and calf. I slipped my socks off one at a time.

I rose to my knees, letting my fingertips drag over my clothing until I reached the hem of my tank top. He tracked every slow movement. Gathering the material, I gently lifted the shirt up and over my head.

Beckett stared, frozen but for his fingers flexing on his half-finished glass of bourbon. My breaths were heavy, nipples tight, skin on fire.

Bourbon and wine swam in my veins, infusing me with a hint of sex kitten confidence I'd never fully embraced. I licked my lower lip and opened the button of my jean shorts. Tooth by metal tooth, I lowered the zipper.

Beckett's palm moved over the front of his jeans. He adjusted himself, and a flush of desire heated my skin.

My hands paused at my hips. "You're really going to make me get naked?"

Untethered darkness swirled in his pewter eyes. "We had a bet, Princess. You lost."

The hard, commanding edge of his voice was more intoxicating than the expensive bourbon. If he'd told me to get on all fours and beg, I would probably do it . . . and like it.

Emboldened, I stood in front of him and let my shorts drop to the floor. Hips cocked, I posed with one hand planted at my side.

Every inch of me was on fire as Beckett held me under

his intense stare. No hiding it, pure appreciation and *hunger* were painted on his tense features.

An achy throb between my legs ratcheted up my confidence. "How about another bet, Beckett?"

Standing in front of him, I watched and waited. His labored breathing was the only sound outside of the rain beating against the windows.

Still leaning back on his arms, he stretched his long legs across the blanket. "What do you got?"

I bit back a smile. Liquid courage swam through me, and I didn't give a second thought to the words coming out of my mouth as I lowered to my knees to be level with him. "I bet you look down."

A muscle in his jaw twitched, but his eyes stayed squarely on mine. "Try me."

Reaching behind me, I unclasped my bra and let it fall to the ground between us. The weight of my breasts bounced, the cold air tweaking my already hard nipples.

Beckett sucked in a sharp breath but didn't look away. "If I can't look, you can't either. Get over here."

Pulled by an invisible tether at his command, I crawled over to him, then lowered myself onto his lap. Through his jeans, his cock was rock hard. Long and firm, and it took everything inside me not to rub myself across his length and moan.

It was too much, too far.

I was straddling my ex-boyfriend's older brother on the floor of my aunt's kitchen, *begging* for him to lose the bet—to look at me, to put his hands on me and *devour* me.

Beckett's breaths came in harsh pants. His eyes roamed over my face but didn't dip lower. His hands flexed at his sides. My chest scraped against his, and a needy inhale sucked through my lips.

But he didn't give in. His hands stayed planted at his sides. The heat from my pussy was unbearable, but he didn't move a muscle. Mere inches separated our mouths. I looked down at his lips, then at where I sat on his lap, admiring how perfectly notched his erection was between my spread thighs.

He let out a grumble, and a smug smile pulled at the corners of his mouth. "You lose."

My eyes whipped to his. They were dark, and the realization that our game was over spread ice through my veins. He'd won when I looked down, and his real prize was leaving me keyed up and absolutely humiliated.

I leaned forward an inch, letting my breath float over his lips. "You're an asshole," I whispered.

In a swift move, I removed myself from Beckett's lap and didn't give him the satisfaction of a backward glance or a goodbye before gathering up my clothing and walking up to my bedroom.

When I slammed the door closed, I listened until, only moments later, I heard his truck start and drive away.

ELEVEN
BECKETT

Truth is, I lost the bet too.

When she'd lifted herself from my lap and turned to scoop up her discarded clothing, I'd gotten more than an eyeful.

A whole lot more.

The memory of the long lines of her legs, that perfect round ass, the way her underwear were damp and pressed to her pussy lips—those were memories I would take to my grave.

I had too much shit to take care of—namely, finding a way to keep my dick in check around Kate.

"What's up, man?" Duke's low voice shoved me from a tangle of thoughts that included what would have happened if I'd let myself touch her, just once. My eyes sliced to the man I claimed was my best friend, and a fresh wave of guilt washed over me.

Kate was his little sister, and I'd just been imagining driving into her while I held her hands down and she wrapped those long legs around me.

"Hey." I cleared my throat and tried to ignore the way

Duke was eyeing me. "I'm going to be back in the city for a few days."

Duke nodded and walked in step with me away from his truck and up the main sidewalk of Outtatowner. "Kate finally got to you?"

I only managed a low chuckle. A sick part of me liked the fire in her eyes when I pushed her buttons, and I hated to admit that it was a turn-on when she called me an asshole. She'd gotten to me, all right, just not in the way Duke was imagining.

I shook my head. "Just work. I need to check in on a few jobs, get them started. Pop into the office so they know I'm alive."

Duke stopped short on the sidewalk. "I know you're giving up a lot to be here. It hasn't gone unnoticed, and I'm sorry if Kate is making things harder for you."

I covered my burst of laughter with a cough. "She's fine. This has nothing to do with her." *Lie.* I stepped toward the entrance to the Sugar Bowl while Duke stood on the sidewalk, staring up at the wooden sign. "What's your deal? Come on."

My best friend stood, silent. His eyes flicked to the busy interior of the popular bakery. A muscle in his jaw twitched.

"Okay, well, I'm going to get a coffee before I hit the road. Do you want anything, or are you planning on getting older while you stand outside?"

My jab got his attention, and he pulled open the door. Inside, the bakery was filled with both townies and tourists. Much like the Grudge, if you knew what to look for, you'd see small groupings of Kings and Sullivans, never intermingled. Tourists made plans for the day or carried bags of knickknacks, while townies casually read newspapers or gossiped with each other.

Although the farm supplied the Sugar Bowl with fresh, local blueberries, in the time I'd known him, Duke almost never visited the bakery. I looked over the menu even though I always got the same thing.

When it was my turn, I stepped up to the register and was greeted by one of the teenage kids Huck typically hired for summer help. "Morning. Large coffee. Black." I turned to Duke, who was looking around the shop with his arms crossed. "What do you want?"

He turned to me just as someone pushed through the swinging doors that separated the kitchen from the front of the bakery. Carrying a tray of freshly baked pastries, she stopped in her tracks, staring up at Duke.

"You."

Duke nodded at her but looked away. "Sylvie."

For a beat, she stared up at him wide eyed before refocusing her attention. "Is . . . is Huck expecting a delivery?"

He only stared at the blonde, looking more annoyed than usual, so I jumped in. "Just getting a cup before I head out." I saluted with the to-go cup I was handed.

Her eyes flicked to mine, and she offered a tense smile. "Great."

Sylvie lowered her head and began arranging the pastries in the glass display case. I paid for my coffee and tossed a few extra dollars in the tip jar before turning back to my friend.

"What the hell was that?" I asked.

"Are we done? I have to get back." Duke stomped toward the door and paused only when he was back on the sidewalk.

I shook my head. "What was that about?" I asked again.

He shrugged. "I have no idea what you're talking about."

I looked at him just long enough to let him know I thought he was being a fucking weirdo.

"What?" he asked. "Your family doesn't hate anyone?"

I smirked. "Oh, my parents hate a lot of people, but the way they get even is by becoming best friends and not so subtly one-upping each other and being generally condescending."

Duke nodded. "Nice."

I spread my hands. "The soul-sucking games of the wealthy."

"How'd you stay normal then?"

I looked over at him. "Guess I had a farmer as a best friend to keep me grounded."

Duke looked down the long road toward Lake Michigan. "You ever think about it? Moving here?" I glanced at him and he shrugged. "Lots of rich vacationers looking for custom homes. The city is only a two-hour car ride away."

I shook my head. "Nah. I love it here, but my business is in Chicago. My whole life."

"Yeah, that's true. I'd probably get sick of having to run interference between you and Katie's bickering anyway."

The mere mention of my best friend's little sister had my pulse galloping. *Did he know?*

"I, uh . . . I think we're finally coming to some kind of agreement. Getting to a place of understanding, maybe."

Duke laughed. "Could have fooled me. This morning she spent fifteen minutes complaining about how hardheaded and arrogant you are. That girl has it out for you, man, and I've never known her to hate anyone."

I shook my head and squinted against the sun. "Yeah.

Not a big fan of the Millers. I can see that." I stuck out my hand, hoping to steer the conversation away from his sister. "The crew knows what to do. I'll see you in a few days."

~

"What's got you smiling?" Gloria, my office manager, lowered herself into the leather chair across from me.

I quickly locked my phone and set it face down on my desk. "Nothing important."

Gloria was a seasoned manager, and there was no way in hell I'd be able to get as much done or be as efficient without her help. Where I could visualize a space and know exactly what needed to be done, she was the queen of spreadsheets and expense reports. Without her, I was sure I would have run Miller Custom Homes into the ground within a year, simply because I couldn't be bothered with things like billing and micromanaging my schedule.

"Well, I didn't mean to interrupt, but since I have you, I wanted to give you a rundown of the current projects."

I nodded and gave her my full attention.

"This Michigan project . . ." Gloria lifted a white eyebrow in my direction. "You realize you're severely undercharging, correct?"

I tried to stifle a smile. Gloria was a fierce business-woman under the sweater sets and pearls she loved so much. "I'm aware."

Gloria continued. "Because of the attention that *project* requires of you, the only other job open is the office space on Madison. The crew should wrap that in the next day or so. I have the punch list." She slid a piece of paper across my desk. It was beautifully organized, and I smiled at her.

"Don't know what I would do without you, Gloria. Marry me?"

She smiled. "You couldn't handle me, sweet boy. It's humorous you think you could even try." It was a running joke between the two of us. It didn't matter that she was happily married and nearly thirty years my senior. She knew as well as I did that I wasn't the marrying type.

"Back to the Michigan project," she continued. "While I stand by my assessment that we could bring in nearly triple what you're currently charging . . ."

"Not about the money." I sat back in my chair, amused when her eyes rolled upward.

"As I was saying." She cleared her throat. "Apparently you have become quite popular on Instagram. I've been fielding calls left and right about people wanting to hire you. We need to discuss your workload and the calendar."

"Send over the requests and I can review them."

"It's a lot."

"How many is a lot?"

She considered. "Fifty-eight, give or take."

I sat up in my chair. "Fifty-eight?"

"That's just in the last few weeks. A lot of people are assuming that you and the woman who runs the Instagram account are a team."

I swallowed past the lump in my throat. "That's the homeowner's niece."

She stood and lifted her hands. "That's what I explained. Seems a lot of people are interested in hiring the pair." Gloria stepped to the open doorway. "For what it's worth, her account is gaining legs. It might not be a bad idea to lean into the whole Brutish Builder thing." Her eyes flicked over me, and I frowned at her. "Not that it's a stretch for you." Her laugh floated through the office as she left.

A pair. Kate and I, working together.

The idea was ludicrous. She knew nothing about building or home renovation outside what she could google or watch on YouTube. I leaned back and opened my phone. When Gloria had walked in, I'd been studying the most recent *Home Again* post Kate had uploaded.

She was sitting on the top stair of the farmhouse with construction debris all around her. Across from her was the local business owner who'd supplied the lumber for the new porch. The snapshot had caught Kate smiling as they shared a cup of coffee in the early dawn hours. Light slanted through the trees in the distance, chickens pecked around on the ground below them, and whatever filter Kate had applied to the picture gave it an ethereal feel.

Nearly two thousand likes.

Kate had used the post to highlight the small business and also to discuss locally sourced lumber versus purchasing from a big-box store. She might not have realized it, but with one post, she'd likely single-handedly boosted sales for a struggling local business.

A wave of pride washed over me as I studied her smiling face. Her head was tipped back in laughter, her long legs tanned by the summer sun.

She should wear jeans in a construction site. She knows this—I've told her a hundred times to stop wearing those goddamn shorts.

The protective thought consumed me, and I wanted to say *fuck this* and drive straight back to Outtatowner just to tell her to cover her damn legs.

I scrubbed a hand over the stubble on my face. *What the hell is wrong with me?*

I was quietly torturing myself with thoughts of my little brother's ex-girlfriend. A girlfriend he'd never seemed to care all that much about, but the wounded look on her face whenever his name came up unsettled me.

I had already crossed a line with her—several, in fact—and I didn't need any more guilt riding my ass. I pulled up Declan's number and fired off a text, asking if he'd be free for dinner. I hoped seeing him would reaffirm the fact I needed to stay far, far away from Kate.

When he confirmed, I sent him the time and location, grabbed the punch list from my desk, and headed out to the Madison Street office space. If I buried myself in work, I wouldn't have time to think about small coastal towns and the irresistible women who lived there.

TWELVE
KATE

"Naked? Like *naked* naked?" Annie's wide eyes looked up from the novel she was reading as we stretched out on the beach.

"Topless? In panties?" I grimaced and peeked out from behind my sunglasses, trying to gauge her reaction to the bomb I'd just dropped. It had been three days since my alcohol-fueled boldness had me straddling Beckett Miller and practically begging him to make a move.

Three days since he'd humiliated me and then disappeared.

"I thought you hated him?" Annie couldn't hide the doubt that creeped into her voice.

"I mean, I did. I *do.*"

"Mm-hmm."

I peeked over at Annie and scrunched my face. "Is it totally terrible of me that I think it's kind of hot?"

Annie shrugged. "Nothing's hotter than something that's forbidden."

"I guess. That has to be it, right? I mean . . . nothing

could ever happen. He's Declan's *brother*. And don't get me started on the epic freak-out Duke would have . . ."

"You know, he totally scared off that clingy guy at the bar the other night." Annie flipped another page of her novel.

"What?"

She grinned. "Oh yeah, Lee told me all about it. Apparently the guy told Beckett that he'd asked the bartender to make your drink extra strong to loosen you up." Annie made air quotes around *loosen you up*, and my stomach soured. "Beckett gave some bro-code Bat-Signal for Lee to intervene, and he was *not* happy about it."

My mind stumbled over the information.

Beckett intervened? Protected me? It was like my brain couldn't compute the new information. My insides were a jumble of nerves and energy. I couldn't think about him another second without wanting to scream.

Instead, I diverted attention from my current garbage fire of a love life and looked over at Annie. "Are you ever going to tell Lee that it was you?"

Annie's eyes were fierce. "Kate . . ."

I raised both my hands in the air. "What? I was just asking."

"It was a really long time ago."

"Yeah, but don't you think he deserves to know?"

"After the accident, those letters were all he had left of her. I couldn't take that from him."

I put my hand on Annie's arm. "Look, it's not my secret to tell, but for the record I think you should tell him. He deserves to know."

Her eyes fixed on the book in her hand and she turned the page. Clearly she was avoiding the uncomfortable conversation as much as I was avoiding having to talk about Beckett.

"So what are you going to do about Beckett?"

An unladylike snort escaped from my nose. "Do? Nothing. Pretend it didn't happen."

"Oh . . . deny, deflect, and completely ignore the situation? Sounds like a Sullivan thing to do."

I laughed and stretched out on my beach towel. Annie had grown up with kind foster parents, but she was a Sullivan through and through. Oftentimes I thought she knew us better than we knew ourselves.

Thankful for a new distraction, I tipped my chin toward the man walking directly toward us. "Incoming."

Annie looked up from her book and a blush stained her cheeks. Charles Attwater was tall and lean and had a swagger about him. A little bookish, but very handsome.

Annie raised her hand in greeting as he walked over. "Hey, Charles, you've met Katie, right?"

Charles casually squatted in front of us and extended a hand. A charming smile lifted the corner of his mouth. "I don't think I've had the pleasure."

I reached out my hand to him, and he held it delicately, pressing my knuckles to his lips. "Charles Attwater. It's nice to meet you."

I smiled and pulled my hand from his. "We've been enjoying your wine at book club."

Charles preened. "I'm delighted that a few lovely women are enjoying the selection."

"Seems like it's more than just a few. Everyone has been raving about the wine shop since you opened."

Charles settled back onto his haunches, enjoying the attention. "Business has been very good. I'm still thinking of new ways to continue to get the word out about the shop. Drum up a little excitement and get people through the door. Maybe highlight a few local business owners." He looked over at Annie and winked. "In fact, there is a certain local artist I had been hoping to chat with about selling a few pieces at the store."

"Wow, Charles. That would be incredible. I could have a few pieces to display. Something to incorporate the wine and the scenery . . . marry the two so that it's mutually beneficial for the businesses."

Charles offered her a slick smile, but it didn't quite reach his eyes. "I am definitely up for something that's mutually beneficial."

I glanced between the two of them, each seemingly oblivious to my presence.

"You know, there's a rumor in town that this fall festival is quite the spectacle," he said.

"The Fireside Flannel Festival?" I asked.

Annie grinned. "It is everything it promises to be. A festival, bonfires, and lots and lots of flannel."

Charles looked down at his chino shorts and short-sleeved button-down shirt. "Looks like I might have to do some shopping."

"You definitely have to wear flannel. That's a requirement."

Charles smiled at Annie, his pale-blue eyes sparking with flirtatious mischief.

"Is there dancing at this festival?"

"Definitely dancing," I chimed in. "Usually several local bands, and after the carnival dies down, it pretty much turns into the entire town having one big party."

"Well, maybe in addition to a new flannel shirt, I'll also have to dust off my dancing shoes. Save a dance for me, Annie?"

She looked up from her lowered lashes. "Of course."

Charles flipped a glance toward me and stood to his full height. "Ladies, I'll let you get back to your afternoon. Annie, it was a pleasure, as always."

The red that stained Annie's nose was no longer from our afternoon in the summer sun. I swatted her arm gently as she watched him walk down the beach. "You have a crush on him! And by the looks of it he's crushing back."

Annie grinned a cheesy smile. "I don't know . . . he seems kind of flirtatious with everyone, but when he turns his attention on me, it's hard to not get that fluttery feeling in my tummy."

My heart squeezed for Annie. She deserved this—a man who showered her with attention and gave her that buzzy, fluttery feeling. For so long she either wasn't interested or her relationship with my older brother tended to complicate things. Most people couldn't fathom how Annie and Lee had remained best friends for so long and never crossed that line.

I suspected I was one of the *very* few people who had protected Annie's secret for so long. At one time Annie's feelings crossed over into *not quite platonic* while Lee was overseas serving our country. But after he got back and everything went down with Margo, it all fell apart. Annie had sworn me to secrecy, and seeing how difficult it was for Lee to recover, I truly believed at the time that it was what was for the best.

But after my own relationship with Declan fell apart, and after coming home from Montana, it was hard to believe that was still the case.

Poor Lee.

~

I KICKED ASIDE an errant piece of cardboard and frowned at the ground. Only days ago, spread out on a moving blanket, I had been topless and straddling Beckett in nothing but my thong.

In the days since he disappeared, Aunt Tootie and I have been busy picking out stain and backsplash tile and materials for a really gorgeous open-shelf concept that I was planning to bug Beckett about.

I also pitched the random idea of adding a row of windows where Tootie could look out of the kitchen into the side yard, where she had her gardens. Sure, it wasn't in the original design, but aside from eliminating two cabinets, it wouldn't mess with the proposal Beckett had already drawn up. To be honest, I was thoroughly looking forward to the scowl he would shoot me when I told him about my amazing new plan.

Beckett's crew had also been hard at work and had removed the center wall, adding in a new header to support what was once a load-bearing wall. His team worked so efficiently I scrambled to track down the man in charge while Beckett was away. I had hoped to salvage the section of wall with my mother's handwriting on it, but when I asked him about it, he shrugged and pointed to the dumpster.

I searched among the nails and debris, but my efforts were hopeless. My chest ached for the loss of my mother, but also for the childhood that at one time had seemed so perfect. Since I didn't have the same memories my brothers did of my mother, her handwriting was a tangible piece of her that I had hoped to keep.

Defeated, and with the crew wrapped for the day, I scheduled my social media posts and decided it would be a good day to finally visit my dad.

Pulling up to Haven Pines, dread rolled through my

stomach. I was the one who had first noticed changes in Dad. It was subtle, him accidentally calling me June, my mother's name. Then he would forget the day of the week or seem more irritable than his typical upbeat self.

For a while I thought I was seeing things that weren't really there. But the subtle shifts became more and more apparent when the relationships with his business partners started suffering. Bills went unpaid. Duke stepped in and quite literally saved the family farm. Tootie and I did our best to care for Dad as his health continued to steadily decline.

Deep down, I knew I could use my father's illness as an excuse to not go away to college and instead hang around Outtatowner in hopes of garnering a real commitment from Declan. What I thought was a committed, long-distance relationship was in fact not. I hated myself for my own naivete.

The lobby of Haven Pines was brightly lit and cheery. I greeted the receptionist, whom I recognized but couldn't quite place. "Hi, I'm Kate. I'm here to see Red? Red Sullivan?"

The older woman smiled at me. "Katie Sullivan? Why, you sure did grow into those eyes!" She clicked her tongue as she assessed me. "Absolutely stunning. To think all the boys ran around calling you Catfish Kate! Who's laughing now!"

My cheeks burned at the reminder of my foolish home-town nickname. I could kill my brothers for coming up with it in the first place. I thought maybe after I left, everyone would just forget about it, but in a place like my hometown, there looked to be zero chance of that happening.

I followed the woman's directions and made my way toward the memory care ward of Haven Pines. After checking in at another nurses' station, they buzzed me into the section where my father was living. The hospital rooms were set up to look like a quaint neighborhood. Doors to the rooms were modeled after front doors to actual homes, and the outsides were landscaped flowers and faux windows and lampposts.

It had been a long time since I had visited my father here. Normally Duke or Lee would pick him up, and we could spend the afternoon with a short visit or a dinner at Tootie's house. His condition was stable, more or less, and we were grateful it hadn't continued to aggressively progress. With the house under construction, it had been hard to find a space that was safe and familiar for Dad.

I lifted the knocker and gently rapped it on the door.

"Coming!" My dad's gruff voice boomed from behind the door. A skittering of panic tickled my belly. *Please be a good day.*

The door opened and my father stood before me. His eyes peered out from the crack in the door. Time had weathered his face slightly, but he was still as handsome as always. Red Sullivan was tall and broad and strong.

My stomach dipped when I realized there was no recognition in the blue eyes staring back at me.

"Can I help you?"

I swallowed hard, but my smile wobbled. "Oh, hi. I'm Kate."

Something flickered over my father's face.

Don't panic. It's fine. This is fine.

"Kate? My Katie?" The door swung open, and my father pulled me into a big hug. "Well, goddamn, Katie. Didn't recognize you at first. You did something different with your hair, right?"

I didn't have the heart to tell my dad that my hair had

remained pretty much the same long brown since my teenage years. The simple truth was that he hadn't quite recognized me at first.

I breathed a sigh of relief as I melted into my father's embrace. "Hey, Dad. Just thought I would come by and say hi. See how you're doing."

"Well, that's fantastic news! I was just headed out for a walk. Care to join me?"

I smiled up at him as he closed the door to his room behind him. We walked down the hallway and around the corner. My dad waved or nodded at other residents and nurses as we walked. It was so much like walking through town in Outtatowner, only this time he was in assisted-living care without the freedom to come and go as he pleased.

"The new neighborhood is different, but it's for the best. I get forgetful sometimes." I looked up at him and wondered how cognizant he was of his condition and prognosis.

"It's really nice here, Dad." I leaned into him as he pulled me in and walked with me tucked under his arm.

"Tootie came by and told me about the updates to the house. Heard you're keeping that cocky builder in line."

My face flushed, thinking about Beckett and how out of line I had been only days before. "I just want it to be perfect for her. There are a lot of good memories in that house."

Dad's gaze grew fuzzy, and I wondered if he was temporarily lost to memories of the past. I wondered if he thought of our mother and how her illness had cut their loving marriage so short. Tears burned beneath my eyelids.

"You're a good one, Kate. I don't care what your brothers say about you," he teased.

I cleared my throat. "I started documenting the work on the house. Would you like to see it?"

I pulled my phone from my purse and flipped to the *Home Again* Instagram page, slowly scrolling through the photos. I stopped to point out the new flooring, how much bigger the new windows in the living room made the space feel, and how quickly the workers had torn apart the crumbling front porch.

"Well, I'll be damned. Your brother has been tight-lipped about the work they're doing on the house. I think he thinks I'm sentimental about it."

Duke was tight-lipped about most things, but he did always try to protect our father. To make sure that he had more good days than bad. As if that were in any of our control.

"Only thing special about that house were the people who lived in it. Your mama, you four kids. Hell, even Tootie, who picked up the pieces when I couldn't." Dad looked at me. "House is just a house."

My father's profound words clung to my ribs. To him it may have just been a house, but to me it was so much more.

My heart ached for that house. It was a monolith whose soul had been ripped from the inside.

If anyone could fix us, it had to be me, and an arrogant, know-it-all builder would not stand in my way.

THIRTEEN
BECKETT

My LITTLE BROTHER sat across from me in a perfectly tailored Tom Ford suit. His blond hair was cut short on the sides, and the longer top had been styled away from his face.

His cold blue eyes stared at me as he leaned back in his chair and pressed his fingertips together. "Surprised to hear from you, big brother. I thought you were holed up in that shitty tourist town."

"We used to love that town when we were kids."

"Sure, twenty years ago when our parents forced us to see how the other half lives."

I shook my head. "Yeah. It was real eye opening in a multimillion-dollar vacation home. I enjoy the coast, and I'm friends with Duke."

My brother adjusted the cuff of his shirt, and boredom glazed over his eyes. "The Sullivans and all their small-town charm." He wiped his hand across his clean-shaven jaw. "Have you seen Kate around? I should give her a call . . ."

My back stiffened, but I schooled my features into a

calm expression. "I don't get it, man. What happened between the two of you?"

Declan sipped his water and glanced around the restaurant. He shrugged. "It was on again, off again."

My brows pinched together. "Did she know that?"

Declan's face twisted like I was not getting his point. "It was casual. You know how it is with tourist-town girls . . . she was always around. An easy lay." Declan sucked in his lower lip and grinned. "You remember Isabella."

"Man, I was seventeen when we met Isabella and her sister in Venice."

Declan shook his head. "Those kinds of girls don't change. When Kate got the scholarship in Montana, it was the best thing that could have happened to me." He leaned forward. "When she started dropping words like *commitment* and *ring shopping* . . ." He shuddered. "Yeesh."

From across the dimly lit table, he studied me. "Why are you asking me about Kate? Is her brother giving you shit? Look, I swear, I didn't know she was going to show up in Chicago."

I ignored his questions, pressing him for more information as I tried to comprehend what he was telling me. "But you two were serious. You brought her to Christmas."

Declan grinned. "Genius, right? I brought her because she's hot and polite enough to keep Mom off my back."

My throat tightened.

Jesus Christ. He'd used her for years, and she hadn't realized it until it was too late. Until her heart was already primed to be shattered. And I thought I was the biggest prick in the family.

An unexpected surge of protectiveness coursed through me as I stared down at my little brother. I had always known

he was an arrogant and entitled little shit, but I was beginning to realize he was also a complete and total asshole—the
cruelest kind of person, and he'd led Kate to believe she was
the center of his world when really she was nothing more
than convenient entertainment.

On the outside, it may not appear I have much in
common with my best friend, but Duke and I shared more
of a bond than my brother and I ever would. There was
absolutely nothing shared with Declan other than a fucked-
up family history.

I despised the fact that Declan knew exactly how soft
Kate's skin felt.

"You know what, little brother? You may see it as a
throwaway town with people who don't matter, but that
town shows up for its people." I stood, my chair scraping
across the hand-hewn wood floors, and tossed a few
hundred-dollar bills on the table, knowing full well Declan
had the money but wouldn't have even bothered to reach for
his wallet. "It's the whole reason the town keeps calling me
back."

∿

It had been over a week since I had finalized the
completion of the build in Chicago. Tootie's farmhouse was
the only open project I had going on, and it was official:
Kate was avoiding me.

She flitted around the jobsite, offering her opinion to my
crew and taking pictures for *Home Again*, but she was very
careful to avoid any and all interactions with me.

Her carefree laughter grated my nerves. I spent my
afternoons sneaking glances, and when the distraction of

her presence caused me to smash my thumb with a hammer, I was done.

"Fuck!" I sucked my thumb into my mouth. While we were waiting for cabinets to be built, I had started crafting custom shutters for the farmhouse.

A car pulled up, and Annie and Lark, Wyatt Sullivan's girlfriend, stepped out. They were both dressed in flannel shirts and denim jeans, as the summer evenings had started their descent into cooler September nights.

"Hey, Beckett," Annie called, raising her hand. Her bright-red curls lifted in the breeze, and she tamped them down with her hand.

Lark offered a bright smile and a wave, and I lifted my chin and grunted a greeting.

"It's looking great out here," Lark called as she surveyed the disastrous construction site. "Everyone is so thankful for the help."

"Yeah, especially Katie," Annie chimed in.

Lark gently hip checked her and whispered something, making them both laugh. I lowered my head and went back to work on the custom shutters.

I could hear the front door open, and I tried not to look up as Kate bounded down the stairs. Tight denim molded to her ass and thighs, running all the way down her legs. They were cuffed at the bottom and stacked on top of short, Western-style boots. She was the epitome of a girl-next-door, small-town wet dream.

I knew what those thighs felt like straddling my hips, and I cursed myself for the millionth time for not having wrapped my hands around those hips and squeezed, just to get an idea of what Kate would feel like bouncing on my dick.

The green flannel shirt she wore was tied up around her slim waist, and the taut bare skin of her stomach made my throat dry. A tiny white tank top stretched across her chest. I knew from being only inches away from them that her breasts would be soft but firm in my palms.

I continued to hammer on the shutters, joining the pieces and ignoring the ache in my gut.

"Are you coming up to the Fireside Flannel Festival?" Annie asked. The three women paused, and Katie popped a hand on her hip, waiting for my response.

I shook my head and looked back down at my work. "Nope."

A disgusted noise shot out of Katie's nose, and the girls piled into Annie's car, leaving me scowling down at my sore thumb.

Duke and Lee would be up at the festival. Hell, the entire town would be. It was an annual kickoff to fall, with beach bonfires and a carnival that turned into a weekend of dancing and drinking. Live bands would play country music classics and Top 40 hits, while townies and tourists welcomed fall with the kitschy charm only a small town like Outtatowner could bring.

The Fireside Flannel Festival was nothing like the elegant galas my parents often frequented. They would be horrified that instead of $2,000 per plate dinners, the folks of Outtatowner would be washing down hot dogs and funnel cakes with cheap beer.

I sat back on my heels and sighed. *A cheap, cold beer sounds pretty fucking good right now.*

I pulled up my texts from Duke and asked him if he was still planning to head out there.

DUKE: *Already saved you a seat, brother.*

Wiping my dirty hands on my jeans, I packed up my tools for the day and secured the farmhouse before loading up my truck. After a hot shower and a change of clothes, I would head up there, and it would have absolutely nothing to do with the nagging desire to keep an eye on Kate Sullivan.

FOURTEEN
BECKETT

Downtown Outtatowner had been transformed from a tourist coastal town to the annual fall festival, with twinkle lights strung between the lampposts that lined the main thoroughfare through town.

The closer to the beach I walked, the more densely populated it became. Kids buzzing from a sugar high of cotton candy and fried Twinkies zoomed between parents. The crashing waves of Lake Michigan were inaudible over the artificial, tinny music blaring from the carnival rides. Cheering and laughter melted together until it was a nearly unrecognizable throb of sounds.

A portion of the main public beach was sectioned off to allow for town-managed bonfires to line the waterfront and draw in those wanting a break from the lights and sounds of the carnival. While I would have much preferred my own bonfire on the private beach in front of my house, there was something charming and inviting about gathering to have a good time with friends and neighbors.

I checked my phone again, confirming that Duke was grabbing food at the Snack Shack, and I headed in that direction. He hated crowds even more than I did, so I was pretty sure I could convince him to close the night out at my place . . . after I got my eyes on Kate again.

"Glad you could make it out." Duke whacked a hand on my back in greeting. "I was worried you were going to work yourself to death over there."

I shrugged and looked over the menu, even though it hadn't changed since I was twelve.

"The progress you've made is phenomenal. I've been following the updates on Kate's posts, but to see it in person doesn't even do it justice."

That was an understatement, considering I'd thrown myself into the work and had doubled our rate of progress over the past week. Being in such proximity to Kate was driving me mad. The sooner I finished the house, the sooner I could forget all about that particular long-legged brunette with enchanting green eyes.

Lee's laughter drew my attention. "C'mon. Do it. Do the face."

From a few feet away, Kate scowled at her brother. "No."

He directed his shit-eating grin at her. "Please? I haven't seen it in so long, and I missed you and that face." Lee was an expert at ratcheting up the charm and poking at Kate to get his way.

Kate's eyes flew to the night sky. She sucked her cheeks into her mouth to form a perfect little fish face. I coughed to cover my laugh, realizing she really did kind of look like a catfish.

Lee cheered and flung an arm across her shoulders.

"I hate you." She playfully pushed him away.

Pink stained her cheeks as she looked at me. Lee loved getting under his little sister's skin and doing what he could to embarrass her, but what she didn't realize was that even with that ridiculous face, she still looked so fucking cute.

I accepted the plastic cup of beer Duke slid in front of me and nodded a greeting at Wyatt. His nose was buried in Lark's hair, and she was wrapped around him, giggling at something he'd said. Something akin to envy flashed through my mind.

I looked down the beach, noticing the crowded bonfires. Lots of unfamiliar faces with only a handful I recognized. Outtatowner was changing, and something about that unsettled me.

Duke wiped his hand on a napkin and tossed it into the trash. "Hang on. I gotta go take care of something."

My eyes moved to the group of Kings, who always seemed to appear as though they were looking for trouble. "Want some help with this?"

Wyatt had already stepped to Duke's side when his shoulders tensed and his voice turned hard. "Yeah, you better."

Together we walked up to the group of Kings, who were shooting the shit near a bonfire.

Duke stepped up to JP King. "Hey, you've been driving through my west pasture?"

JP and his brothers looked over at Duke. "Man, I have no idea what you're talking about."

Duke took one step into his space.

Here we go.

"That's bullshit and you know it. This is the second time I have found tracks near our land, and you're the only one with a shiny new four-by-four."

A guy I didn't recognize stepped forward. "He said it wasn't us."

Duke looked him over as we started drawing the attention of a crowd. "It better not be. If I find out that you're up to something or messing with our land, we are going to have issues. Filling my truck with balloons or towing Royal's car across town is one thing, but messing with a family's liveli-hood is low. Even for a King." Duke spit their last name like it tasted foul in his mouth.

"Why don't you back the fuck up?" Royal King stepped between Duke and JP.

My fist clenched. I was ready to pop someone in the jaw if it came down to it. The town may be divided, but my loyalties were firmly planted in Sullivan territory.

Ever since I was a kid, the Kings had been known to be dangerous. Reckless. The fact that they had more money than God gave them a sense they ran this town, when in reality it pissed them off that the Sullivans were the back-bone of Outtatowner.

"Hey, guys, seriously?" Lark stepped next to the men, seemingly unafraid of the crackling tension. I looked at Wyatt, who stood with his arms crossed and a smug, self-satisfied look on his face.

Apparently he thinks Lark can handle it.

She looked at Royal. "Come on. I thought we came to an understanding."

Duke's eyes flashed to Wyatt and then to Lark. "What the hell is that supposed to mean?"

Royal smirked, and it should've been enough for him to earn that fist to the jaw. "Don't worry about it. That's between me and Lark."

Wyatt barked a laugh, and Lark rolled her eyes. "Stop stirring shit, Royal." She focused on Duke. "When a few of Wyatt's players got into trouble, he talked to Lucian and asked him not to press charges. *That was it.* Nothing more happened, and you all know it." She pointed her finger and chastised the group of adult men with a single look.

JP lifted his chin. "I told you before, Duke. Wasn't any of us."

Duke looked the small group over once more and spat on the ground. "It better not be."

He looked at me and tipped his chin. "Come on, let's go."

I pinned Katie with a glare as she stared wide eyed from the sidelines. I didn't want to make a scene, but she damn sure wasn't staying near the Kings with the tensions between the families at an all-time high. Annie looped her arm around Kate's and pulled her with us as we all walked back toward the pier.

Jutting out into Lake Michigan was a restored lighthouse that served as the backdrop for Outtatowner and a popular tourist spot for pictures and fishermen. The marina stretched along the pier, and tucked into an artificial alcove was a small stage. A local band was deep into a set of country classics, and a local brewery owned by the Kings sold drinks.

"All right." Lark sighed. "If you boys are done comparing dick sizes, I want to dance."

In agreement, the women walked together toward the makeshift dance floor. Lee brought over a round of drinks, and I gazed into a lukewarm beer, trying not to stare as Kate's cheers and poorly sung lyrics floated above the crowd.

After a few songs a blonde stepped up next to me. She tapped her hand against the outside of her thigh in time to the beat. I looked over at her and caught her eye.

Her grin widened. "I like this song."

"Yeah, it's a good one."

She nodded toward the dance floor. "Would you like to dance?"

My back tightened. "No, thanks," I grumbled. "I'm content here, just holding up this table."

She laughed at my shitty joke and nodded. "Well, if you change your mind, I'll be just over there." She pointed toward a nearby table and a group of women who pretended to not be taking in our conversation.

When she was out of earshot, Duke knocked me on the shoulder with his fist. "Hell is wrong with you, dude?"

I shot a quick glance toward his sister but lowered my eyes to my drink before taking a healthy gulp. "I don't know, man. Just don't feel like dancing."

Duke looked back over at the group of women. "Well, I don't recognize them. So if you want your chance, tonight is probably all you've got."

My thoughts ran back to Declan's comment about easy women and vacation towns. Whether it was a tourist or a townie, I wasn't interested in being that kind of man.

"What about you?" I asked.

Duke only scoffed and drank another sip of his beer. "No, man. That ship has sailed."

As close as we'd become over the years, we'd never really talked deeply about our relationships. We both seemed content in our solitude, and besides the occasional short-term relationship or weekend fling, we never really talked about women.

He certainly would be shocked to find out about the incessant thoughts I had been having about his little sister.

When the music slowed, I let my eyes roam over the dance floor.

"Who the fuck is that?" I asked without thinking.

Some douchebag in Dockers and a tight flannel shirt spun Kate and pulled her into an overly dramatic dip.

Duke followed my gaze and smiled. "Oh, hey. That's John Mercer. Went to our high school. I think either Lee's class or maybe the one right after." Duke shrugged. "Don't worry about it. He's a decent guy."

Jealousy burned through my gut as I watched him step on her toes. Katie giggled, then swatted at his chest.

I didn't give a shit if he was the nicest guy on the planet. I didn't like his fumbling arms around her.

I scowled as he stumbled through another song, and instead of feeling pity for her incredibly left-footed dance partner, her cute smile grew wider, and she pulled him into an affectionate side hug.

When the music slowed again to a sad country ballad, I finished my beer and set it on the table with a plop.

I cleared my throat and wiped my hands on the front of my jeans. "I'll be right back."

I didn't bother looking back at the table as I headed straight toward Kate. I ignored the hopeful smile of the blonde from earlier as I breezed right past her.

Standing next to Kate and her dance partner, I towered over him by at least six inches. My eyes burned into hers. "May I have this dance?"

Kate's eyes widened, and I was fully prepared for her to laugh in my face, but she stood silent.

"I . . . I think we were . . . ," John stammered.

"It's okay," Kate cut in. Her palm landed gently on his chest, and she smiled sweetly at him. "Thanks for the dances, John. Let's catch up again soon."

His eyes moved to mine as his jaw clenched, but the man knew when he had lost.

With a resigned nod, he took one step back. "You two have a good night."

As the music floated around us, Kate stared up at me with stunned eyes. I opened my arms, and she silently stepped into my embrace. Her palm slid into the expanse of mine, and I curled my fingers around her delicate hand. My other hand slipped around her trim waist, my calloused fingertips smoothing across the soft, exposed skin above her hip.

Kate tipped her head back to meet my eyes, and her brunette waves tumbled over her shoulder, exposing the delicate column of her neck. Her heartbeat hammered beneath the thin skin, and I wanted to plant my mouth on that pulse point until I could feel her heartbeat radiate through me.

I stared down at her.

Kate blinked. "Suddenly felt like dancing?"

A soft smile teased the corner of my lips as I looked down at her face, flushed from dancing and laughing. "I've been watching him step on your feet for the last three songs. I couldn't stand it anymore. Figured maybe you were looking for someone who can dance."

Kate squeezed my hand, and her smile had my heart banging against my ribs.

"By all means, show me what you got."

At her challenge, I started moving her around the dance floor. Not quite a two-step, but I managed to guide her and move her to the beat. The inches disappeared between us as we swayed to the music. Soft, golden light bounced off her radiant skin. Her delicate floral scent filled my lungs, and I pulled her closer.

"Are we ever going to talk about the poker game?" Her voice was barely audible above the music.

I paused to stare down at her. "We can. Just not tonight. Not right now. Let's just enjoy this."

Kate exhaled and leaned in, melting into my embrace. "Okay."

I held Kate against me until the song ended. When the band transitioned to something new, we stayed planted, staring at each other.

Unmoving.

Her eyes dipped to my lips, and I almost did it. My hand was ready to capture the back of her head, tilt her at the perfect angle until I could take her mouth.

Claim her.

Never let her go.

Instead, I ground my teeth together and left her staring at my back as I walked away.

FIFTEEN
KATE

"WHAT THE HELL WAS THAT?" Annie stepped up next to me as I watched Beckett stomp off and disappear into the crowd.

My heart hammered against my ribs. My legs wobbled. "I have absolutely no idea."

Lark planted her hands on her hips and pointed in the direction of his exit. "That man wants you. *Bad.*"

A lump formed in my throat, and I swallowed hard. Flushed, I fanned my hot skin. "I think I need something to drink."

"I need a bucket of ice water. The way you two moved together? How he held you like there was no one else in the world? Holy fuck, that was hot." Lark laughed as we moved through the crowded dance floor and back toward the outskirts of the alcove.

We each got a cup of water from the bar area, and I gulped mine down in three chugs. Annie and Lark stared at me as I continued to scan the crowd for any sign of Beckett.

Together Lee and Wyatt walked up, and Lee threw a

friendly arm over Annie's shoulders. "I saw Beckett storm off. What did you say to him now, Katie?"

Lark snorted and covered her laugh with a cough as Wyatt scowled down at her.

I looked, wide eyed, at my brothers and shook my head. "Why are his pissy moods always my fault?"

Duke walked up, slipping his phone into the back pocket of his jeans. "Beckett texted. He headed home."

Coward.

Duke scanned the crowd one last time. "I'm out of here. Anyone need a ride?"

Irritated, I tossed the plastic cup in a nearby garbage bin. "I'll go with you."

After saying our goodbyes, Duke and I walked up the long sidewalk, past the marina and toward his truck, which was parked on a quiet side street. My eyes peered into the heavy darkness, knowing only three blocks up was Beckett's house.

I wanted to storm over there, bang on his door, and demand he talk to me. Instead I climbed into the cab of Duke's truck and folded my arms over my chest like a petulant child.

Silence filled the truck as he headed toward the farmhouse. When he cleared his throat, I looked over at my brother.

"So, uh . . . you and Beckett."

My stomach dropped, and my eyes flashed to his.

When I stayed quiet, Duke sighed. "I'm not an idiot, you know."

Heat flooded my cheeks. I wanted to dissolve into the seat of the truck and disappear altogether. I suddenly felt thirteen again, having to listen to Duke lecture me about crushing on his friends and how uncomfortable that made everyone.

"I know it's difficult, with him being Declan's brother. You have every right to be hurt, but I really wish you'd give him a chance to do this renovation right. You've been really aggressive. What Declan did to you wasn't his fault."

Wait a minute . . . what?

"Just don't ride his ass so hard," Duke continued. "He's doing us all a huge favor."

Riding his *ass* was not at all where I thought this conversation was going. I shifted in my seat, my eyes lowered to my hands. "Yeah, I know."

"Can you please talk to him? Try to get along—for me?"

I offered a small smile as my stomach swirled. "Of course. He and I will work something out."

Duke pulled into the long, darkened driveway to the farmhouse. I was more determined than ever to figure out what the hell was really going on between Beckett and me. There was something brewing between us that I couldn't fully explain, but I was determined to peel back the layers of our complicated *situationship* and get to the bottom of it.

Like the dutiful brother he was, Duke waited until I was up the steps and had unlocked the front door before offering a wave and heading home.

Duke didn't want me riding Beckett's ass, but I was pretty sure riding his dick wasn't an option either.

Unless . . .

With renewed giddy anticipation, I brushed my teeth and headed to bed, ready to see just how many buttons I could push before Beckett Miller finally pushed back.

∾

ON THURSDAY the crew flew into a fervor when I dropped the bomb that I wanted to make a few changes to the original design plans. New wiring was underway for the entirely updated layout to the kitchen. With the center wall removed, the space was already more open and airy. Beckett had caved and agreed that the additional windows helped brighten the space.

Add one point for Kate.

Beckett had barely grumbled two words to me, but he was going to have to toughen up, because despite the simmering tension between us, we needed to make forward progress, and I had an idea that was perfect.

His back was to me, and he was checking something off his metal clipboard when I walked up. "Okay, so don't be mad."

His back stiffened, and he slowly turned to face me.

I offered a bright smile. "I have an idea."

He immediately sighed and dropped his hands at his sides.

I raised my palms. "Hear me out . . ." I walked in a wide circle around him. "What if"—I stepped through the small doorway from the kitchen to the large mudroom at the back of the house—"we borrow half of this space for a walk-in pantry?"

I clamped my fists together and planted them under my chin, infusing hope into the look I gave him.

His nostrils flared.

I stepped farther into the space. "It's just a matter of opening this doorway and adding a wall to separate it from the back entrance. This area is huge and doesn't really make sense. Why have this huge mudroom taking up a perfectly good back entrance? A smaller entryway is plenty for Tootie to shuck off her boots and a *walk-in* pantry?" I blew air between my lips and casually swatted that air between us. "Come on. A simple build for you and the crew."

Instead of obsessing over the dance I'd shared with him, I'd chosen to fall down a Pinterest rabbit hole instead.

"Let me guess. You saw it on Pinterest."

A laugh shot out of me. "What? No."

Beckett looked back down at his clipboard, then glanced around me into the large back entryway. "Does Tootie know about this?"

Excitement danced through me. "She enthusiastically gave the green light."

A delicious muscle ticced in his jaw. "I suppose the space could be more efficient, and a large pantry would modernize it." He looked through the paperwork on his clipboard again. "But we're not cutting this area off."

His eyes scanned the large area and went slightly unfocused, as they often did when he was designing in his head. "The back entryway will open up to here." He gestured with his hands, and the corded muscles of his forearms flexed and danced. "Instead of a walk-in pantry eating up that space, we can borrow from the back bedroom closet to get a better footprint. That way, everything flows—one room into the next. I'm thinking, in order to transition the spaces, instead of hardwood, we do exposed Chicago brick for the utility space. Rustic and durable."

Beckett painted a gorgeous picture of a functional, modern farmhouse. It was absolutely perfect.

"That's how we'll do it." He made a few notes on his clipboard, and irritation crept up my spine at the finality in his tone.

"Why do you always have to do things your way?"

He glanced up at me and scoffed before looking back over his notes. "Because, Princess, my way is usually the right way."

"I haven't agreed to it."

Beckett sighed and tossed his clipboard on the old utility bench with a clatter. "Kate, I'm not going to argue with you about this again. You wanted to make the changes in the first place. I know what I'm doing, and you talk too much."

I narrowed my eyes as I glared at him. Beckett was the most frustrating human on the planet. I sucked in a deep breath, ready to toss in a few jabs and argue a little bit before ultimately agreeing to the updates exactly as he'd laid them out.

"First of all—"

A flash of darkness swept across Beckett's gray eyes before he took one step and crowded my space. One hand clamped around my jaw as he advanced and pressed my back against the wall. His mouth swallowed my argument in a hot, rough kiss.

Stuck between the wall and his hard body, a shocked gasp slipped between my lips. His hand was rough, demanding. My body reacted, and one leg lifted to his hip. Beckett's free hand gripped my thigh, driving my back harder against the wall.

Every inch of him was solid and tense. His tongue swept across my lips, demanding I open for him. His rough palm moved lower, circling my throat. I opened for him with a gasp, and he groaned into me. The rattle of his deep grunt vibrated through me. His lips were soft but firm, and there was no tenderness in the kiss, only a steady demand of Beckett completely claiming me.

He pulled himself off me, and my breath was ragged. The back of my hand flew to my swollen lips.

Beckett smirked down at me, still invading my space. "Well, that's one way to get you to shut the hell up."

I lifted my chin in defiance, trying like hell to ignore the fact my panties were soaked through from one kiss.

"We can't kiss every time we disagree."

Beckett's eyes roamed over my face, completely unconcerned that anyone could walk in and see us making out in the back hallway. "I know that. But every time we argue, all I can think about is how good it would feel to have your lips on mine."

My cheeks flushed, and I tried to regain my composure and not dissolve into a needy puddle at his feet. I had never been pushed up against a wall and *taken* before, but holy hell if I didn't like it.

His intensity was palpable. "You like to push my buttons." My knees wobbled at the sharp edge in his voice as he continued: "If you're not careful, I'll show you exactly what happens when you push me too far."

My jaw dropped open at his dangerous promise. I tipped my head up, hoping for another kiss. Instead, Beckett wore a cocky, self-satisfied grin and pulled back, his hand still gently pinning me against the wall by my throat.

Annoyance warred with desire as my blood thrummed under his hands.

"If we cross this line, you have to know this is all I can give you."

Sparks of electricity crackled under his touch. Anyone could walk in and catch us. The thought alone sent heat pooling between my legs.

I swallowed hard. "It's enough. You are enough."

Beckett smirked and lowered his face. Before I could react, his tongue stroked up the side of my throat before he planted a rough kiss on my mouth and stormed out the back door.

SIXTEEN

BECKETT

I was losing my goddamn mind—that was *exactly* what I was doing.

I had told myself that I wouldn't touch her. One dance and I was mentally seeking out ways to run my fingertips against the back of her hand, brush past her in a hallway, get just close enough to earn a hit of her heady perfume.

All while being totally pissed off that she'd managed to get under my skin. I hated to admit that a sick part of me enjoyed getting under her skin. Her fire was a turn-on.

I can't believe I almost missed out on this side of her.

A quiet, pettier part of me reveled in the fact that Declan hadn't seen this side of her either. Using the nail gun, I drowned out my thoughts, driving nails into the wood with heavy slams. I didn't need to think about how wrong I may have been about the woman who'd chosen my brother. How different that person was from the Kate I was getting to know.

It's enough. You are enough.

Her breathy words rattled around inside my skull. I hadn't pegged Kate for the kind of girl to agree to a fling, but if we could work something out, I'd be more than willing to bend my rules for her.

But first I needed to figure out how to get this job done when my focus was shot to hell.

I had known Kate would come up with a dozen half-cocked ideas during the renovation, especially after her Instagram page blew up. I'd already mentally adjusted the budgets and timelines, but I was surprised that all her ideas truly did improve the renovation. The walk-in pantry would be a perfect utilization of the unnecessarily large back foyer.

The crew and I went to work immediately, reworking walls and framing out the new space. I'd personally torn down the wall that I'd pressed Kate up against.

Christ. I'm lucky she didn't knee me in the balls and tell me to go to hell.

I needed to destroy the memory of that kiss—how pliable and needy she was under my hands. I scoffed at the idea I would ever forget that kiss.

Fat fucking chance.

Which was why, after a punishing day of manual labor at the farmhouse, I wanted to drown my sorrows with a hot bath and maybe even a bourbon on the beach.

After the bath did fuck all, I turned to the bourbon.

I couldn't have Kate, that much I knew. She was my brother's ex and my best friend's little sister, two lines I'd been more than willing to cross when Kate started to run her mouth, and I wanted nothing more than to find decadent ways to shut her the hell up.

There was a bang at my front door, and heat prickled at my neck. I glanced at my phone. Typically Duke texted before showing up at the house, but there was nothing. Awareness washed over me, and a small part of me knew it was Kate before I even cranked on the handle and pulled open the door.

The gust of air from me jerking the door open lifted the dark ends of her hair. Her green eyes were wild with the inky, starry sky behind her.

One look at her and I snapped.

Before she could even speak, I reached out, cupped the back of her head, and pulled her mouth to mine.

I swallowed her gasp. Her hands clawed at my shirt, and she pulled me closer. I bent down, smoothing my hands over the curve of her ass, and I gripped her thighs, hauling her up. Her long limbs wrapped around me as we crashed together.

Needy mewls vibrated in her throat as I devoured her. My hands squeezed and massaged her thighs. One step backward and we were in my house. I kicked the door closed, slamming us into the door as I continued to feel every inch of her move against me.

Our kisses were deep, sloppy, and *hungry*.

Kate tasted like mint, and her floral scent folded over me. My cock hardened, begging to plunge inside her and finally—*finally*—claim her as mine.

One hand moved over her hip and up to her rib cage. My hand wound around the hem of her shirt, diving under to tease the underside of her bra. I flicked a thumb over the pointy tip of her nipple, and she moaned into me.

I pulled my head back. "Needy fucking girl."

Kate's hands went to the sides of my face. "Beckett."

My name on her lips was all it took—the sweet, breathless sound of my name and the last bit of the tether holding me back snapped.

I swiveled, and with long strides I carried her through the house toward my bedroom. When my knees hit the mattress, I dropped her onto the bed. My body followed, covering hers and using my thighs to push her farther up the mattress. Her legs wrapped around me as her hips pushed into me.

I ground my hard cock against her. "Tell me to stop."

Her brunette hair fanned around her. She sucked her swollen bottom lip into her mouth, fire dancing in her eyes. "No."

I traced the line of delicate muscles in her neck and stopped, flattening my palm against her chest. Her heartbeat pounded beneath my hand.

"Such a fucking brat."

A smirk pulled at her puffy lips. "Then maybe you should put me in my place."

A low growl rattled in my chest as I sat up to get a better look at her. Her tiny denim shorts were shoved high between her legs. Through the leg opening, I could see the smallest scrap of smoky pink fabric covering her pussy. On the bed, her baggy sweater rode high on her ribs, covering something that looked like it was half bra, half shirt. I pushed the sweater up to get a better look.

The outline of Kate's dusky pink nipples was barely visible through the lacy fabric. I scooped her breasts out, and her bra pushed the pointy little tips of her nipples into the air.

I loomed over her but lowered to suck her breast into my mouth. Using my tongue, I nipped and teased her. Inside I was screaming to punish her, devour her for making me lose control, but I could never hurt her. Using her gasps and moans as a guide, I tortured her with pleasure. My mouth sucked at her skin, marking her as mine.

"Oh my god, yes." Kate's hands slid into my hair, tugging at the roots. I shifted my hips into her, my aching cock pressing against the zipper of my pants. If she kept touching me and moaning like that, I was going to blow my load all over her before I was finished with her.

I wrapped one hand around her wrist, then the other. Using my weight, I pinned her hands above her head. "Easy now."

"I want it. I want you."

"Then you'll be a good girl and take what I give you."

Kate's hips shifted up to meet mine. I held her hands a second longer, shooting her a silent warning with my eyes.

My hands found the button of her jean shorts, and I opened them and slowly slid down the zipper, tooth by tooth. Beneath the scrap of denim was a thin pair of pink underwear, the front soaked through with her arousal.

I slid the denim down her thighs and off her legs before tossing her shorts onto the floor. I bent forward, nuzzling my nose against her pussy and taking in her sweet scent. "Fuck, you smell good."

Kate brought her knees up but kept her arms above her head like she'd been told. I planted my hands on her inner thighs, stretching her legs wide. The silky fabric barely covered her sweet little cunt.

"That's it. Open up for me, baby."

"Jesus, Beckett. I need you inside me."

"That's right," I soothed, my hands kneading her soft inner thighs, spreading her even wider. "Tell me how bad you want this cock."

I lowered my head, licking and teasing the seam of her underwear, inhaling the scent of her arousal and feeling my cock pulse in response. Every fiber of me wanted to be buried deep inside her warm, wet heat.

Kate's hands moved down to her breasts, kneading and twisting her nipples. I should have punished her for moving her arms without permission, but the sight of her head back, mouth open, while she played with those perfect tits was painfully gorgeous.

"Please, *please*, Beckett. I need something inside me."

A low chuckle moved through me. "I like it when you beg."

Starting with my teeth, I pulled the smooth fabric of her underwear down until I could yank it the rest of the way off. Kissing and teasing her, I let my hot breath move over her skin. She was slick, ready, and eager. I teased her with my tongue, gliding over her silky inner lips. The tip of my tongue circled her entrance. I swirled my tongue higher, finding her clit and sucking gently.

Kate called out and ground her hips higher, begging for more. I moved lower, plunging my tongue into her, reading her cues and giving her exactly what she needed as I ate her pussy.

She clamped around my tongue, gentle rhythmic spasms telling me I was pushing her closer and closer to the edge. I thumbed her clit, demanding more.

"Give it to me. Give me that cum, baby."

I buried my face into her, licking and lapping while my fingers played with her clit and my other hand kneaded her ass. Kate's hips pumped into me, fucking my face as hard as I was eating her. It fueled me, and I planted my mouth on her clit.

Kate cried out, and I shoved two fingers inside her, feeling her inner walls clamp down around me. "Good, good. That's a good fucking girl."

I swiveled my fingers, stretching her and making sure she would be ready when I took her with my cock. Her panting slowed, and I looked up at her.

Flushed. Breathless. Absolutely gorgeous.

Overwhelmed by her beauty, I pulled my fingers from her and sucked her cum from them with a moan of appreciation. "So fucking sweet."

Kate swallowed hard as I sat up and pulled my shirt off. I made quick work of removing my pants and underwear as Kate remained limp and satiated on the bed.

"More, Beckett. I need more. I need you."

I crawled back toward her, letting her thighs rest on top of mine as I pulled her body toward me. "I'm right here, baby. Are you ready to take this cock?"

Kate wiggled her butt, and I palmed myself. One long hard pump did nothing to alleviate the ache. I reached toward the nightstand to pull out a condom. Quickly rolling it on, I dragged the head of my cock through her wet pussy.

"You're still soaked for me."

Kate lifted her head, and her eyes went wide at the sight of me. Her mouth dropped open, and she licked her lips. "Holy hell," she panted.

"It'll fit." Kate squirmed as I notched the head of my cock against her entrance. Looking down, I watched as her perfect pussy stretched around me. Despite having been primed, she hissed at the way I filled her.

My hands found her plush hips as I slowly pushed into her. "That's it, baby."

Her head fell back. "Jesus. I'm so full."

My heart beat faster as she squeezed around me. "That's only about half. I have more for you. You can take it."

"Beckett. Yes. Oh . . ."

Stuffing myself into her tight little pussy was ecstasy.

Hot. Wet. Snug.

I stilled, letting her adjust, and when she started to

move her hips, I began pumping. Sliding through her little cunt, over and over, I fed her every solid inch of me.

The more I moved, the more I felt my soul separate from my body. Kate was perfect—strong, pliant, *illicit*.

Mine.

She had no idea, but she had completely ruined me for any other woman, and all it had taken was *one touch*. As I moved, I gently dragged my fingertips down her torso, committing every smooth line to memory.

I wound my hand around the back of her neck. "Look at me."

Kate's eyes fluttered open, and her emerald-green gaze captured me. I swallowed thickly, my declaration lodged in my throat. I wanted to tell her I was sorry for being an asshole. Sorry for the heartbreak my brother had caused her. Sorry for anything in her life that caused her sadness. And I wanted to vow to make right anything in her life unworthy of her.

Kate was everything, and somehow I hadn't seen it. I had been too stubborn to see the warrior hidden beneath the pretty princess.

A soft smile graced her lips as I brought us closer to the edge. As her pussy clamped down on me again and she called out my name with her release, my own orgasm broke free. I collapsed on her, breathing in the soft perfume of her hair and gathering her in close.

SEVENTEEN
KATE

I HAD THOUGHT Beckett was about to say something when he applied gentle pressure to my neck and ordered me to look at him. The expression on his face was soft but tortured. Instead of sweet words, he looked at me with reverence.

It was enough.

His sticky, chiseled body was draped over mine. I'd never been so spent—*so used up*—in my entire life. I ached with the most delicious kind of soreness, from head to toe. His heart beat in his chest, galloping in time with mine.

When I had stormed over to his house, I had every intention of chewing him out for ignoring me, *again*, all day, because he was in a pissy mood. I fully planned on giving him a piece of my mind and letting him know that he couldn't just kiss me and then bark orders the rest of the day.

Little did I know he was going to snap and the domineering, controlling part of him would be so goddamn hot. I always knew I liked when a man took charge in the bedroom, but holy smokes. Beckett was next level.

That's a good fucking girl.

Praise kink unlocked? Check.

My body hummed with contentment. I let out a satisfied sigh, and Beckett shifted to lie beside me. His large arms wound around my body, pulling me close and snuggling into my hair. I never would have guessed Beckett Miller was a cuddler.

The wall of the bedroom faced Lake Michigan, and the panoramic windows were closed, but they still allowed for an unobstructed view of the water. Against the dark night sky, the crashing waves were barely visible in the distance. The bedroom itself looked as though it was hanging off a cliff. I peered into the darkness, but not at the water. Instead, I admired the reflection of Beckett's muscular body wrapped around mine.

In another world, a life with Beckett could be heavenly. For now, whatever kind of affair this was turning into would have to be enough.

"Mmm." Beckett sighed into my hair again. "I didn't even ask you why you came over."

A soft laugh bubbled up in my chest. "I came to yell at you."

He pulled me closer. "You can still yell at me if you want to. I like seeing you all riled up."

I rolled my eyes. "You're insufferable."

"I know."

A few moments passed, and we lay in comfortable silence, our slow breaths the only sounds that filled the quiet bedroom. My mind began to swirl.

What now?

What are we?

Is there a we?

Oh god. How do I explain this to everyone? To Duke?

This is Declan's brother. *What the hell did I do?*

"I can hear you thinking." Beside me, Beckett propped himself up on an elbow and peered down at me.

I did my best to smooth my expression and appear unaffected by the cosmic shift that was happening inside me.

He stared down at me. The demanding, brash edge to his voice was gone. "Let's get you cleaned up."

Before I could argue, he moved from the bed. I watched the muscles of his butt flex as he walked, unashamed of his nakedness, to the en suite bathroom.

I heard water running, and his head popped back into the room. "You coming?"

I unpeeled myself from the bed and placed my toes on the rich hardwood floors. My legs were tingly and unsteady, so I took a cleansing breath to brace myself. Carefully, I walked to the bathroom.

There the expanse of panoramic windows continued, exposing the bathroom to the outdoors. My hands moved to cover my breasts.

"Don't worry. It's one-way glass. No one can see you but me." Beckett moved behind me and planted a kiss on my bare shoulder. The simple, harmless peck sent warmth spreading through my chest.

I looked around the elegant bathroom. The ceiling was high, and an ornate crystal chandelier glittered in the light from the vanity. Double sinks lined one wall, and what looked like a steam shower was tucked in the far corner. The focal piece of the bathroom was the enormous soaker tub. It looked big enough to host a party in, and as the steam from the water rose up, thick, luxurious bubbles threatened to spill over the top.

Beckett turned off the water and faced me. My eyebrows lifted. "What?" he asked.

I slowly walked toward him and took in the array of bath salts, bubbles, and candles arranged neatly on the countertop. "This is a pretty well-stocked bathroom for a bachelor."

Beckett lifted a shoulder. "I like a bubble bath. Sue me."

The image of broody, grouchy Beckett sinking into the freestanding tub and disappearing beneath a cloud of bubbles was ridiculous. But also endearing.

"Just get in," he commanded.

Aaaaand he's back.

I stepped toward the bath. My muscles ached from working on the farmhouse, but also from the vigorous romp with Beckett I had just experienced. He took my hand as I stepped into the tub. I lowered myself into the hot water and sighed.

Perfection.

I opened my eyes to find Beckett staring down at me.

"You're not coming in?"

A soft grin started at the corner of his mouth, as though I'd surprised him by wanting him to soak with me. "I'll be right back."

Still naked, Beckett left me in the bathroom. I wiggled my toes and breathed in the relaxing scent of mint and eucalyptus. If it weren't for the risk of drowning, or the absolute embarrassment of Beckett finding me passed out in his bathtub, I could have drifted off to sleep right then. Nothing had ever felt so decadent, so utterly relaxing.

I peeped open one eye at the sound of Beckett returning. He was carrying a tray with water, a bottle of wine, two glasses, and a plate filled with crackers, cheese, and some kind of cured meat.

When he caught me staring, he shrugged and placed the tray on the nearby countertop.

Beckett filled a glass with pale, golden wine. "Domaine de la Romanee-Conti Montrachet." His voice flowed over the French words with ease, and butterflies erupted in my stomach. Beckett's rough exterior during the renovation made it easy to forget that he was a Miller—born into ridiculous old family money. Of course he only drank fancy French wines, but the way he poured and sampled it with ease was a total turn-on. Satisfied with his selection, Beckett poured us each a glass, placing mine on the white marble counter beside the tub.

"I think the snacks will get soggy."

Beckett took a sip of his wine and smiled. "Those are for later."

Later.

My heart pumped at the prospect of more time here, lost in the cocoon of this house. *With him.*

"Scoot up."

I did as I was told, and Beckett stepped into the bath, settling in behind me. He placed his wineglass next to mine and pulled my body into his. My back nestled into his front as we sat together in the tub.

His hands glided over my thighs beneath the water. I concentrated on the slow, steady beat of his heart against my back. He rested his chin on my shoulder, and I nearly melted.

Beckett sighed. "Are you okay?"

I moved my head to try to look at him, but he only squeezed me tighter. "Yeah . . . I'm great. Why?"

"I just . . ." He cleared his throat. "I just thought maybe I got a little carried away, was a little too rough without making sure you were okay with it first."

My heart squeezed and I smiled. "I'm good."

He planted another wet kiss on my shoulder.

I sighed and let the weight of my body lean into him. The blackness of Lake Michigan through the windows was vast.

"I always thought this house was too garish for the Michigan coastline, but there's no denying this view . . ." My voice drifted off as I appreciated the luxury around me.

"I hate this house." He harrumphed behind me. "The design is totally wrong for the location." Beckett was quiet for a moment. "I didn't realize you had been here. Stupid since . . . you know."

Since you thought I was in a committed, years-long relationship with your brother?

I cleared my throat. *Might as well put it all out there.* I tried to infuse lightness into my voice, but it came out sounding more nervous than anything. "Yeah, I've been here a few times with him. I, uh, lost my virginity in this house, actually."

Beckett tensed behind me. "Jesus, Kate . . ."

I turned around to face him. His knees were bent, and my legs were over his, our centers nearly touching.

My hands went to his face. "Hey. We both know it happened. But if this"—I gestured between him and me—"is going to be a thing? We've probably got to talk about it."

His face was moody and dark. "I meant it before. There's nothing beyond this that I can give you."

My eyes went wide. My heart beat wildly. In my mind, I willed him to keep going, to finally open up more.

I hoped my smile didn't look as forced as it felt. "Our hooking up is totally messed up."

He grunted.

"But also totally hot," I continued. "I'm good with it if you are."

He nodded to himself before running a warm hand up

my thigh. "I'm good with it. Your past doesn't matter to me. He didn't deserve you, Kate. He didn't deserve to be your first of anything."

My throat was tight, and tears burned at the corners of my eyes.

Beckett looked me over. "Maybe I should have been gentler. Made it special."

I shook my head. "If I wanted you to be gentler, I would have said so. With you, it was perfect."

"With me." He repeated the words softly, as though he couldn't believe I would be pleased with how perfectly aggressive and in control he was.

What he didn't realize was that he had unlocked some deep part of me, and I craved more. When he was in control, I didn't have to think or make decisions or worry.

"In fact," I said, scooting closer, our mouths only centimeters apart, "I'm more than happy to mouth off to you again, just so you can put me in my place."

Beckett's eyes narrowed as he lowered his chin. "I knew you were a brat." He nipped my lower lip and kissed me.

I inched forward, sliding my hands into his hair and working my way up his body as I deepened the kiss.

Beckett's arms wound around me. "You know what happens to brats? They get punished."

Before I could tease back, he slid his body down, dragging us both underwater. I pushed off him, sputtering and wiping a thick layer of bubbles off my face. "Beckett!"

His long fingers tickled my sides. Shocked by this new, playful side of him, I couldn't do much but struggle against his flirtatious assault and try to get away. Wet and slippery, we slid around the tub as our legs tangled.

Breathless, I wound my legs around his torso to hold him in place. I wiped at my eyes. "You're the *worst*!"

"I know, baby. But if anyone could bring out the best in me, it just might be you."

∿

WE OPTED to take the tray of snacks and wine to the living room. Beckett had started a fire, since neither of us wanted to bother with the clothes that going to the beach would entail. On a cozy blanket, he lay across from me, completely unashamed of his nakedness, his long, muscular body sprawled across the soft blanket. I had a throw blanket wrapped around me as we laughed and ate our weight in gourmet cheeses. The wine was heavenly, better than any I had ever tried.

I swirled it in my glass, appreciating how it clung to the sides and how the firelight danced in the reflection. "I wonder if Charles Attwater would carry this in his shop."

A little laugh escaped through Beckett's nose, and I scrunched my eyebrows at him.

"I don't know that he'd move a lot of bottles. That particular year goes for about four thousand dollars."

I nearly choked on the sip I had been taking. "A *bottle*? Four *thousand* dollars?! I can't drink this." I set the glass down.

He laughed and picked his up to take a sip. "Too late now. You drank nearly half of it, and it doesn't keep. Might as well enjoy it."

I narrowed my eyes at him. "How is it that your work boots are scuffed and some of your jeans are threadbare, yet you casually drink four-thousand-dollar bottles of wine just because."

"The boots are finally comfortable, and the jeans are just pants. And this is not *just because*."

"It's not?"

"Of course not. We're celebrating."

Intrigued, I leaned forward. "What exactly are we celebrating?"

He swirled his glass as he considered his words, then shrugged and swallowed the last remnants. "You. Us."

Warmth spread through me, and it was not the ridiculously expensive wine. Beckett had a way of irritating me one moment, then turning me on my head and completely buttering me up the next.

It was infuriating, but I loved it.

My cheeks warmed as I struggled to find the right words to tell him that somehow he'd changed things. I had been so wrong about him and was enjoying getting to know the real Beckett behind his grumpy exterior and all the misinformation I'd been fed over the years.

He sighed and dragged a hand through his hair. "Look. I don't really do the whole *pillow talk* thing."

A laugh burst out of me at how uncertain he was. "It's fine. I don't need that. We can talk about something neutral —no feelings allowed."

He popped a bite of food into his mouth. "What did you have in mind?"

I considered. "How about . . . what's the weirdest thing you did as a kid?"

His face crinkled with a small laugh.

I rolled my eyes. "Fine. I can go first. I used to tell people I was born in France. At one point I started pretending I knew French. It wasn't purple. It was *aubergine. Fraises. Bluets.*" I laughed at how I had once believed the story was plausible. "I was a weird kid. Then I'd watch the tourists and imagine where they came from. Sometimes I'd dream they'd take me with them. Though back then it was a lot less kidnappy and a lot more exciting."

He leaned into me. "You were a weird kid."

I pushed his hard shoulder and he barely moved. "You mean to tell me you never did anything dumb as a kid?"

"I used to pretend to be sick." He shrugged.

"Like, *sick* sick?" I asked.

He shook his head. "No, not really. Little things like a fever or bellyache. When one of us was sick, it was the only time Mom took off work to be with us instead of the nanny. I even made notes to rotate my sicknesses."

Jesus, that's sad.

When a knock sounded at the door, my eyes went wide, and my sudden sadness for Beckett's loveless childhood evaporated. "Hello?" a female voice called out as we heard the front door opening.

"Fuck." Beckett stood and stormed out of the living room.

Stranded and still naked, I pulled the blanket around me and stood up.

I could hear murmuring down the long hallway toward the home's entrance, and moments later Beckett came walking in, wearing only gym shorts and a strange expression.

From behind him, dressed in a flowing silky top, wide-leg pants, and heels, was his mother.

"Oh, Kate. Hello, dear."

EIGHTEEN
BECKETT

IF KATE COULD SHOOT daggers from her eyes, she would have killed me where I stood. Not that I blamed her. The unexpected arrival of my mother was enough of an inconvenience, topped off by the fact that Kate was wearing nothing but a fur-lined blanket.

There was no denying what was happening at the Miller vacation home.

"If you'll please excuse me, Mrs. Miller." Kate offered a strained smile as she continued to stare at me like I was the devil himself.

Hurrying past us, Kate disappeared down the hall.

"Well," my mother started.

"Don't," I interjected. Tension wound itself through my back and shoulders.

My mother raised her hands and innocently lifted her eyebrows. "I didn't say a thing."

I looked at her and at the smug smile she tried to hide. "You were about to. What are you doing here?"

Mom blinked twice. "Well, that's silly. Is this not my house?"

I sighed. "You haven't been here in years. You hate this town and this house."

"Precisely." Her smile grew. "We're finally doing it. Selling it. My assistant will be up tomorrow, so I can have her label and box anything I might want to keep." Her eyes slid over the house with bored displeasure. "Not that I imagine there will be much."

A soft throat clearing had us both turning to see Kate, dressed now and with her eyes cast to the floor. "Excuse me."

She was nervous. Scared. Not at all like the spitfire I had been getting to know. I fucking hated it.

"I wanted to say goodbye before I left."

I took one step forward. "Don't go."

Kate lifted her chin. "I'm leaving. We can talk tomorrow." She looked past me. "Good night, Mrs. Miller."

Ever ready with the polite facade, my mother smiled brightly. "Good night, dear. Lovely to see you."

Kate sneaked one last look at me and hurried toward the front entrance, then slipped out the front door. My chest ached at the sight of her leaving, and it pissed me off.

My mother cleared her throat. "I'll give you the same advice I gave Declan."

I turned to look at her.

"Just don't get her pregnant. Lord knows you don't need to be tied to a woman like her the rest of your life."

My molars ground together. "A woman like her?"

Mom rolled her eyes, and she swatted at the air. "Oh, you know what I mean. Below our station. Stop being so dramatic."

You know she will never change. It's not even worth trying.

I sucked in a breath and changed the subject as I stalked

over to the discarded picnic Kate and I had been sharing. I scooped up the tray and dumped the contents into the trash. "I'm staying here until the renovation is done. Can the move wait until then?"

Mom looked around the open living room and faced the large bank of windows overlooking the lake. She sighed. "I suppose . . ."

My shoulders relaxed. "Thank you."

"If," she continued, and nerves roiled in my stomach, "you promise to bring Kate to Thanksgiving. Della's is catering again, and the whole extended family will be there. *Lakeshore Living* magazine is doing a spread on our family and the holiday, so it'll be decorated for Christmas, but you know how those things go. I need you there. Declan insists on bringing his flavor of the month. Kate's presence will ensure an even number. Plus, she's a good girl. Quiet. Does as she's told." My mother looked up at me. "Agree, and this place is yours until you're done playing house in this godforsaken town."

My stomach dropped. There was no way Kate would ever agree to yet another Miller family holiday, *especially* since "the whole family" would inevitably include my pain-in-the-ass brother, Declan, and his new girlfriend. "Agreed. Fine."

I'll just have to come up with a last-minute excuse for her absence.

"Wonderful." Mom pulled her phone from her purse and began pushing buttons.

"What are you doing?"

"Shh. I'm calling my driver and telling him I've changed my mind. He can drive me back to Chicago tonight." Her eyes flicked over the home, and her lip curled.

She spoke to her driver with direct, unfriendly words.

I'm sure his salary ensured he would do exactly as he was told, despite my mother speaking to him as though he was less than human. Drivers, much like lint and children, were entirely disposable in the eyes of Talia Miller.

"Can I make you tea while you wait?"

Mom tucked her phone back into her purse and smiled. "That would be lovely."

As we waited for her driver to return, I made polite conversation and wondered how the hell I was ever going to make this right with Kate.

NINETEEN
KATE

"That rooster's a real asshole."

An abrupt laugh burst from me as Wyatt scowled at his seven-year-old daughter, who had the mouth of a sailor. "Pickle, watch your language."

"Sorry," she grumbled and looked up at me with guilt-ridden eyes.

I winked at her and wrapped an arm around her little shoulders. I leaned down to whisper as we walked deeper into the yard and away from the family gathering. "It's all right. Bartleby Beakface *is* an asshole. But last week he did steal Beckett's ham-and-cheese sandwich, so he's got *some* redeeming qualities."

Her giggles were infectious. "Team Beakface." Penny held out her fist, and I bumped it before dropping a kiss on her head.

"Do you want to pick some flowers for Lark and Tootie? They might like that."

Together we circled the edge of the yard, where it transitioned from lawn to wild grasses to farmland. While most of the spring and summer flowers were slowly dying back, little pockets of black-eyed Susans were standing tall. While Penny fussed over the perfect arrangement of flowers, I stepped into the blueberry field to pluck a few ripe berries from the bush.

Sweet, tart juice washed over my tongue, and I sighed. Supermarket blueberries couldn't hold a candle to the fat, juicy crops Sullivan Farms grew. "Want one?" I held up a ripe berry for Penny, twirling it between my thumb and forefinger.

Her eyes lit up, and she popped open her mouth. With a laugh, I tossed a berry toward her and hit her square in the eyeball.

We laughed as she squinted. "Ow!"

"Again. Let me try again!"

I lined up another berry and totally missed as Penny moved her head to try to catch it, making a dramatic show of chomping at the air.

"Last one, I promise. I'll get it this time." Lofting it higher in the air, the berry made a perfect arc and landed in her mouth.

She cheered in triumph, and love swelled in my chest. Because of her dad's NFL and coaching career, Penny had spent her early years traveling the country with Wyatt. At the beginning of summer, they'd finally set down roots and come home.

I'm so glad I'm not missing this.

I had been so blinded by what I thought was love that I had willingly left my hometown when Declan urged me to take the scholarship. I hadn't even realized how much I missed having everyone together—how comforting it was to be surrounded by people who really knew you, but loved you anyway.

Only you're a different Kate now.

It was true that the little sister who'd left Michigan with a heart full of adventure and hope had changed. Broken-hearted and without them, I was forced to pick up the pieces and do the mending without the comforts of my family. As a result, a sister who had found her voice and was willing to stand up for herself was proving to be an uncomfortable change for my big brothers.

Penny beamed her blueberry-stained smile at me. *This kid gets me.*

I pulled Penny in for a hug and pointed us back in the direction of the farmhouse. From across the yard, it didn't look like the half-done mess it was up close. Sure, the paint was dulled, and the half-full dumpster was an eyesore, but *damn* she was a pretty house. A sprawling farmhouse surrounded by blueberry fields and a three-legged dog chasing chickens in the yard.

Wyatt called to us, and we started walking back toward the family, chatting about what was going on in her life. Penny had started her first school year in Outtatowner, and I enjoyed hearing her take on it.

Apparently Mrs. Crumbly was still mean as a snake, and the lunchroom still served rectangles of cheese pizza that tasted like cardboard. When we had made a wide loop around the yard, Penny walked toward a large oak tree. Beside the tree was a decent-size rock, awkwardly placed with *Eggburt* painted in her little kid handwriting. She bent to place one happy, yellow flower in front of the rock.

I had heard all about how Penny had thrown an impromptu chicken funeral for little Eggburt. Turned out it was *not* one of Aunt Tootie's beloved chickens, but a store-bought roaster that the family had eaten at dinnertime.

That kid was a *nut*, and I loved her for it.

When we turned, Tootie was pulling a box marked

cobbler from a take-out bag. Despite not having a working kitchen, the farmhouse was still the largest place to have us all together, and take-out dinner in the yard was better than nothing. Penny presented the rest of the flowers to the women. Lark looked like she was going to cry, and Tootie fussed over them before pulling Penny into a tight hug.

I straddled the bench of the large picnic table and listened quietly as my family's conversations overlapped with each other.

Duke caught my attention when he cleared his throat. "I invited Beckett over, but he said he couldn't make it till later. So . . ." Duke's eyes shifted warily to me. "He may come by."

Heat flamed in my cheeks. Beckett and I hadn't spoken since last night, when we'd had sex and his mother caught me naked in his living room. I wanted to die of embarrassment and never think about it again, but reminiscing about Beckett and the night we shared seemed to be *all* I could think about.

"He's a dick, right?" Penny asked around a large bite of cobbler.

Water shot out of Lee's mouth as he covered a laugh.

"Pickle. Mouth." Penny slinked back as her dad shot her a very serious look. "Sorry," she whispered. "That's what Aunt Kate called him . . ."

Accusing eyes turned my way.

"Penny, I shouldn't have said that. It was not nice. I don't think that anymore, and he and I are . . ." I looked at the faces of my older brothers, who were each staring at me in anticipation. Lark's grin only widened.

Shit.

"We're friends," I stated simply.

Wyatt frowned. Duke crossed his arms. "Since when?"

"Hey, I think it's great, Sis." Lee scooped another serving of blueberry cobbler and smiled at me.

"You think what's great?" Duke pressed.

"Come on. Kate's a total smoke show. He was bound to notice. I've been making threats at the fire station for weeks, telling those dogs to back off." Lee winked at me to defuse the tension as Wyatt mumbled something akin to *Jesus Christ, Lee.*

I unfolded myself from the bench. "I am not talking about this with my *brothers.*"

"We just don't want you getting hurt again," Wyatt added, concern laced in his voice, but instead of being comforting, it grated my nerves.

"I'm fine! Will everyone please stop treating me like I'm going to fall apart at any moment?"

"Hey." Duke raised his hands in a misguided attempt to calm my bubbling temper. "Calm down. We can take care of it."

"Calm down?" I pointed a finger at him. "Don't you dare tell me to calm down. And take care of *what*? I am a grown woman, whether you want to believe it or not. Oh my god, you are all so frustrating."

"We know you're a little fragile after what happened last time . . ." Duke was really stepping in it now.

"I am *not* fragile! It was just sex!" My hand flew to my mouth.

Yep. I had just yelled across the family dinner table that Beckett and I had had sex.

"Daddy, what's sex?" Penny looked up at Wyatt as Lark stifled a laugh.

"It's something we'll talk about when you're older, Pickle." Wyatt shot daggers in my direction as he stood and guided Penny away from the table.

I sighed and called after him. "I'm sorry. Wyatt, I'm sorry." I ran my hands through my hair, and frustrated tears burned at the corners of my eyes.

"This a bad time or . . ."

My head whipped up to see a freshly showered Beckett standing in the yard, looking devastatingly handsome and overhearing the entirety of my declaration, all while holding a small bundle of wildflowers.

Duke's eyes moved between me and his best friend before flicking down to the flowers.

"Nope. Welcome aboard, champ." Lee laughed as Tootie took to clearing up the remaining paper plates.

Beckett stepped forward. "These are for you, Ms. Tootie." He held out the tiny bundle as she fussed over him.

"I'm going to help her clean up." Lee stood and gathered his plate.

"Good idea." Duke stood before Beckett and me, his face marred with confusion. "Seriously? You two?"

I wanted to argue, tell him it was nothing, but the words were lodged in my throat. Beckett spoke up. "It was unexpected. I respect you and our friendship. You know that. I want to talk about it, but not before I have the chance to discuss a few things with Kate."

I was stunned into silence. I had thought for sure Beckett would smooth things over with Duke, deny what happened, or even suggest we keep what happened between us a secret.

Duke's brow furrowed. "Yeah, I get it. I'm not mad, I'm just . . . surprised. And mad." He sighed. "Yeah, I guess I don't know how I feel about it."

I stepped toward my oldest brother. "Duke, I—"

His hand shot up and my steps halted. "Just let me take a fucking minute."

"I understand." Beckett stood quietly, giving time for Duke to process what just happened.

"I'm going to go," Duke said at last with a sigh. "'Night, guys."

I opened my mouth to speak, but he'd already turned his back to us. Duke whistled to his dog, and Ed climbed into his truck.

I looked at Beckett. "Well, then. That was fun."

He stepped forward into my space. He loomed over me and kept his voice low. "Are you okay?"

I hummed. "Besides blurting out that I had sex with my brother's best friend at a family dinner? Yep. Fantastic."

His large palm smoothed down my arm. "Hey, it'll be fine. I'll talk with him."

I finally looked up at him. Beckett's gray eyes bore into me, and flashes of our night together flipped through my mind. I stepped back to give myself some space to breathe.

"It was sweet of you to bring Tootie flowers."

A smirk lifted the corner of Beckett's lips. "I used to bring some to your mom from time to time."

My heart did a little tumble, and I tamped down the irrational disappointment that the wildflowers weren't really for me.

"I also didn't want Duke to break my nose again."

I smiled. "He did not."

"The hell he didn't! First summer we met. I can't believe you didn't know that."

"Apparently some of us Sullivans are better at keeping secrets than others." I sighed and looked around. "Well, I think I successfully ruined dinner, but there might be some cobbler left over. Do you want some?"

Beckett shook his head. "No, it's all right. I do have a question for you, though."

When I lifted my eyebrows, he continued: "There's a lighting manufacturer in the city. I have an appointment to look at some options for the back entryway and thought you might want to come along. We'd be gone overnight." My stomach clenched in anticipation and he lifted a shoulder. "You know, for the Instagram page."

I slowly nodded. "For the page."

He grinned. "Of course."

Worry gnawed at me as I thought about my brothers and the shit show that had just gone down in the backyard.

Cat's already out of the bag, I guess.

I shrugged. "I'd love to. When do we leave?"

Beckett looked at his watch and smiled. "Be ready tomorrow at seven."

I scowled at him. "In the morning?"

Beckett leaned down, his face only inches from mine. "Yes, Princess." The deep grumble of his voice sent chills racing through me. He pecked a kiss on my cheek before turning his back and stalking toward his truck. "Don't be late."

My hand covered the spot where I could still feel his lips on me. I turned to see my family standing on the top step of the porch. Wyatt scowled. Tootie wore a smug smile. Lark, Lee, and Penny all grinned down at me.

Shit.

TWENTY
BECKETT

I KNEW there was no way in hell Kate would be ready by 7:00 a.m., so I made a loop through town to stop in at the Sugar Bowl. It was crawling with people, which was expected, since it was a Saturday morning and the Sugar Bowl was known to have the best pastries in town.

When it was my turn, I stepped up to the register, and the blonde woman, Sylvie, offered a tight smile.

"Welcome to the Sugar Bowl. What can I get started for you?" Her tentative smile didn't quite reach her eyes.

"Do you know Kate Sullivan?" I asked.

Her eyebrows lifted. "Of course I do."

"Great. Do you happen to know what her favorite is?" I pointed to the glass display case full of scones, muffins, and danishes.

Her face softened, and a small smile overtook the scowl. "Katie likes the cheese danish but usually only lets herself get it once a week."

I grinned. "Perfect. Two cheese danishes for her, whatever her coffee order is, and the blueberry crumb muffin with a black coffee for me, please."

The woman nodded and rang me up before relaying the coffee order to the teenaged barista working the espresso machine.

As the woman handed me the small white paper bag with the pastries inside, another woman came through the swinging double doors from the back.

"Sylvie . . . there's an issue with this week's produce order. Huck isn't here, so someone needs to talk with Duke Sullivan. Can you do it?"

My eyebrows lifted as her cheeks stained pink. She looked pissed off. Inconvenienced. "Right now?"

The woman grimaced. "He's waiting in the back."

Sylvie sighed and wiped her hands on her apron. "I'll be right there." She turned to me and painted on a thin, forced smile. "Have a good day."

With my hands full of coffee and pastries, I offered a small salute and headed toward the Sullivan farmhouse.

To my surprise, Kate was not only awake but looked gorgeous in the early autumn light. She sat on the top stairs in jeans and a cream blouse with short, fluttery sleeves. Next to her was a small overnight bag with a sweater looped through the strap. As my truck rolled down the driveway, I raised a hand to the three crew members who were working on a Saturday to keep us on schedule.

As I opened the driver door, Kate stood, stuck out her thumb like a hitchhiker, and lifted a knee to wiggle it in the air. I laughed at how damn cute she could be when she wasn't at my throat all the time.

I rested a forearm on the top of my open door. "Need a ride, Princess?"

"I mean"—she batted her lashes playfully—"if you're offering up round two." The thinly veiled promise of giving Kate a different kind of *ride* sent tingles of anticipation through me. We may have had the best sex I had ever experienced, but I wasn't done with her. Far from it.

"Your chariot awaits."

As she hooked the strap of her overnight bag onto her shoulder, I rounded the truck to open the passenger door for her.

"Oh, and he's a gentleman," she crooned.

To prove to her just how *un*gentlemanly I was, I smacked her ass hard as she climbed in and was rewarded with a yelp and her giggle.

The drive from Outtatowner to the city was just over two hours if traffic was light. Instead of pushing it, I opted for an easy pace, and for the first time in a long time enjoyed the winding roads and tree-lined views as we drove.

Kate hummed along to the radio. It didn't seem to matter which station it was or even if she knew the song. Her low, thick voice vibrated as she hummed the melodies. For a while she looked out the window as the lake raced alongside us. Then she took to staring at the side of my face.

When I didn't give her the satisfaction of a reaction, she finally spoke up. "It's weird."

"What? My face?"

She laughed. *Christ, that had to be the best sound in the world.*

"No, idiot. It's weird to not be fighting with you."

"Oh, I can give you some solid design advice. Get some work done. Maybe even breathe a little too loudly? Those things seem to piss you right off."

She rolled her eyes and gently pushed my shoulder.

I smirked. "It is kinda fun, though."

I winked at her, and a sexy blush bloomed on her cheeks. Reaching across the truck, I laid my palm on her upper thigh. Absently I rubbed and enjoyed the tight quarters of the cab. It was wrong to have my hands on her, but there was no denying how *right* her body felt under my hands. When she didn't push me away, I let my fingers drag in slow, sensuous circles.

"Did you talk with him yet? Duke?" I could tell Kate was nervous about everything between us being unexpectedly out in the open. Though, surprisingly, the thrill of being with her seemed to only grow the more time we spent together.

I shook my head. "Not yet. I was giving him some time to come to terms with it."

From the corner of my eye, I watched Kate pick at her nails. I figured she was uneasy that her brother might complicate things. Hell, I was nervous about that, too, but I knew Duke was a straight shooter. He might be pissed that I moved in on his little sister—not that I could blame him— but he would come to understand we were both consenting adults.

I hoped.

"I really hadn't planned to tell anyone."

I raised an eyebrow at her. "Keeping me your dirty little secret? I'm scandalized."

She shifted in her seat to lean against the door and face me. "You know what I meant. I wasn't going to tell them like *that*. It's strange and complicated . . . you being Duke's best friend. Declan's brother . . ."

She trailed off, fully expecting me to pick up the conversation, but I stayed quiet. I didn't have flowery promises for her. In all honesty, I had no idea where anything with Kate could possibly go. Before she came knocking on my front door, I had fully decided that she was off limits.

Now I couldn't seem to keep my hands *off* her, as evidenced by my hand creeping higher up her thigh and

rubbing dangerously close to her middle. A sick part of me
got off on how wrong it all really was.

"Let's just take the next couple of days, have a good
time. We don't have to figure anything out right now."

I could guess that at one time my brother had offered
her empty promises and false hope. I wouldn't do that to
her. We'd both have a solid understanding of what this was.

The miles stretched on, and I finally asked a question
that had been dogging me. "What's the deal with Duke and
the woman who works at the bakery?"

Kate tipped her head to the side. "Sylvie King? What do
you mean?"

"I don't know. Couple of times he acted weird when she
was around. It seemed . . . different than before somehow."

She shrugged. "You'd probably know more than me.
Believe it or not, despite my screaming about my sex life
over cobbler, we don't really talk about it."

I thought for a moment. I'd never suspected anything
strange between the two of them before, but now that I had
seen how easy it was for me to cross a line with Kate, I was
curious about it.

"Honestly? She's a King. The only one Duke can
tolerate is MJ, and that's just because she is a nurse and so
good with Dad. I've never even seen him speak two words to
Sylvie King."

I looked out onto the highway. "Hmm. Yeah, it's probably nothing. I overheard there was some issue with the
berries he sells them."

Kate shrugged and shook her head. "I don't know. I've
only just started getting to know her at the book club. She
keeps to herself a lot. Honestly, if they weren't Kings, I'd say
MJ would be perfect for Duke. She's probably a little young
for him, but she's sweet, funny, and has a kind heart."

I lowered my voice. "Is this the book club where King and Sullivan women conspire against the menfolk?"

Kate laughed again and relaxed in her seat. "More like uncomplicating all the problems the menfolk create. Did you hear the latest? Someone put up a *No Trespassing* sign along with a small fence on a stretch of public beach and marked it as King territory. There were some very confused tourists and a few very angry Sullivans. Apparently some of our distant cousins are threatening to go to court over it."

A laugh broke free from my chest. "I never understood how this feud has stood the test of time. It seems so . . . asinine."

Kate snorted. "Because it *is*. But any townie will tell you they know more about the feud than each other's real names. It started so long ago but just self-perpetuates. People pick sides, draw literal lines in the sand, and are too prideful to cross them."

"Bound to happen one of these days."

Kate shook her head and looked out at the passing trees. "Not in our lifetime."

Traffic slowed around the tip of Lake Michigan, but as we headed back north toward the city, a sense of familiar comfort came over me. I knew the bustle of the city—the rhythm and demands of honking horns, one-way streets, and throngs of pedestrians. While it lacked the slow, easy pace of a small town like Outtatowner, it was familiar.

I pulled up to my building and took the side entrance to a private garage. I wound down to a gated area and scanned my card to gain entrance.

The sun was blocked by concrete, and only small lights illuminated the lower portion of the private garage. I pulled into one of my parking spaces, turned the truck off, and hopped out.

Kate followed as I led the way. Both the underground glass foyer and the elevator itself required the key card.

"Fancy," Kate whispered in the darkened space.

Sweetheart, you have no idea.

I used the card to gain access to the top floor—my penthouse. The buttons I pushed didn't go unnoticed, but Kate didn't comment on the fact that my place was a penthouse on the North Shore.

As the elevator door opened, I swept my arm out, signaling for her to walk before me. The private elevator opened to a formal foyer. Kate stood in the middle of the room and turned in a slow circle. Her eyes ran over the living room, where my housekeeper had started a fire in the wood-burning fireplace. She took in the dining room and the sunroom to the right. She didn't know it yet, but tucked away in the corner was even a library.

"Are you kidding me right now?"

I smiled, and a smug part of me liked that she appreciated my home. "What?"

She shot me a flat look. "What, please. You know what. This place. It's . . . wow."

Pride swelled in my chest. "Thank you. It was a gem I had found. There were plans to tear down the whole building, but obviously I couldn't let that happen. The original plan was to renovate and sell, but once I was done with it . . ." I shrugged. "I don't know—"

"It felt like it was yours all along?" Her soft smile and the bright sparkle in her eyes were arresting.

I swallowed hard, taken aback by the fact she understood so easily. "Something like that."

"Can I look around?" Giddiness slipped into her voice.

"Of course. Explore all you want. I'll put the bags in our room."

Her smile widened. *Our room.* She didn't miss the slipup either.

I made quick work of depositing her overnight bag and my duffel in the primary bedroom. As I had requested, my housekeeper had also lit the wood-burning fireplace in the corner, and in the bathroom she had set out a beautiful arrangement of bubbles, soaps, and candles.

I smiled to myself, knowing I could easily pamper Kate in my home.

"What's upstairs?"

I followed the muffled sound of Kate's voice until I found her in the all-white chef's kitchen. She looked soft and dainty against the marble countertops and custom cabinetry.

"Couple of bedrooms, a media room, and a living room that leads to the outdoor terrace."

"Holy shit." Her eyes were wide.

"What?"

"I mean, I knew you were rich but . . . this is like *rich* rich." I didn't miss the hint of disgust in her voice.

"Is . . . that a problem?"

Her brow furrowed. "No, I mean, I guess not. Though you did shatter my dream that you were some down-on-his-luck black sheep that I could take pity on."

I scoffed. "Oh, I'm still the black sheep." I shrugged, feeling slightly embarrassed. "Just maybe not so much the *down-on-his-luck* part."

Kate lifted her hands to take in the open space. "Clearly. With money like this, why even take the farmhouse renovation? We could have found someone else."

I suppressed a smile. "I'm sure you would have loved that."

She blinked in innocence. "Is it too late to hope?"

I shook my head and stuffed my hands into my pockets. "Wasn't about the money."

Kate walked across the kitchen and stepped into my space, wrapping her arms around my middle. I lowered my lips to her hair and wrapped her in a hug.

"Thank you," she whispered.

The sudden shift in intensity clogged my throat. I couldn't speak, so I simply dropped a kiss on the top of her head.

As much as my body was screaming at me to lift her up, let her wrap those long legs around me and finally have my way with her here, we had an important appointment to make.

"Tour's over. We have to get across the city to meet with the lighting guy."

"Already?" she asked, looking up at me with mischief in her big green eyes as she smoothed her palms across my chest. A look that told me she'd be more than happy skipping the appointment and finding some new ways to fill up the hours.

"'Fraid so. I had to call in a favor to even get a Saturday appointment. We can't be late."

Kate reached around and grabbed my ass. "If you say so . . ."

She turned to walk away, and I caught her arm, spinning her and pressing her into me. "I do say so."

A hum vibrated low in her throat. "So bossy." She sauntered away, locking her eyes with mine and knowing exactly how her ass curved and swayed in those jeans.

What a fucking brat.

Peering out of the windshield, Kate asked, "What the hell is this place?"

I had opted to take the Land Rover rather than my beat-up work truck, and I turned the key off. The ride was decent considering typical urban traffic, and we'd ended up across the city, past the university and into the heart of the Chicago Arts District.

Storefronts gave way to rows and rows of lofts, studios, and retail spaces for artists and galleries. Not only were there art vendors lining the sidewalks and quirky shops jammed next to each other, the architecture itself was amazing. Down a few narrow streets and past what looked like empty buildings, I had come to a stop. Kate had yet to make a move to exit the car.

"That is an abandoned warehouse. Nice try, Ted Bundy." Kate crossed her arms and stared at the looming gray building.

I shot her an annoyed look. "If I was going to kill you, I'd do it when the entirety of your hometown didn't know we were together. What do I look like, an amateur?"

A laugh shot out her nose, and she pursed her lips, considering.

She narrowed her eyes at me and pointed a long, painted fingernail in my direction. "Fine, but no weird stuff, or I'll tell Beakface about it. You don't want to be on his shit list."

I laughed as I got out of the car. "Trust me, I'm already *on* his shit list. And, Princess? Sooner or later you'll be begging for the weird stuff."

Heat flamed in her cheeks as the front entrance to the warehouse opened up. "Hey there!"

I smirked at Kate and then focused my attention on the man we were set to meet. Sylvester Stormbrewer, though I'd be shocked if that were his real name, offered his hand, and I snatched it up in a friendly handshake.

"Who do we have here?" He turned to face Kate, who was still stunned speechless.

"Sly, this is my friend, Kate Sullivan. Kate, Sly."

"Hi." Kate offered him her hand, but instead of shaking it, he made a dramatic show of bowing, touching his forehead to the back of her hand, and sweeping one long arm out to the side.

"Mademoiselle."

Kate found him endlessly amusing. Everyone always did. Sly turned to me. "This couldn't possibly be the homeowner you were telling me about."

I steadied him with my glare. He was a shit stirrer if I'd ever met one.

Still holding her hand, he turned her in a half circle. "Why, I don't see a stick shoved up her ass at all!"

A shotgun burst of laughter erupted from Kate. "*I'm* the one with a stick up my ass?" She dropped her chin as though she and Sly often shared secrets. "Surely you know that's not true. Just look at his face." She popped her thumb in my direction. "The tight bunch of his shoulders. That man hasn't let his hair down in a decade, at least."

He turned to me. "I like her, Beck."

I sighed, feeling a pinch at the tightness in my shoulders that Kate loved to point out. "Can we please just go inside?"

Amused with himself, he tucked Kate's hand into the crook of his arm and led her to the doorway of his impressive studio.

I grumbled behind them and ignored the pang of affection for her blooming under my ribs.

TWENTY-ONE
KATE

"Look at this one!" I stood in a huge lofted warehouse, looking at the ceiling and turning in a slow circle.

It was pure magic.

Beckett's friend Sly was a master craftsman when it came to designing and executing designer lighting concepts. Everything from large chandeliers to table lamps and free-standing lighting was jammed into his studio. Parts of the building were sectioned off to look like a kitchen or bedroom or outdoor living space—all to give you an idea of how to use his quirky, sometimes unusual, concepts.

One particular flush-mounted light captured my attention. The base was a matte silver color, and the globe of the fixture was made of delicate white pieces, fitted together to look like blooming flowers. The material looked like pearlescent paper or shells.

Sly stepped next to me and looked up at it. "Mmm. She is pretty. Naturally harvested capiz shells from my trip to the Philippines." He lifted his hands for emphasis as he pointed to the light. "Each petal is hand cut and shaped into the petal forms. The fixture should, quite literally, bloom from the ceiling. An interior designer recently installed a cluster of them to create the effect of a warmly glowing flower garden. This is the only one left of the series I made."

"Wow." It was feminine, delicate, and whimsical. *Absolutely stunning.*

"It won't work." Beckett's growling voice came up behind me. "We're lighting a turn-of-the-century historical farmhouse. It doesn't fit."

I sighed and dropped my hand. "Well, obviously." A disgusted noise shot out of me. "You're such a fun-ruiner. I just thought it was pretty."

Sly laughed. "Unfortunately, I have to agree with your grouchy companion. For a modern update, while still maintaining the integrity of the farmhouse, I have a few options over here."

As he led me to a back corner of the warehouse, I let my eyes linger a second longer on the shell light fixture. I was sure it was outrageously expensive, and I sighed as I wistfully dismissed the hope it could ever be mine.

"These are all strong options for you." We entered a space that was glowing with golden light. "Wood, black metal, and glass will all be strong, traditional options. If you like something that leans a bit more interesting, something like a drum cage or strung wooden beads could do the trick."

My hands glided across the cool metals that warred with warm woods. It shouldn't have worked, but the lines and curves melded perfectly together. "I kind of like this one." I stopped in front of a chandelier that was understated and had a softness to it. Worn wooden beads were strung in an intricate pattern around the glowing bulb. Subtle metal accents added a bit of modern flair to the whole thing while still allowing it to have a rustic sort of charm.

"A lovely choice." Sly remained quiet as I continued to look at his designs.

"What do you think about this one, Beckett?" I pointed at a pair of chic sconces. "Maybe for the back foyer."

His full lips pursed, and I wanted them on me. Apparently spending a shit ton of money on luxury lighting was *also* a turn-on.

"I like it. Is that all?"

I swallowed hard and nodded.

"Great." He turned toward Sly. "We'll take them both. My assistant can call with the shipping address and details." He held out his large palm. "Pleasure, as always."

Beckett and Sly shook hands as I processed exactly what had happened. Seemingly, at the flick of my wrist, Beckett had committed to an extravagant purchase and barely batted an eye.

Suddenly, the hard, demanding way *Is that all?* rolled off his tongue had a new, exciting connotation to it.

No, sir. That's not all. Not by a long shot.

"Is this place haunted?" I pointed at an ornate vase of flowers as we stepped from the penthouse elevator. "Because those were definitely not there earlier."

"A flower-delivering ghost?"

I looked up at him. "Could be. That or a burglar whose calling card is leaving flowers for his victims." I glanced around. "Does it look like anything important is missing?"

He scoffed. "No." Beckett slipped off his jacket and held out his hand to take mine, so I did the same. He hung our jackets together in a closet in the foyer. "That would be

Marita. She's the housekeeper and manages things like that."

I buried my nose in the bouquet. "Mmm." I sighed. "Now *that* I could get used to." I stepped into the large living room and stretched. After visiting Sly, Beckett had taken me driving through the city. He pointed out significant architecture and buildings he claimed had unique character. The low, warm melody of his voice was fascinating—far more fascinating than any of the actual buildings, in my opinion. He was so *into it* that hearing him talk about design and architecture was like peeking behind the curtain of his surly, grumpy facade.

Beneath the bluster, he was passionate, smart, and really clever when it came to marrying design and function.

It should have annoyed me, but really? It was a huge turn-on. A lot like how the mere fact that being with Beckett was so *wrong* was its own turn-on. By the time the car ride was over, my body was humming for him. For his touch to linger a few seconds longer.

Afternoon shifted to evening, and the autumn sun hung low in the sky, hiding behind the skyscrapers and casting shadows through the large windows of Beckett's house.

He came up behind me and reached around to hold out a glass of white wine. "For you."

I looked between him and the wine. "Oh . . . thank you."

He flattened his lips and nodded. "There's something I need to take care of." He guided my shoulders down a small hallway and stopped in front of a closed door. "It'll take a little bit, but I figured you could spend some time exploring in here."

Beckett pushed open the french doors to reveal a gorgeous in-home library. Curtains hung delicately over large windows, which would be perfect for natural daytime light. My mouth popped open at the rows and rows of book-shelves. Two plush couches were angled toward each other with a fireplace as the focal point. It was the perfect place to sink into the soft fabric with a hot cup of tea and a new book. The only thing it was missing was a bookshelf ladder. Add that and the whole place could have been plucked from my dreams.

"Holy crap."

Beckett chuckled and kissed my shoulder. "Spend some time here if that makes you happy, or freshen up. I've got a surprise for you in"—he glanced at his watch—"an hour, give or take."

I pursed my lips and narrowed one eye playfully. "Hmm . . . very suspicious, but if you say so."

"I do." He flicked a knuckle on the top of my nose. "Be good and I'll find you when it's ready."

He slapped my ass and left me alone and reeling at this playful, sexy man who was surprising me at every turn.

TRUE TO HIS WORD, almost sixty minutes on the dot, Beckett came looking for me. After drooling over the vast selection of books in Beckett's library—a healthy mix of classics and contemporary fiction—I'd made my way down the hall and into the primary bedroom to freshen up a little.

I had piled my long hair on top of my head and taken a quick shower to rinse the day off my skin. I applied a few dabs of my favorite perfume and slipped on a *very* racy pair of underwear I had procured while in Montana. For a tiny nowhere town, my favorite boutique had the naughtiest lingerie sets, and during one shopping trip I couldn't resist. I may have never had the opportunity to wear the set before, but now I was doing mental backflips because the sheer, feminine mesh was *perfect* for Beckett.

Knowing the soft, delicate set was underneath my blouse and jeans was enough for me to have tingles racing down my back. I couldn't wait to see Beckett's face when he realized what lay under my clothing.

A soft knock at the door startled me. "Come in."

Beckett had cleaned up too. I shouldn't have been surprised, as there were multiple bedrooms in the house, but I loved seeing him in fresh jeans and a white button-up with a tight gray T-shirt underneath. The sleeves of his crisp shirt were rolled up, displaying the corded ropes of muscles in his forearms. The tips of his hair were still slightly damp, and he hadn't bothered to shave.

My insides clenched at the image of feeling his stubble rasp against my inner thighs.

"It's ready," he said.

I swallowed hard and could barely get the words from my scratchy throat. "Okay."

I placed my hand in his outstretched one as he guided me through the main floor. Instead of stopping at the kitchen, as I'd expected, we walked up the staircase in the center of the penthouse to the second floor. I hadn't explored this part of the house yet, and it was just as luxurious as the downstairs. A large open area that could have been a second living room had a pool table in the center and a large television mounted on the wall. Doors, which I assumed led to the additional bedrooms, lined the perimeter. A larger set of double doors was tucked into one corner.

I pointed at them. "Media room?"

He nodded. "Six rows, projection screen. On impulse I bought a popcorn machine, too, but haven't used it yet."

"A popcorn machine?" I couldn't help but smile.

He scrubbed the back of his neck with his hand. "Yes. One too many late-night infomercials suckered me into it. There's a matching one at the lake house."

The thought of serious, hard-nosed Beckett buying something as whimsical as a popcorn cart was endearing. I wasn't surprised he hadn't used it yet and made a mental note to change that immediately.

Well, maybe not immediately, but very soon.

We continued through the upstairs, my hand wrapped in his, until we came to a set of doors that led to the outdoor patio. Beckett stopped and looked down at me. His eyes shone with unspoken words. Words I desperately wanted him to voice.

Instead, only a soft smile lifted at the corner of his mouth. With his free hand, he turned the handle and swung open the patio doors.

My eyes went wide, and I sucked in an overwhelmed breath. The upper terrace was open and airy. Partially covered with a pergola-style structure, the space was illuminated by warm, glowing twinkle lights.

Soft music played from hidden speakers as the gentle breeze from the lake lifted the ends of my hair. In the center of the patio was a table with two chairs, set for an evening meal. Off to the side were covered dishes and a bottle of unopened wine.

"Beckett . . ." My voice trailed off as I took in the incredibly romantic scene in front of me. "This is . . ."

"Too much, I know," he cut in. "But I figure it beats Chinese takeout again. And I wanted to do something different for you. For us."

Us. Why does that word feel so heavy?

I swallowed down my nerves and smiled up at him as I moved into the space. The table was simply set with plates, silverware, and glasses. A small arrangement of flowers, ones he must have clipped from the larger bouquet in the foyer, were placed in a squatty white vase in the center.

Beckett reached into his pocket and produced a lighter, illuminating the candles on the table.

I breathed out. "You are full of surprises."

He leaned down. "It's just dinner, Kate."

Tingles raced through me as he pulled out a chair and guided me to sit. *Then why does this feel like so much more?*

I watched as Beckett, completely in his element, effortlessly arranged our dinners. He took the seat across from me, and I couldn't help but feel a mix of nerves and excitement. Beckett had cooked us a beautiful meal, and the Chicago skyline provided the perfect backdrop to our dinner. Two large propane heaters tucked into the corners of the patio warded off the chill, and the autumn sun splashed gold and raspberry shades across the sky.

Beckett also surprised me with his culinary talents. "I have to admit, I didn't think you had it in you," I teased, taking a bite of the perfectly cooked steak.

He raised an eyebrow at me. "You think just because I can swing a hammer, I can't cook?"

I laughed. "I didn't say that, but I'll be honest. I pegged you for the bachelor-food kind of guy."

"Bachelor food?" He leaned forward. His intense eyes held me like an embrace, dragging me closer and closer.

I shrugged and lowered my lashes. "Yeah, you know . . . Spam mac and cheese or tuna from a can."

Beckett's face twisted. "That's disgusting."

His inner rich boy was showing, and his obvious disgust tickled me into giggles. "Keep in mind, my brothers are my primary points of reference. But I will say, the Spam mac and cheese is surprisingly delightful. Lee makes all kinds of weird shit at the fire station. I consider it one of his hidden talents."

Subtle amusement danced in his eyes. I loved that Beckett understood the nuances of the Sullivan family so easily. No long explanations, just . . . understanding.

He chuckled, his eyes crinkling at the corners. "I have many hidden talents."

My stomach tightened as my mind raced to dark and dirty thoughts about Beckett's many, *many* talents. "Is that so?"

He leaned forward, darkness seeping into his stormy gray eyes as the candlelight flickered between us. "Would you like to see one?"

From under the table, his hand caressed my knee. With our eyes locked, I could only muster a jerky nod.

A sly grin spread across his face as he leaned back in his chair. He cleared his throat and slowly sucked in a breath. "Z-Y-X-W-V-U-T-S-R-Q-P-O-N-M-L-K-J-I-H-G-F-E-D-C-B-A."

I blinked at him, a bubble of laughter fighting to be free. "Did you . . . ? Did you just recite the entire alphabet backward?"

He smiled before sipping his wine. "In one breath."

A laugh burst out of me. "That is the most useless talent on the planet!"

Beckett scoffed and flicked a dismissive wave. "You can't do it."

"That may be true." I was fighting a fit of laughter as I dabbed at my eyes. "This is unbelievable! Beckett Miller . . . you're a *nerd*."

His deep rumble of laughter joined mine. I had learned his laugh was a rare thing, and its warm, rich timbre washed over me. Pulling a genuine laugh from him was precious.

Special.

And right now, it's mine.

"Fine. Your turn." He gestured at me with a haughty sweep of his hand.

"My turn what?"

"Show me your hidden talent." As he leaned back, he crossed his arms over his chest, waiting for me to impress him.

I propped one arm under my elbow as I tapped my lip and thought. I didn't really have any hidden talents, as far as I could recall, but then it hit me.

I lifted a brow, determined to nail this. "Can I use your phone to put on a song?"

Beckett reached into his pocket, unlocked his phone, and slid it across the small table. I found what I was looking for as nerves swept through me.

I gently pushed myself back, standing beside the table. "Okay, take your chair and put it here." I pointed to the open space on the patio.

His jaw flexed, but he did as I asked. I dragged my own chair across from his so the two faced each other without the table between us.

Standing across from him, I smoothed my hair back and took a deep, fortifying breath.

Oh my god, I can't believe I'm going to do this.

"Ready?" I asked, nerves simmering beneath my skin as I slipped off my pointed-toe flats and wiggled my toes.

He sat back in the chair and smirked. "Still waiting to be impressed."

This is wrong. Wrong, wrong, wrong. But oh my god . . .

Cloaked in the safety of near-darkness and the sides of the high-rise buildings around us, I pushed play.

Low notes flowed from the speakers as the song began. I

closed my eyes, letting the music move over me and willing my nerves to melt away.

My heart hammered as the intense, sensual beats of "Desire" by Meg Myers filled the air. Gathering my courage, my body began to roll. I didn't risk opening my eyes, but my hands moved across my chest and hips as I let myself be lost in the sultry music.

The heat from Beckett's gaze seared into me. When my eyes opened and flicked to his, he pinned me with his stare. Tension rolled through his body as he watched me move.

Dance for him. Show him what you've got.

With slow, sensual movements, I allowed my hand to explore the vertical line of my leg, bending at the waist to highlight the curve of my ass. The bold lyrics were like gasoline on the burning ember inside me as I grew bolder with every lyric.

His eyes seared into me.

A fresh wave of sensual confidence moved through me. Fueled by how deliciously wicked it was to be dancing for Beckett, I lowered myself to the ground, moving and flowing with the music. I'd be lying if I didn't admit I was thinking of all the things I wanted Beckett to do with me.

To me.

I let those thoughts run wild as my eyes moved over him and appreciated the hard lines of his body.

Sitting back on my heels, I moved my torso in small circles and gently unbuttoned my cream silk wrap blouse, revealing the delicate mesh balconette bra beneath it.

My fingertips grazed down my neck and lower, across the hard points of my nipples.

The low drone of the bass thrummed through me as I vibrated with want and need. From the ground I looked up at him, my back arching and working in time to the music.

"Get your ass over here," he growled as my gaze sliced to him. God, it was so wrong how much it turned me on when he used that harsh tone with me.

I didn't stand, but rather slinked on my hands and knees toward him.

"That's it, Princess. Crawl to me."

His demanding words sent a fresh wave of desire coursing through me, settling between the moisture pooling between my legs as I moved for him. Stopping at his feet, I ran my hands up his spread legs and over his firm thighs.

Beckett reached down to catch my chin. His hand moved to cradle the side of my face. "Fuck, you look pretty on your knees for me."

Emboldened, I held his hand and guided his arms back to the armrests on the chair. He settled back as I stood, towering over him, and continued my dance. I pulled out every trick and sensual move I could recall, letting the music take over my body. Every ounce of self-consciousness faded away as his appreciative eyes roamed over me.

I teased and slowly removed my jeans. Beckett's eyes flared as he took in the equally sheer mesh of my french-cut underwear. My creamy silk blouse hung open, and I let it slide down my arms before gracefully tossing it to the side.

I desperately wanted to feel his hands on me, but drawing it out—the anticipation—nudged me dangerously close to the edge.

As the final notes of the song faded, I hooked one knee, then the other, around his hips and settled on his lap. Fisting my hands into the strands of his hair, I brought his mouth to mine.

When we broke our deep, sensuous kiss, Beckett's voice was tight as he pressed his forehead to mine. "Princess, I'm going to tear you apart."

TWENTY-TWO
BECKETT

PRIMAL NEED TORE THROUGH ME.

I'd intended for our dinner on the warmly lit patio to be romantic. Tender. Sweet. I may not have been able to give Kate everything she deserved, but at the very least I could cook her a nice meal.

Kate on her knees, watching my cock push through the soft pillows of her lips as she took me deep was not exactly what I had envisioned.

But goddamn . . .

No man could have resisted the most erotic, sensual lap dance I'd ever experienced. Throughout the song, Kate's long limbs were strong and moved with elegance and grace. Her dance wasn't overtly explicit but left just enough to the imagination to have me crawling out of my skin, begging to be buried deep inside her.

When I demanded she crawl to me, she not only listened but did so with a sexy little smirk on her face. I was done for.

As Kate licked and sucked my cock, I looked down at her, consumed with need. I held her steady, gently forcing her eyes to meet mine. She smiled, hunger shining back at me. A perfect match for mine. As I held her face, Kate turned, sucking two of my fingers into her mouth, her tongue working the digits.

"Fuck, you'd let me put anything in this mouth, wouldn't you?"

A playful smirk bloomed across her gorgeous face as she tilted her chin to me and dropped her mouth open further, flattening her tongue.

I knew exactly what she wanted.

What she needed.

I willed her to understand everything I was aching to tell her. "You're mine, Princess."

I looked down at her lowered lashes and let my spit fall on her tongue. Her eyes closed with a throaty moan as I guided her mouth back onto my cock. The hum in her throat rattled through me as she took me even deeper. My hands held her hair and let her set the pace.

There was no doubt Kate was the one in control.

Despite my harsh tones—the way I took her body in any way she was willing to offer it—I was lost to her.

Determined to please her, I shifted our weight so I could stand, then swiveled Kate at the hips so she could brace herself on the chair. I sank to my knees, not bothering to take her gauzy underwear with me. Instead, I ran a finger down the thin elastic that trailed the seam of her ass. Pulling it to the side, I buried my face between her legs.

Kate's cry floated out into the night air. I didn't give a fuck if every neighbor within a five-mile radius could hear us—I would draw out every last drop of her orgasm before I stopped.

Let them listen.

I worked her with my tongue, using the gyrations and

tilt of her hips as my guide to giving her exactly what she wanted.

When her legs trembled, I slowed my pace and lifted off my knees. Using my body weight, I guided her legs wider.

"Spread for me."

My hand ran up her back and around her ribs to tease her nipples.

"Please, Beckett."

"I've got you, Princess." I fished out a condom from my pants pocket and, once it was on, lined myself with her entrance. Her hips tipped backward, urging me to fill her.

I drove into a bent-over Kate. Balls deep, I reveled in the fact that her flimsy panties stretched and tore around her thighs. My hands held her steady as she held on to the chair, and I sank into her.

I pulled her hips down as I drove into her at a demanding pace.

Words tumbled out of me without hesitation. "You are everything. *This* is everything."

I would process those words and why I couldn't seem to hold them back later.

I was too lost in her.

"I need you. I need to see your face." Swiveling her around, I gripped her thighs and hauled her up to gently place her on the ground. I pulled her underwear down her legs as my body covered hers. I wasted no time sliding back inside her.

We moaned in unison as we reconnected.

My hand traveled a path down her face and neck. One of her arms hugged around my back, holding me close, while the other raked over my chest. I captured her hand and pressed it against the beating of my heart.

"Your body is mine, but this"—I planted my hand on top

of hers to trap it, to make her feel the erratic thumps beneath her palm—"this is yours."

Kate's hips moved beneath me, matching my fevered pace as she tumbled over the edge. I swallowed her cries with a kiss, following right behind her and pouring every ounce of myself, every emotion I was too afraid to feel, into her.

I was drowning in her, but if someone had tried to hand me a life raft, I would have refused to take it.

Awareness slowly came back to me as my senses began working again. Our heavy breaths. The smooth melody of whatever song was still playing through the speakers. The whistles and claps from across the alleyway.

Shit.

Kate heard it, too, because she immediately buried her face in my shoulder. "Oh my god," she hissed. "Can they see us?"

I lifted my weight from her, still shielding her from any possible viewers, and looked around. The patio had a privacy fence, but high-rise buildings loomed over us. It was *possible* someone could see us if they really wanted to, but it sounded like the whoops and applause were coming from behind the cover of the privacy wall.

"I don't think they could see us, but they definitely heard what was going on." I couldn't help the goofy grin that spread across my face as I looked down at Kate.

She blushed under my assessment and huffed out a breath. "You know, it would be really nice if I wasn't embarrassed immediately after every time we had sex. First your mom, now this?"

At that, I laughed. "We can work on that."

I rolled off her, careful not to crush her any more than I already had. The concrete floor of the patio was made barely more comfortable by the outdoor rug, but it certainly wasn't suitable for lying on.

As I unfolded myself, I held out my hand. "Come on. Let me take care of you."

A deep, contented sigh filled the air, and her arms reached high above her head. "Mmm. You already did. But," she continued, "I did have plans for that bathtub."

Smiling, I pulled her from the ground and did my best to smooth the knotted hairs on the back of Kate's head. A sharp pang sliced through me at the sight.

Damn it, man. She deserves better than a kinky fuck on the outdoor patio.

I ground my teeth together, determined to pamper her in a way she deserved.

TWENTY-THREE
KATE

My head was spinning as I lowered myself into the warm bath. Beckett sat across from me, only the ghost of his signature scowl at his lips.

He shook his head.

"What?" I asked.

His hands dipped lower, running down my calf until he captured my foot. His thumb pressed into the arch. I moaned and closed my eyes.

"Nothing. You're just cute."

I opened one eye. "Cute?"

"*Very* cute." His hands continued to rub and melt away the aches in my foot as ribbons of steam swirled around us.

I lifted my chin. "Did you think my lap dance was *cute*?"

He locked his eyes on mine, intensity darkening his gaze as he recalled my performance. "*That* was sexy as hell. Right now you're cute. You can be both."

When I rolled my eyes dramatically, he continued: "I happen to like both."

Any compliment from Beckett was a rare and beautiful

thing. It left me speechless.

"I'm glad you liked it," I managed. I recalled how Declan chastised me for taking the dance classes in the first place. *Cheap*, he called it.

What a dick.

"Your hidden talent was very . . ." He thought for a moment. "Impressive." He inched closer to me, his muscular body slicing through the water. "But it better stay fucking hidden. You only dance for me."

A giggle threatened to escape as I wiggled my toes. "So grumpy."

In a quick move, he grabbed my ankle and tickled the bottom of my foot. I screamed in surprise and tried to pull my foot from him, splashing water and bubbles over the side of the tub.

"Stop!" I cried.

"Tell me. Tell me your dances are only for me."

Laughing, I relented—anything to get him to stop tickling me. "Yes! Fine! They're only for you!"

He moved through the water, pulling me into an embrace and holding me close. "That's what I like to hear."

I wrapped my arms around his back and held him close, my head resting on his broad shoulder. "You're the worst."

"I know," he whispered and nuzzled my wet hair.

You may be the worst, but I'm falling in love with you anyway.

I COULDN'T HELP but smile as I watched Beckett's serious expression while he painted the old farmhouse's exterior. He was so focused on the task that he didn't even notice me walking up behind him.

"Hey, Grumpy Bear," I teased, tapping him on the shoulder.

He turned with a scowl, but I could see the faintest glimmer of amusement in his eyes. "What do you need?"

I grabbed the paintbrush I had tucked into my back pocket and dipped it into the bright-white paint. While I'd fought him on the paint colors—I really, *really* wanted to turn the farmhouse into one of the historical "Painted Ladies" I saw splashed all over Pinterest—ultimately Aunt Tootie agreed with Beckett and opted for a fresh, clean white with creamy undertones to complement the home's natural surroundings.

Of course, this was not before a healthy online debate and Beckett insisting on educating the followers of *Home Again* on the history behind white-painted farmhouses.

If I had to endure another lecture on lime paint, white-wash, and *purity*, I was going to drown myself in one of the many, many five-gallon buckets of paint lined up in the shed.

But, with every stroke—yes, he also insisted it be done by hand to ensure the integrity and authenticity of brush-strokes—I knew they had been right in choosing such a fresh and welcoming palette.

"The materials for the back entryway still haven't arrived." I mirrored his slow, steady strokes. "I wanted to help."

He grunted and took a step to the left to give me space. "Fine. But don't mess it up."

I stuck my tongue out at him and he smirked, falling into an easy silence as we worked together.

Side by side, each of us was lost in our own thoughts and the steady rhythm of painting the broad backside of the house. From the corner of my eye, I saw the paintbrush in

Beckett's hand start to shake, and when I sneaked a glance, he was fighting back a smile.

"What?" I asked.

He shook his head. "It's nothing."

I turned to face him and planted my free hand in a fist on my hip. "Seriously. What is it?"

"You've just got something." He turned to look at me. "Here."

Without warning, Beckett's paintbrush swiped across my forehead, and I gasped in surprise.

Oh, it's on.

On a yelp, I flicked my brush in his direction, splattering droplets of paint on his sexy, grumpy face. Heat flamed in his eyes, and I realized I was totally fucked.

I screamed again and ran into the open yard, paintbrush still in hand and flying above my head like an Olympic torch.

Beckett chased me around the yard, playfully yelling and gaining ground with every one of his long strides. As I ran, I flung my arm, splattering paint behind me with abandon, laughing and dodging as he came for me. Members of his crew stared and smiled as they continued working on the house and we ran circles through the yard like children.

"No!" I shrieked as he effortlessly closed the distance between us.

His muscular arms wrapped around my waist, trapping my hands at my sides. "That's it. You messed up, Katie-girl."

"You started it!" I shouted through laughter. Heat bloomed in my stomach at the new, unexpected nickname.

With one arm still banded around my middle, Beckett reached up and rubbed his face on me, transferring and smearing the splatters of paint from his face to mine.

Together we tumbled to the ground, collapsing on the

soft grass.

The sun rode high in the sky, and my heart raced as our laughter filled the air. Panting and laughing, I turned my head to Beckett.

His eyes crinkled, and a deep laugh rumbled from him as his chest rose and fell with each breathless pant.

I leaned over and kissed the side of his face, unable to hold back anymore.

He responded eagerly, rolling to loom over me and pull me close.

The tension between us melted away, and a warm, fuzzy feeling spread throughout my body. Beckett peered down at me, his eyes moving over the soft lines of my face.

He smelled like soap and leather—a scent I found myself missing when he wasn't around. I pulled the comforting smell deep into my lungs.

From overhead, we heard a low, grumpy bawk.

"What the hell is that?" Beckett looked over my head and out into the yard.

I lifted my chin. Though upside down, I spotted Bartleby Beakface only feet away, looking annoyed and ready to attack.

"Don't. Move." Beckett's tone was intense and measured. He slowly started to lift himself off me, his eyes never leaving the rooster.

Crouched, Beckett raised a palm in surrender and slowly lifted himself off the ground. He took a step forward, attempting to scare the rooster away, but Bartleby was undeterred.

As if it were his war cry, the rooster let out a loud crowing.

"Fuck," Beckett muttered. He glanced at me. "When I say run, *run*."

My eyes went wide.

"Run!" Like a shot, Beckett took off across the yard. I didn't listen but only rolled to my stomach, watching the ridiculous scene in front of me unfold.

Determined, Bartleby squawked and chased after Beckett. I held my breath and covered my mouth to keep the laughter from escaping.

Beckett zigged and zagged, but Bartleby was relentless. "You mean motherfucker! I will bury you next to Eggburt!"

That did it.

I lost it and dissolved into a fit of giggles, rolling onto my back. I only pulled myself together and stood in time to shield Beckett as he ran past me.

I spread my arms wide. "Shoo! Go!" I flapped my outstretched arms toward the rooster, and Bartleby skidded and hopped to a halt. "Go on. Go!" I stepped toward him, and with a low, grumbly bawk-bawk, he gave up the fight.

Bartleby finally retreated, leaving Beckett breathless as he brushed himself off and tried to act like he wasn't embarrassed by the whole ordeal.

I couldn't help but grin at the sight of him, my tough and confident contractor, wearing smeared paint and looking shaken up by a yard bird.

I knew I shouldn't tease him too much, but I couldn't resist. "Huh. I don't think he likes you."

Beckett shot me a scowl that nearly threw me into a fresh fit of laughter, but I bit it back.

"I hate that fucking bird."

My sides ached from laughing. Despite his broody disposition, there was a playful side to Beckett that was endearing. A side he tried so hard to keep hidden. There was so much more to him that I hadn't seen before, a side I was falling for and could no longer ignore.

TWENTY-FOUR
BECKETT

THE CREW HAD LEFT for the day, Kate was off at her book club, and I was in a shit mood.

It terrified me that I already missed her—the sound of her voice, her laugh, the way she carried herself with my crew, doling out compliments one minute and confidently giving instructions the next.

This is not good.

The materials for the back entryway had finally been delivered, and their late arrival had put us behind schedule. Not that it mattered. I didn't mind drawing out this project to spend more time with Kate, but Tootie deserved to live in her home, and I was getting tired of coming up with excuses whenever my assistant, Gloria, asked me why I wasn't meeting our deadlines.

When I heard the front door open, my heartbeat ticked up, hoping Kate had changed her mind about going into town. I popped my head out of the back room and saw Red Sullivan slowly walking in, inspecting the renovations.

Shit.

I glanced around, not seeing any of the Sullivans who

might be accompanying their father.

"Hey there, Red." I walked over confidently, offering my hand. "I'm Beckett, a friend of Duke's and working on the house."

I knew quite a bit about his condition through Duke and knew providing him with cues and information in a way that didn't come off as condescending was often helpful.

"I know who you are." Red took my hand and gave me a proper once-over, hiding the shadows of uncertainty that still lingered in his eyes. "You got tall."

I smiled at the man I'd known since I was a teenager, a man who often felt more like a father than my own. "Yes, sir."

A pang of sympathy shot through me. Red's memories often faded or got confused. Some were downright forgotten. I could imagine it would be disorienting to see so many changes to the house he grew up in, started a family in. Maybe that was why Duke had been hesitant to share the details of the renovation despite Lee's subtle urging to include him.

I was reminded of when Kate had put me in my place about the farmhouse. It wasn't just a reno job. For them, this home was the keeper of their memories—good and bad. It was a testament to what the Sullivans had gone through, what they were still going through.

It was why I needed to make it perfect for them.

For her.

Duke came through the door with a rap of his knuckles. "Hello? It's me."

I tipped my chin in greeting, and Duke looked over at his father. "Hey, Dad. I thought you were going to wait in the truck."

Red scowled at his son. "Why would I do that?"

I stepped toward Red. "Can I walk you around? Show you the work we've done?"

Duke offered me a flat smile. We still hadn't talked about the fact that I was sleeping with his little sister. He didn't know that whatever was happening between Kate and me was a hell of a lot more than fucking for fun, but I was not yet prepared to have that conversation in front of her dad.

It would be hard enough to look Duke in the eye, knowing the kinky shit Kate and I had gotten ourselves into.

"I don't need someone walking me around my own damn house." Red walked past me and ducked behind the long plastic sheeting that protected the living room from construction dust.

Laughing softly, I followed him. Room by room, we walked as he took in the subtle changes Kate and the crew and I had made to the farmhouse. He seemed to like the addition of the windows in the living room and didn't have an opinion on the wall color Tootie had chosen. The kitchen was still in a bit of disarray as we waited for the countertops, but the walls were freshly painted, new windows had been installed, and the custom cabinets were spectacular.

"This is different." A deep furrow settled in Red's forehead.

"Yes, sir. It is. The wall that was here"—I gestured to the now wide-open space that allowed room for a kitchen island —"was taken down."

He examined the work we'd done. His arms crossed over his chest. "Juney always wanted me to fix it up." He shook his head. "Never found the time."

My mouth felt dry. Red loved his wife deeply, but when

she passed, he was consumed with busting his ass to raise the kids and keep the family farm afloat. Duke had been old enough to recall life *before*, and it was painful. Back then, the Sullivans were close, happy, *complete*.

"Well, you're welcome to give me a hand anytime." I glanced at Duke, whose eyes looked wary, but I was unaffected. Surely I could handle a few hours here and there. I had known Red to be handy, and he had a wealth of knowledge and experience. It was the least I could do for a man I had so much respect for. It might make Kate happy, too, to spend some time with her dad.

Red nodded. "I might do that."

Duke cleared his throat. "Okay, Dad, we should get the box for Tootie and head over to drop it off." He looked at me. "Looking for a box marked *Hooker Supplies*?"

A laugh burst from me.

"I don't know," Duke cut in. "She promised it was knitting supplies, but I'm not looking in that box."

I nodded. "According to your sister, they got bored when packing up." I tipped my head down the hallway. "They stacked a bunch of things in the back bedroom."

"I'll look." Red strode off down the hallway.

"We need to leave in five!" Duke called behind him.

Red waved his hand in dismissal. "All right, don't rush me. And keep your voice down," Red hollered back. "You'll wake the baby."

My heart sank, and a prickly ball formed in my throat.

The baby. Shit.

Some days—like today, apparently—it was easy for Red to fool you into thinking his memory was less affected than it truly was. Sometimes he seemed so unchanged from the man I knew growing up. Other times his memories crashed and melted into one another and it was hard to tease out where his mind was. I couldn't imagine how scary and confusing that must have been for him.

Duke sighed. "One of those days."

I nodded. "A bad one? He seemed okay at first."

"Not great, but we've had worse. Just mostly irritable."

My eyes cast downward. There wasn't much else to say about it. Awkward silence settled over us.

"Got a call from Haven Pines. Dad was having an off day and could use familiar scenery. Figured he could tag along for a few errands." Duke was rambling, but I knew it was only because neither of us wanted to talk about his sister.

"I meant what I said. He's welcome to come here and help out. We can find something for him."

Duke nodded but surprised me when his eyes went hard. "Were you going to tell me?"

Guess we're done talking about Red.

I cleared my throat. I'd mentally practiced what I had to say to my oldest friend. He deserved to know the truth.

My voice was steady as I looked at Duke. "I'm not asking for your permission."

His nostrils flared, and I raised a hand.

"Listen. This wasn't my intention," I continued. "I was perfectly fine with Kate hating me and my family. I took this job for you. But things changed."

He stared at me. "Obviously." Duke ran a hand through his dark hair and sighed. "She's been through a lot. Katie's . . . fragile. I don't want to see her get hurt. I've got enough to deal with." He gestured down the hallway.

I knew Kate would bristle at hearing her brother call her fragile. Duke had yet to accept that his little sister had been through hell and had grown more resilient while she'd nursed her wounds in Montana. He either couldn't see it yet or didn't want to.

"I have no intention of hurting her. And I hope it goes without saying that I tried my hardest not to go there, but it happened. Somewhere along the way things shifted between us."

Duke was leaning into the tough-older-brother routine when he crossed his arms, but I recognized the furrow in his brow meant he was actually listening—taking in what I was trying to tell him.

Duke's assessing eyes were hard to read. "I've never held you accountable for what your brother did. I just don't want to see her heart broken again. Especially not by you."

I scoffed. "You know she won't end up with a guy like me, man. Not in the long run. She'll find some banker or a good guy who makes her laugh, brings her flowers after work, and never disagrees with a word she says. Eventually she'll get sick of me, and it'll be back to business as usual."

The words were a sharp lance beneath my ribs as the utter truth of my statement settled over me.

Because Kate *did* deserve someone who was light and fun and normal. Even though I was just a stepping stone for that man, and my feelings for her were growing deeper every day, I wouldn't stand in her way when he came along.

Eventually Kate would set me aside for the man she deserved. A better man. It was inevitable. Like the women before her. Hell, even my own family thought they could do better.

Tension and silence stretched between us. I held out my hand, a peace offering and promise to my best friend. "She'll get her happy ending."

And I will never love another woman again.

TWENTY-FIVE

KATE

"Yes, ma'am. I would love to walk you through it." Excitement danced through me as I listened to the reporter on the other end of the phone. "I can get back to you on that and to confirm the time. Thank you!"

The call ended, and I stared down at the phone.

"Holy shit!" A giddy squeal erupted from me as I shook out the nerves that lingered in my limbs.

"You all right in there?" Beckett's head popped up from his crouched position on the floor in the back entryway.

"More than okay!" I lifted my phone. "That was *the* Barbara Holland from News Channel Three. They saw the Instagram page and the renovation, and they want to do a television interview about the remodel, the house, *our team*."

He smirked at me. "We're a team now?"

My shoulders lifted. "Apparently," I teased.

Beckett continued to pull up sections of the old, beat-down flooring as crew members hauled off the debris. "What's the catch?"

I swallowed. *He is not going to like this . . .*

"The catch is that they want us both to do the interview." I offered him a hopeful smile.

"Is that all?"

I nodded. Hope and excitement and full-body chills raced through me.

"That's fine." He didn't bother looking up.

"Seriously? You're okay with an on-television interview about the house?"

He sighed and sat back on his heels. "If it's what you want to do, then yes. We can highlight the local businesses that we've worked with, and you clearly want to do it. It's fine."

My heart swelled for that crabby, sweet man.

He gestured toward the floor. "Now get off your ass and help me. This floor isn't going to tear up itself."

I laughed, knowing his teasing was part of his many charms. I snapped a picture of the Brutish Builder hunched over the flooring, his muscles taut and large as he pried a floorboard up.

Oh yeah . . . fans are gonna love that one.

Dressed in adorable overalls and armed with heavy-duty kneepads, I sank down next to Beckett. I pulled my leather gloves on and lifted a pry bar. The wood floors had been chipped, scuffed, and beaten down by years of my family's use of the back entrance. Beckett's vision of Chicago exposed-brick flooring would provide warmth to the space but also durability. I couldn't wait to admire the variations in color on the pallets of brick veneer that were waiting for us in the shed.

The ancient nails were thin, but tough, and I had to use my muscles and back to pry them free.

"Be careful," Beckett warned.

I strained, wiped my brow, and tried again. "Yes, boss."

With a squeak and groan, the boards began to lift. Once the first got started, a renewed sense of determination flowed through me. Music played on the Bluetooth speaker, and I hummed as we worked alongside one another, prying up the flooring bit by bit.

When a popular song came on the radio for the third time, Beckett lowered the volume and sat back on his heels. "Did you ever imagine you'd be sweating your ass off, ripping up hundred-year-old floorboards, and that it would feel this satisfying?"

I raised an eyebrow. "I thought you said you didn't do pillow talk?"

Beckett's shoulder lifted, and I could see he was fighting a smile. "I can't listen to that song again. Besides, this isn't pillow talk, it's . . ." He shrugged. "Plywood talk."

My head tipped back and I laughed, enjoying the playful energy flowing through me. "Well, in that case, is it safe to admit that I know fuck all about renovating hundred-year-old farmhouses?"

"Princess, I knew that the day you walked out wearing a pink tool belt and those tiny shorts."

I stuck my tongue out at him. "Well, what about you?" I waved my pry bar in a small circle. "Is this living the dream?"

He grinned. "Damn close to it. I don't mind the solitude. I like the sense of accomplishment when a project is done, but the solace of the day-to-day is what keeps me going."

I smiled at him and hummed in agreement. Everything about it suited him. We continued working, board by endless board.

When I came to a particularly stubborn plank, I looked at Beckett. He pried and moved across the space with quick efficiency. All those muscles made it go nearly three times as fast for Beckett.

"I can't get this one." I pushed and pried and couldn't seem to wiggle the board free.

"Try again."

I shot him an annoyed look and put my weight into it. The board popped up, and I looked over at a grinning Beckett.

"Knew you could do it."

I stifled a self-satisfied smile. When I looked at the exposed subflooring, I paused. "Hey. What's this?"

Underneath the flooring was what looked like a cut into the subfloor. Beckett settled in beside me to examine it. "Huh. No idea. Let's pry up some more boards and get a better look."

I scooted over to give him room, and he pried up three more floorboards. The line continued and then took a sharp ninety-degree turn.

Beckett frowned down at it. I sent up a silent prayer.

Please don't be an issue with joists or rotted subfloor. We really, really *don't need that kind of setback.*

Beckett removed several sections of flooring until a large square was visible in the subfloor. On one side was a latch.

"What the hell is that?" I asked.

He looked around the space, orienting himself. "It looks like a trapdoor." He pointed to the wall. "It would have been covered by the closet space we borrowed from the back bedroom there. Then, at some point, someone added the flooring over the top." His frown deepened. "Hang on."

Beckett stood and stomped out of the room. My eyes traced the four sides of the possible door. He returned with blueprints in hand. He unrolled the yellowed paper in front of us.

"These are some of the original plans that your family maintained." He pointed to the sketches and faded architectural plans. "This could be an old well from a basement offshoot . . ."

I shook my head. "The house doesn't have a basement."

He looked at me. "Exactly."

My mind raced. "Maybe a root cellar or something?"

He nodded. "Could be." In the air his finger traced the outline of the rectangle. "Seems really big for a cellar opening, though."

Beckett flipped through several pages of plans, many of which had been changed or updated throughout the home's many, many years.

"We should open it," I announced.

Beckett quietly studied the floor beneath us.

"Come on . . . it probably is an old cellar. Maybe someone hid a duffel full of money in there!"

He frowned. "Or a dead body."

A nervous laugh shot out of me. Beckett looked around. "I don't know what we're going to find in there, if anything. More than likely it's an empty space and a waste of our time, but I don't want to open up something that someone went to these lengths to conceal. It's probably nothing, but we need to talk with your aunt first to see if she has any knowledge of what this could be."

I sighed. "Fun-ruiner."

He lowered his chin to stare at me. "Safety. First."

I rolled my eyes and snapped a picture of the trapdoor before dialing my aunt's phone number.

~

"It probably is a dead body."

"Tootie!" I scolded, staring at my aunt as she, Beckett, and I stood staring down at the trapdoor. Once I'd called her to ask about the mysterious door, she'd immediately come over.

"I'm guessing it's a crawl space to access plumbing or electrical. Most likely this is a waste of our time." Annoyance laced in Beckett's voice, but there was something else there, too, a subtle hint of uncertainty, that had excited energy buzzing through my veins.

Tootie would never miss out on being the first to know something—especially something as exciting and cryptic as a hidden door. A door that she claimed she had zero knowledge of.

From what she could recall, and that we could confirm with the plans that Beckett had, the addition of the back bedroom and entryway had been completed sometime in the mid-1930s.

We could assume the addition to the farmhouse was due to a growing family, but then why would the door exist, only to be covered over? It didn't make sense.

"Only one way to find out." Beckett lowered to his knees and wedged the pry bar between the small gap in the flooring. With a hard yank, the wood groaned and came free.

Carefully, Beckett stood and folded back the door, revealing what had been hidden underneath.

Stairs.

I peered into the darkness. "What the actual fuck?"

"Katie!" Tootie scolded, but her eyes were as wide as mine.

Beckett folded the small door on itself, expanding the opening. Excitement and nerves danced through me as I stepped onto the top stair. "Let's go look."

Beckett's hand closed around my arm. "Wait."

I paused.

"We don't know what's down there, or if the stairs are safe enough to hold our weight. I'll go first." He clicked on a flashlight, and specks of dust danced in the beam of light.

I stepped back onto the main floor and watched as Beckett stepped down, gently testing his weight on the slightly curved stairs. Slowly, he descended and disappeared into the darkness.

I gripped Tootie's hand as we stood together and waited. Finally, his voice floated up the stairwell. "You're going to want to see this."

Tootie and I looked at each other with wide eyes, and each sucked in a deep breath. One by one we started down the darkened stairwell.

My heart raced. Dust floated around me, and the musty smell of earth and decay filled my nose.

Please don't be a dead body. Please . . .

A shiver ran down my spine as we went toward Beckett's light.

As we descended the narrow staircase into the hidden room, my mind raced. Tootie kept her hand clasped in mine.

Smells of old wood and damp stone filled the space. My eyes struggled to adjust to the dim lighting, and I gasped as I looked around the room.

It was like stepping back in time.

The walls were made of brick and wood paneling. One was lined with shelves stocked with dusty bottles of all shapes and sizes, and there were tables and chairs scattered around the room. A bar stood against one wall, complete with a vintage cash register and an array of glasses and bottles.

Beckett stepped over to the bar and ran his hand over its smooth surface. "I think this was a speakeasy," he said, his voice filled with wonder.

Tootie nodded. "How could this be here the whole time and we never knew it?"

I turned to Beckett. "When was the addition to the house completed?"

He ran a hand over his chiseled jaw. "Mid-thirties is my best guess, based on changes to the architectural plans. Back then things weren't documented as well as they are today."

"Mid-nineteen thirties would mean the end of Prohibition, right?"

He nodded. "Sounds about right."

Tootie walked around the space, carefully examining the items forgotten in time. She tucked a chair under one table. "Seems like the perfect place to hide from the law and enjoy a drink."

My mind raced. We had discovered a hidden piece of history, something that had been tucked away for almost a century. I ran my fingers over the rough surface of the wall, trying to imagine what it would have been like during those days.

As we explored the room, more treasures revealed themselves. A few old records stacked on a shelf. A small jukebox in the corner. A stack of newspapers dating back to the 1920s and a vintage roulette table.

A sense of history hung in the air. It was like the room had been frozen in time, waiting for us to discover it.

"We have to tell your brothers about this." Aunt Tootie set a record back on the shelf. The movement kicked up dust, and she began to cough.

"Hey, let's put a pause on this for a bit." Beckett pointed to the ceiling. "There was electricity at some point. I'll see if it's connected somewhere and safe to use. Then we can figure out what all this means."

I nodded. The dust and dirt weren't good for Tootie. I guided my aunt toward the stairs, making sure she didn't trip or stumble. Before I took a step onto the staircase, Beckett's hand landed on my forearm.

My eyes turned to his, and he tilted his head to be sure Tootie was making her way safely up the stairs.

He turned to me and whispered, "Look at this."

I glanced down, and in his hand was an old, dusty liquor bottle. The label was faded and peeled, but the words stamped across it were clear as day: *King Liquor*.

IN ALL MY years of renovating, I had never unearthed anything so valuable—*so fucking cool*—as what we uncovered at the Sullivan farmhouse.

While Kate was in awe and her mind spun with ideas of how to share our incredible find with her *Home Again* followers, I worried.

Tensions between the Sullivans and Kings were already high, and this discovery only added to the mystery behind the generations-long feud.

Did the Kings have ties to this house?

Would Kate be safe in the house if word got out about the hidden speakeasy?

What the hell do we do with it now?

Seemingly overnight, the tiny town of Outtatowner, Michigan, just got a hell of a lot more mysterious.

"There's nothing in the house plans about this?" Duke rubbed a hand on his chin. He and Lee had explored the speakeasy. Wyatt was busy with football games and work, but we had filled him in on our discovery.

I shook my head. "Nothing."

"Makes sense if someone was trying to keep it a secret." Kate ran a rag over the smooth bar top.

"Don't they have old, local newspapers stored digitally at the library? I could look through those and see if I can find anything," Lee offered.

"Not a bad idea," I said.

"Especially about King Liquor," Duke added. "That's what's not adding up for me. Far as I knew, Kings have always been businessmen, but bootleg liquor? I don't know."

Kate shrugged. "Would have been a good way to make some money in the early days."

We all agreed.

"I don't want this getting out and them causing us problems." Duke was thinking the same thing I had—we needed our find to stay quiet until we knew what we were dealing with and what the family planned to do with the discovery, if anything.

I sighed. "We had a full crew working when we found it. Unfortunately, this really isn't a secret."

"Especially in our town," Lee scoffed.

"Exactly." Duke's mouth turned down into a frown.

Kate's chin lifted. "So we own the narrative." Her brothers looked at her. Swallowing, she continued: "We need to control the rumor mill. I can post about it on the Instagram page. Document the whole thing. Information we *want* to get out about it can be out there. If people hear about it and we *aren't* talking about it, that will definitely make people think we're hiding something."

I considered her plan—share our find, but only details the family didn't mind getting out there.

"I think it's a great idea." Lee winked at his little sister.

Duke, still frowning, looked around the space, apparently considering our limited options. "I think so too." He stepped toward her and put an arm around her shoulders, pulling her in for a quick hug. "Good thinking, Katie."

A smile bloomed across her face. So often I watched her brothers try to protect or coddle her, and here she was making plans and kicking ass. I loved that they were getting a chance to see Kate shine.

I smiled at her. "It's settled then. Are you ready to blow the minds of your *Home Again* followers?"

~

HOLY. Fuck.

Not only did the reveal of the hidden speakeasy instantly go viral on Kate's Instagram page, but she was fielding calls from news stations clamoring for more interviews. Even reporters from across state lines were interested in the story.

Some were even showing up on the jobsite.

Irritation rolled through me as my crew worked to establish a line of rope and sawhorses in an attempt to create a blockade and keep trespassers off the Sullivan property. The local Outtatowner police had increased their patrol and helped in shooing people off the property.

It was a mess we hadn't anticipated and made me uneasy that Kate was staying at the house by herself.

Thankfully, Lee was helping with that.

On his day off, he installed seven high-tech security cameras around the perimeter of the house and property to monitor anyone who came and went. Kate rolled her eyes when Lee insisted, but I wholeheartedly supported her overprotective brothers.

I'd been short tempered all day, frustrated with the

spiraling situation and my inability to maintain a controlled jobsite. I took it out on a few inexperienced crew members, which left me feeling like shit.

When I finally closed the door to my temporary home behind me, the cold, dark greeting of the house only soured my mood further. A long soaking bath would only make me think of Kate, so instead I opted for a scalding shower and a small fire on the beach.

The lull of crashing waves surrounded me as I peered into the fire and let the warm, spreading heat of a good bourbon fill my chest. Tossing a few dried pieces of driftwood into the fire, I watched as the sparks rose and danced above the flames until they transformed into the tiny specks of starlight above me.

The distant slam of a car door caught my attention. I paused to listen. A faint banging could barely be heard over the gentle waves on the beach. Annoyed, I set down my glass, unfolded myself, and trudged through the soft sand toward the back of my home.

The banging on my front door continued, and my heart leaped to my throat when I heard Kate call out. "Beckett! Please, are you home?" More banging. "Beckett!"

"Kate!" I called out. My heartbeat ticked faster as I broke into a run. The panic in her voice was very real. I rounded the house, and her body crashed into mine. My arms wound around her shoulders, and she buried her face into my chest. Her heart was pounding nearly as fast as mine.

"Kate, what is it? What happened?" I gave her a quick once-over. "Are you hurt?"

She shook her head but pulled me close again. A sob racked out of her, and instinct took over. I bent at the knees and scooped her into my arms, making my way to the front door. I quickly pressed the key code to unlock my door and muscled my way through it, then kicked it closed, still bundling a shaking Kate in my arms.

"What is it, Princess? What happened to you?"

Kate's large green eyes shone with tears as she looked up at me. A big fat droplet raced down her cheek, and she bit down on her lower lip to keep from crying. A fresh bruise was blooming above her right eyebrow.

My blood simmered. "Who did this to you?"

A weak laugh tumbled out of her. "I did." Her eyes squeezed tight. "I'm sorry. I got freaked out. I shouldn't have come here."

"The fuck you shouldn't have." I pressed her into me. Whoever did this to her was going to pay. "I'm glad you did. What happened?"

Still holding her in my arms, I walked us to the kitchen and deposited her on the island. Stepping between her knees, I held her face in my hands. My thumbs swept over her cheeks, drying the sad trail of tears that stained her gorgeous features. The bump above her eyebrow was puffy and starting to bruise.

"Kate." Her eyes flew to mine as I steadied my breathing. "Tell me what happened."

Kate swallowed hard and lowered her lashes. "I was down in the speakeasy, cleaning it up and staging it for the pictures I have planned for tomorrow. I had music on and wasn't really paying attention. I thought I heard something above me, so I lowered the music. When I listened, I heard voices."

My jaw clenched. "Voices?"

She nodded. "Yeah, or something like it. I went upstairs and heard it again. They were low and murmured . . . but then the door handle jiggled like someone was trying to get in."

My thoughts went to dark places. Thoughts that included her unaware in the below-ground space. Alone. Vulnerable.

My throat burned as I swallowed back the bile that threatened to rise up. Someone had been on the property when Kate had been there alone. They'd been only a door's width away from the most precious thing in my world. I shook off the thoughts and why I shouldn't be having them before I let my anger consume me.

"I grabbed a knife." Kate looked up at me sheepishly.

My grip on her thighs tightened. "Jesus Christ, Kate . . ."

"I grabbed it," she continued, "but it was dark. I was fumbling around and freaking out. I stumbled over some tools and caught a toolbox to the face."

A wave of possessiveness rolled over me. I didn't care that she was Declan's ex-girlfriend or Duke's little sister.

She was mine.

Heads were going to roll when I found out who left the tools out for her to trip over.

"My palms and knees hurt, but I got to my feet, and when I yanked open the door, there was no one there."

Images of a knife-wielding Kate looking brave but scared flashed through my mind.

"The lights Lee installed were on," she continued. "I thought maybe it was a raccoon or stray dog or something."

"Raccoons don't talk. Or try to open door handles." Fun fact. Raccoons can open doors, but I didn't need to provide that oddly specific nightmare fuel when she was already freaked out.

"Exactly." She nodded. "Then I heard squealing tires as

they kicked up gravel and sped away. It all happened so fast."

"You didn't see a vehicle or how many people there were?"

Kate shook her head and looked at where my fingertips were digging into her thighs. I softened my grip but couldn't seem to let her go. "I think they were parked up the road, because I didn't hear the car start, just them burning rubber as they drove away."

"Did you call the police?"

She shook her head, her voice barely above a whisper. "I came here."

I pulled her into me. "Good. You did good, Katie-girl."

I couldn't ignore how witnessing her pain and fear had unleashed something feral inside of me. A deep, frightening part of me that would stop at nothing to keep her safe.

Kate's wobbly sigh nearly broke me. I held her closer to me, whispering tender reassurances and letting my lips brush over the soft strands of her hair.

When I finally felt like I could speak without losing my shit, I pulled back to look at her face. "You're staying here." Her plush mouth had opened to protest when I swept my thumb across it and continued: "You're staying. Leaning on me doesn't mean you're not strong. You chased trespassers off your property with a knife, for Christ's sake." I let my fingers trace the delicate lines of her face. "It was probably just an overeager reporter trying to get a scoop."

It was a lie and we both knew it. No reporter cared that much about a historic property, but for the time being, we could pretend until more information came to light.

I rubbed my hands up and down her thighs to comfort her. "It'll also keep your brothers from stepping in, because you know once they find out about this, they're going to be all over you."

Kate pouted as the truth of my words sank in. She knew damn well each of her brothers had an overprotective streak when it came to her. Her privacy and autonomy would shrink to *zero* if they thought there was a chance she was in any kind of danger.

Finally, she lifted her chin. A spark of steady determination replaced the wariness in her eyes as she sighed and settled her shoulders. "I could use a drink."

"Yo, Catfish Kate. Can I get you anything?"

I tamped down an eye roll as I turned to see Lee looking me over. As Beckett had predicted, as soon as word got out about the incident at the house, my brothers were all over me. Wyatt texted so often it was a wonder he had a job at all. He'd even sicced Lark on me, and she was incessantly trying to set up more "girl time." Duke was constantly *just swinging by*, and Lee hadn't worked a shift at the fire station all week and opted to be up my ass instead. Top it all off with the lookie-loos who made it their business to stop me in town and ask endless questions.

The only place I found peace was in the quiet comfort of Beckett's obnoxious beach house.

"All good!" I infused my voice with as much cheeriness as I could muster when really I wanted to punch Lee in his stupid face.

"Okay, well, I brought you a lemonade anyway." He lifted a can of my favorite drink and shrugged.

Ugh, why is it so hard to stay annoyed at him?

"Thanks." I sighed. "You can put it over there." I

pointed to the freshly polished bar top as I readjusted the tripod to peer through the new digital camera I had purchased.

When Lee didn't move from behind me, I turned to him again, my eyebrows up. "Everything okay?"

"Yeah. I just . . ." He tucked his hands into his pockets and sighed. "I've been thinking. The house is getting close to being done, you know? I was just making sure you're sticking around when it's all over."

My mouth felt dry. Sullivans were known for shoving down feelings and avoiding *those talks*, but in the cramped space of the speakeasy, Lee had me cornered. He and I had always been the closest. As kids, we had relied on each other after Mom died, and despite how "well adjusted" everyone said he was, I knew his time overseas had permanently changed him. There was a weariness, a sadness, that never let up despite the wisecracks and easy smiles.

Lee was hurting as much as the rest of us, only he was much, much better at hiding it.

I stepped forward and pulled him into a hug. When he sighed and sagged into me, my heart squeezed for him.

I held Lee at arm's length and smiled at him. "You're a great brother." His white smile beamed down at me. "But get out of here. You're messing with my lighting."

He laughed and threw up a jaunty salute before ducking and trudging up the stairs.

SOFT RAIN PATTERED against the massive glass windows of Beckett's house. In the darkness, I could just make out the angry, churning water of Lake Michigan. Water slammed against the beach, dragging bits of it back to disappear beneath the surface.

The swirling chaos matched the unease that rolled through me. As the autumn temperatures dipped, our list for the renovations shrank. *Home Again* had another huge uptick in popularity once images of the hidden speakeasy were posted. I struggled to keep up with the questions and comments, but overall I was *loving* the interaction with people from all over the world. More and more questions started rolling in about the Brutish Builder and our next project.

What is the next home renovation reveal?

Where will it be?

Come to my hometown!

In all honesty, I mostly avoided those comments. Not only were there zero plans for anything beyond renovating my aunt's home, but a part of me enjoyed living in the fantasy where renovating and documenting the journey was an actual part of my life.

While taking pretty pictures was fun, the real joy came from hearing about the history of the home, talking with the small business owners who had perfected their craft, and uncovering hidden secrets of a historical space. Our local library was a treasure trove of information now that I knew what to look for. Plus, the physical labor was giving me some very nice definition in my arms.

The thought of this phase of my life coming to a close was depressing. It didn't help that after each day wrapped, Beckett and I went back to his house and pretended there wasn't an end date to whatever was happening between us. He didn't talk about Chicago, and I didn't talk about the end of the renovation.

Ignorance is bliss.

Only I wasn't ignorant. I was willfully finding more work around Tootie's home—a garden bed here, new molding there, an enclosed area designed to keep the hens and Bartleby happy, occupied, and away from his nemesis, Beckett.

Even that was a stretch. Earlier today I caught Beckett sitting with his crew in the yard, enjoying lunch. When I walked up, I spied him pulling vegetable scraps from his lunchbox and tossing them to Bartleby Beakface, who happily pecked at his offering. Apparently they had come to some kind of arrangement. An arrangement where Bartleby didn't attack so long as Beckett kept him fat and happy. Though I didn't miss it when Beckett had called out, "I'd still eat you."

"How does a movie sound?" The deep rumble of Beckett's voice pulled me from my thoughts. As I turned from the large windows, I appreciated the long lines of his physique as he strode toward me.

A delicious shiver danced up my spine.

He's mine, even for a little bit.

"A movie would be great, but first . . ." I reached for a small metal box I'd set on the table beside me. "Look what I found."

The rectangular metal box was dark green and heavy. The simple latch on it was sticky, but once I'd pried it open with a screwdriver, I couldn't believe what was inside.

I handed it to Beckett, who looked it over. "Where'd you find this?"

"It was tucked under the bar. Like, on a special shelf up under the bar top. Definitely hidden."

He examined it closer. "How in the hell did you find that?"

I laughed. "Lee wouldn't leave me alone, so I bet him

ten dollars he couldn't squeeze into the cabinet underneath the bar. It kept him busy for a whole five minutes as he tried to contort himself to fit. He's the one who found it."

Beckett lifted the latch. Inside were several loose bits of brittle, yellowed paper, a small notebook, and a ring of mismatched keys. His eyes lifted to mine.

Excitement coursed through me. "Cool, right?"

"Did you look through it?"

I scoffed. "Of course I did. Curiosity got the best of me." I reached in and took out the small notebook. "I'm pretty sure this is a ledger of the bootleg alcohol deliveries."

The pages were stiff and brittle, so I turned them carefully. My fingers gently raked down the smooth pages and over the faded pencil markings. "There are some names I still recognize—families that still live in Outtatowner—who were getting regular deliveries."

Beckett grinned. "Scandalous."

"Apparently us townies liked to party, even then."

His finger stopped on the upper corner of the page. "What's that?" Circled at the top of each page were a pair of letters—either *JK* or *PS*. "A bootlegging code, maybe?"

I lifted my shoulders. "I haven't figured it out yet. I wanted to do some research in the archives at the library first. See if it maybe matches any kind of name or something."

"Philo Sullivan is one of the early owners of the home. That name is on one set of plans your aunt had." He shrugged. "Could be something."

"Huh." I ran my finger around the letters *PS* circled at the top of one page. "Could be." I beamed up at him. "Thanks."

Beckett set down the metal box. "But for now let's leave

work at work." He stretched his back and groaned. "I'm ready to settle in with a movie at home."

Home.

A warm melty feeling spread through me. Beckett had already turned his back to me, so he didn't see my heart eyes forming as I watched him turn and walk away.

I mentally shook myself. Leaning into the big, complicated feelings I'd been battling for weeks wasn't going to do me any good. We had a house to finish, and he had a fancy, important job waiting for him in Chicago.

After changing into a soft cotton pajama set, fluffing my hair, and brushing my teeth with hopes for more of a *Netflix and chill* kind of night, I met Beckett at the entrance to the upstairs media room.

He opened the double doors to reveal the huge flat projector screen against the far wall. The interior room had no windows, and as my eyes adjusted to the darkness, I walked forward. I ran my hand across six rows of buttery-soft leather couches. Tucked in the corner was a kitschy popcorn cart.

I pointed to it, eyes wide and mouth open. "Pretty please?"

A soft smirk graced his face. "Of course."

He made quick work of plugging it in and measuring out the kernels for popping. "Extra butter?"

"Definitely," I fired back as I scrolled through a ridiculously long list of movie choices. "There are an obscene amount of romantic comedies on here."

I didn't miss the soft blush that tinted his cheeks as the light from the large screen illuminated the room.

I gasped. "Beckett Miller! You are a closet rom-commer!"

His face screwed up as he scoffed. "Okay."

I kept scrolling, giddy laughter bubbling in my chest. "You are!" I accused. "These are all under 'Recently Watched.' 27 Dresses? My Best Friend's Wedding? The Holiday?"

Beckett spun and pointed the popcorn scooper at me with a scowl. "That movie is a national treasure."

I erupted in a fit of laughter. "I can not handle this information."

"It's not that funny," he growled.

"Yes. Yes it is. Beckett Miller, permanent grump, secretly loves sappy movies with happy endings. I can't get over this newfound information about you. This is why pillow talk is vastly underrated."

Beckett rolled his eyes and focused on the machine. As the popcorn started popping and bouncing over the kettle in the center, warm buttery smells filled the media room.

"So what's your favorite?" I asked.

Beckett stirred the freshly popped corn and started scooping it into a large red-and-white-striped bucket, stopping every few scoops to lightly dust the top with salt.

"Come on, you can tell me."

More silence.

I cleared my throat. "Fine . . . I'll just guess."

Scrolling down the list, I called a few out as I looked for any reaction. "Hitch . . . Maid in Manhattan . . . Twilight." I gasped. "Yes, please tell me it's Twilight. Are you team Edward? You'd make a hot vampire."

Beckett walked toward me with a fresh bucket of perfectly popped movie-style popcorn and a scowl furrowing his brow. He motioned for me to scoot over. I did and tucked my feet beneath me.

"Please," he scoffed. "I would never sparkle."

Giggles tumbled out of me.

I popped a piece of popcorn into my mouth as Beckett sat and sighed. *"You've Got Mail."*

"Aww . . . ," I crooned.

Beckett shook his head as though he couldn't believe he was actually admitting it. "I am fully in my Meg Ryan era."

"As you should be." I grinned at him, loving the complex layers I was uncovering about him on what felt like every single day.

After I grabbed another handful of popcorn, he moved the bucket just out of reach, setting it on the table beside him. "Besides, what's not to like about two people who really should hate each other falling in love? Plus, if you really think about it, Tom Hanks's character really is a prick. She never should have forgiven him, but she did."

"Hmm." I smiled at him but tried to hide the flutter that settled low in my belly. Maybe Beckett and I had done just that—been two people at odds with zero chance of a romantic connection, yet there we were, laughing and sharing secrets. I scrolled until I found a movie and decided it was perfect.

I playfully pushed his shoulder to cut through the mounting tension. "Such a softie."

Beckett lifted the armrest that separated us as he adjusted the seats to recline and settled in next to me. He raised his arm. "Get in here," he ordered.

I snuggled in next to him, breathing in his warm, freshly showered scent. It wasn't until he opened his mouth again that the fantasy burned away like the reel of an old-fashioned film getting stuck and melting away the world you'd just been immersed in.

His arm banded around my shoulder as he whispered over the opening credits. "Hey, come to Thanksgiving with me."

TWENTY-EIGHT
BECKETT

I shouldn't have let the tension and panicked silence that radiated from Kate bug me. When I'd asked her to join my family for Thanksgiving, I really wasn't thinking. We'd had a grueling week, I was tired, and I was captivated by her laughter as she discovered my secret for sappy, unrealistic love stories.

My guard was down and the words slipped out.

I held my breath until I heard her soft, sweet voice breathe out, "Okay."

I swallowed hard past the lump in my throat and pulled her closer as we watched Tom and Meg fall in love despite many obstacles. While we watched, I was determined to one day treat Kate to New York in the fall.

If we survived a Miller family holiday.

When I pulled up to the Sullivan farmhouse the next morning, I couldn't help but smile.

The home was gorgeous, standing proudly against the stark November landscape with a fresh coat of crisp white paint that gleamed despite the overcast day. The roof had been replaced with black metal sheets that would likely outlast all of us. The addition of front windows not only brightened the inside, but added interesting details to the exterior of the home.

The large wraparound porch was my favorite detail—not just because every time I looked at it I thought of the fire in Kate's eyes when she'd demanded I fix it. The porch was truly stunning. It had been meticulously restored to its former glory, with sturdy wooden columns that had been stained a rich brown to pop against the white exterior. Per Kate's request, there were no railings but rather a beautiful unobstructed view of a warm and welcoming home.

Soon it would be adorned with the cozy furniture Kate and Tootie had picked out, including an extra-wide swing that my crew would hang as a quaint finishing touch.

I turned at the low clucks behind me. That fucking rooster was nowhere to be found, but I still palmed a few pieces of dog kibble in my pocket. After some internet sleuthing I found that Bartleby, like many other chickens, liked the treats. He and I had come to an understanding—I'd toss him a few pieces and he'd leave me the hell alone.

The coop was painted a fresh, cheerful shade of yellow. While the cleanup of the speakeasy took some time, Kate had hauled over a few buckets of paint and refreshed the outside. The hens were content, and seeing how happy something as simple as a coat of paint made Tootie, I'd also had a few of the guys build simple planter boxes around the outside that she could adorn with flowers come springtime.

I couldn't remember a job I'd been more proud of. A dull ache formed in my chest when I thought of the Sullivan job coming to a close. Once we discovered the speakeasy, we'd pivoted and redesigned the entire back entrance, making accommodations for easy access to the lower level. Tootie wanted to keep it accessible and the design in line with the 1930s, so besides updating the electrical and making it safe to use, I let Kate have free rein with the design elements. Her followers on *Home Again* were eating it up, and Gloria was still fielding calls almost every day, asking if we were a team and if we'd consider their home for our next project.

In fact, there were several unread emails and a string of voicemails left by Gloria, demanding I answer her questions about my open calendar and potential upcoming jobs. I clicked off my phone and pocketed it. I didn't want to think about Chicago or work without Kate hovering by my side to snap a picture or ask for me to explain what I was doing.

Sometimes I'd still pretend to be annoyed and like I wasn't sucking in a breath to hold her scent in my lungs a while longer.

"Okay! I got it!" Kate broke me from my thoughts as she bounded down the porch steps with a duffel braced against her shoulder and a garment bag slung over her back. She'd needed to return to the house to pack for our overnight stay in Chicago.

I stepped forward, taking her bags from her and guiding her into the passenger seat. After stowing her bags in the back, I climbed behind the wheel.

Kate let loose a heavy sigh.

"Ready for this?" I asked.

She chewed her bottom lip, and my nerves fizzled in my gut.

Please don't back out. I don't think I can make it through this without you.

"Definitely not," Kate said, but immediately laughed.

I chuckled and shook my head. "They know you're coming. I called Declan to give him a heads-up, and he sounded . . . indifferent." I laced my fingers with hers. My brother was a fucking moron to have ever let Kate go. I'd at least have the decency to mourn my loss when this was all over. I sure as hell wouldn't be as epically stupid as my brother.

She pressed her lips together. "Sounds about right."

I shifted to face her. "Hey." Her soft eyes lifted to mine. "We don't have to do this. Say the word and I will call my parents and back out." I shrugged. "Fuck 'em."

That made her laugh, and the band around my chest loosened. She swallowed hard and shook her head. "No, it's okay. You've done so much for us. It's the least I can do. What's one family Thanksgiving?"

I let out a gentle laugh. "Christmas, actually."

Her brows pinched together.

It was a minor detail I had intentionally left out. "Mom is using the rare occasion we're all together to stage her Christmas photos, but don't worry. She'll be so busy being the center of attention that she'll forget all about us."

Kate blew out a steady breath and faced the windshield. "Awesome."

IT WAS NOT AWESOME.

I gripped Kate's hand as chaos erupted in front of us. My parents' house, a five-thousand-square-foot Tudor along Chicago's Gold Coast, looked as though the North Pole had vomited all over it.

Swags and garlands hung across every available surface. Tasteful orchestral Christmas music blaring over the in-home speakers could even be heard outside, and the array of cars lining the driveway told me the *intimate family gathering* my mother had promised was anything but.

A woman with a headset and iPad was directing people to their designated spots as she attempted to coordinate the chaos.

My mother had hired a *coordinator*.

A low throb hammered behind my eyes.

I tightened my grip on the steering wheel. "Let's just go. I can get us back in less than three hours, or we can stay at the penthouse. I don't care. Anything is better than this."

Kate looked over and smiled. It was the kind of demure, put-together smile I'd remembered from the holiday or two she'd arrived on Declan's arm.

Not her real smile.

"It's fine." She gently cleared her throat and left me in the truck as she held her head high and opened the back door to retrieve her clothing. "You coming?"

"Yep." I climbed out and stifled an annoyed grumble.

As we walked up to the house, my mother, adorned in a long, body-hugging green velvet dress, spotted us. She flapped her hands in excitement but didn't leave the front entryway, and she let us walk to her. "You made it!"

"Mom, what is all this?" I gestured to the chaos around us.

Her eyes went wide. "What? I told you they were doing a featured spread for *Lakeshore Living.*"

"You said it was just the family."

She swatted the air between us. "I never said that. Don't be so dramatic." Her eyes swooped over me and flitted to the casual jeans and warm, puffy coat Kate was wearing. "There's plenty of time to freshen up."

Mom's fake smile brightened as she set her sights on Kate. "Katie, dear! It's so lovely to see you. Declan will be eager to catch up." Mom added a playful wink that made my stomach roll.

I went to step forward, to speak up and set her straight that neither of us had any desire to *catch up* with my brother. I was fulfilling an obligation, and then we'd be gone.

"I'm looking forward to it, Mrs. Miller. Thank you."

I stared at Kate as she preened in front of my mother. I had never regretted a trip home as much as I did at that very moment. Mom clutched Kate's hand and sighed. "Oh, I forgot how sweet you are. Let's get you inside to warm up. You can take one of the upstairs bedrooms to change into something suitable."

Two hours and about eight million photos later, we still hadn't eaten. Apparently the opulent display of charcuterie was *for the photos*. Short of gnawing my own arm off, I was desperate for anything to eat and keep the tension in my gut from coiling.

"Here." Kate leaned over to whisper, and the soft hit of her perfume settled around me. She leaned in close, dropping something into the pocket of my suit jacket. My hand followed hers, quietly reveling in the way her fingertips dragged against the inside of my wrist as she pulled away.

Inside my pocket, Kate had deposited a small fun-size bag of peanut M&M's—one I recognized from one of the many little treats she often carried in the mysterious depths of her oversize purse.

When my mother called her over, she turned to me and winked, pressing her index finger to her lips. "Shh."

I watched in awe as she moved through the busy great room, smiling at strangers as she made her way toward my mother. I tore open the package and shoved a handful of candy into my mouth.

"She always did have a nice ass." My brother's smug voice came up behind me.

I shoved the remaining M&M's back into my pocket and glared at him. "Watch it."

Declan scoffed. "I should have pegged you for the sloppy-seconds type."

My head snapped toward him. "The hell did you just say to me?"

He raised both his hands in defense. "Okay. All right. I'm just busting your balls. I had no idea it was like that."

I pinned him with a furious stare. "It is."

He let out a low whistle. "You've got it bad, big brother." He let out an obnoxious laugh as his hand pounded down on my shoulder before he walked straight toward my girl.

I sighed as I steeled my back, and my molars ground together.

You've got no fucking clue.

TWENTY-NINE
KATE

NESTLED between Beckett and the weird uncle that kept trying to look down my shirt, I was in hell. It was surreal to be spending Thanksgiving, disguised as Christmas, in a house full of Millers who were putting on a show.

In the dining room, I was across from Declan and his date, because *of course I was.*

I had thought seeing him would be difficult. That maybe I would have a pang of longing for what could have been or that deep sense of disappointment would settle over me.

Instead, all I could focus on was how sickly slimy his grin was and whether it had always looked like that. His date was dressed in a skin-hugging, cherry-red dress that looked amazing on her figure but sent Mrs. Miller into a tizzy when it clashed with her decor.

I had learned a long time ago that at a Miller family function, you show up, you shut up, and you wear beige. Declan's date seemed unfazed, and the odd angle of her arm under the table made me almost certain she was trying to give him a not-so-secret hand job.

When I realized my hands were tense and clasped in my lap, I reached for Beckett. In a sea of Millers, he had somehow become my anchor.

Mid sip, he lowered the crystal tumbler of water and winked at me. Butterfly wings flapped wildly in my belly as warmth spread through me, and I relaxed against the back of my chair. Beckett had a knack for looking at me with heated eyes that told me exactly what dark, delicious places his thoughts were heading in.

All day his smile had been forced, and between the two of us, I couldn't tell who wanted to bail more.

Why had I ever agreed to this in the first place? How did I even get to this point?

Sitting at a Miller family holiday next to brooding grump Beckett and wanting nothing more than to grab his hand and run *home.*

As I stared at his profile, I heard a subtle click and was reminded that, even during dinner, we were being photographed. My eyes landed on my lap, where Beckett gripped my hand and gently brought my knuckles to his lips for a kiss.

There are those butterflies again.

"So, Katie, I see another son of mine has captured your attention." Beckett tensed beside me, and I swallowed hard at his mother's rather uncouth and obvious dig.

Speculative, busybody eyes from down the long table immediately swung our way as Beckett's voice rose above what would be considered *polite conversation.* "Mother—"

I squeezed Beckett's hand and steadied my breath. "Beckett has been friends with my oldest brother Duke for a very long time. He was gracious enough to undertake renovations to our aunt's farmhouse."

Mrs. Miller tilted her head in a cool, calculated smile.

"I've heard your little social media page has gotten quite a bit of attention thanks to my son. I get to hear all about it when I brunch with the ladies."

At that I let out a soft laugh. "He is a favorite of the ladies."

Her perfect face tipped down into a subtle frown.

I know that look. It's the dreaded disapproving mother look.

Trying to recover, I added, "Beckett has truly outdone himself with the renovation. If you're a follower, you may have seen we uncovered a speakeasy that was hidden away. Beckett was able to modify the original plans to preserve the space while making it a functional part of the house."

"A space for criminals and alcoholics. How charming." The twitch in her lip made it look like she was swallowing a gag. "More mashed potatoes?" His mother slid the dish in my direction.

"Kate doesn't like mashed potatoes."

My head whipped in Beckett's direction. *How the hell did he know that?*

"Of course she does. She asked for my recipe last Christmas."

"You mean Aunt Maude's recipe," he said coolly, adding his own subtle dig to the conversation.

I reached for the serving dish. "It's fine," I whispered to him.

He stopped me mid reach, my arm outstretched across the massive table. "It's not fine. You don't like them. You don't have to eat them just because she told you to."

Heat flamed in my cheeks as my eyes flicked among Mrs. Miller, Declan, and the rest of the table guests. I forced myself to smile, but I could feel it wobble at the edges.

Old Kate—the one with the deep, innate desire to please everyone and smooth things over—reared her head. I'd worked *so hard* to never be that girl again, but under the cumulative frosty stares of the Miller family, I shrank back.

My eyes pleaded with Beckett to not make a scene. My nerves frayed at the edges, and when I looked up at him, concern darkened his features. The conversation continued around us, picking up wherever it left off as the silent, ninja camerawoman continued to document the fake family holiday.

Mr. Miller was a man I'd heard speak only a handful of times. Typically he was relegated to work meetings or had his nose in his phone, busying himself with an important email or phone call. When he focused his attention on Beckett, the temperature in the room dropped twenty degrees.

"This social media page . . ." He leaned back in his chair, quietly assessing his oldest son. "You've been smart enough to monetize it, haven't you?"

My eyes flicked between Beckett and his imposing father.

Beckett slowly looked up. "It's Kate's page. Those are her decisions."

Mr. Miller scoffed. "Nonsense. I've seen the posts. She's made an impression by exploiting you. Whoring out your image to lonely women on the internet."

My mouth popped open as a low noise rumbled out of Beckett. His fist clenched beside me.

I tried to laugh off his comment. "I've been having a good time documenting the renovation. Teasing Beckett was just part of the fun."

"Fun you're making money off of." Mr. Miller crossed his arms.

"Dad." Beckett's harsh tone was a warning, and the tiny hairs stood tall on the back of my neck.

Mr. Miller tossed his linen napkin beside his plate. Mrs. Miller slipped on a strained smile as she gritted through her teeth and glanced at the camerawoman. Everyone stopped to stare and listen. "Now is not the time, Frank."

He gestured across the table toward us. "I'm helping. He wants to stop getting passed over, opportunities like this are it."

My brows pinched together. "Passed over?" The words slipped out, but as they settled in, my temper sizzled.

Mr. Miller's bored gaze moved over me. "He'll never be anyone's top choice when he lacks a killer instinct."

Never be anyone's top choice—including his father's.

I shrank back at the realization that despite his privileged upbringing, Beckett had never managed to gain his parents' approval. It was no wonder he pushed himself so hard.

"Father, don't make a scene." Tension rolled off Beckett as his eyes flicked to the camera aimed at our end of the table.

He looked at me and my stomach tightened. "We aren't making a scene, are we, young lady?" His cold eyes slipped back to Beckett. "She knows her place, unlike you, who—"

My head snapped up. "My place?"

Mrs. Miller cleared her throat and smiled thinly. "That's quite enough, Frank. We are having a lovely family dinner. Now is not the time to discuss the career path our son chose."

Mrs. Miller could barely hide the disgust as the words flowed out.

And I couldn't stop. It was unfathomable how they could dismiss and minimize their own son. I lifted my chin.

"Do you know he's fielding calls *daily* for people begging to work with him? Not only is he extremely talented, but he's a great boss. The people who work for him show up and work hard for *him*. Because he's a leader they trust, and he works hard right alongside them. No, I'm not monetizing *Home Again* at the moment. That's not what it was about."

Mrs. Miller smiled. "Kate, dear, this outburst—"

"I'm not finished." I stood from the table, and my heart hammered as shocked eyes locked on me. "Do I tease and poke at him? Yes. Do my followers like it when I snap a candid picture of him? Of course. But we're using the page to also highlight the local businesses. It's been good for my community."

Their blank, bored faces were too much. Nothing I said made the slightest impact. I was drained.

"If you'll excuse me," I said to no one in particular, then took a breath and placed my napkin on the chair. Without looking back, I exited the dining room and excused myself past the other waitstaff just outside the room.

I knew Beckett would be coming after me, so instead of retreating to the powder room on the first floor, I bolted up the stairs and hid behind the first unlocked door I could find.

Pressing my back to the door, I placed my hand over my racing heart.

This whole situation is completely fucked up.

Tears burned at the back of my eyelids. In our little bubble of Outtatowner, I didn't have to face the fact that I have deep, stupid, impossible feelings for Beckett Miller. Or face the harsh reality that not only had I dated his younger brother, but, despite my best efforts, I would never fit in with their lifestyle. The Millers fundamentally misunderstood me and everything I stood for.

Fake holidays and photo shoots and swanky uptown penthouses were *not* for someone with a name like Catfish Kate.

My heart jumped when I heard the pounding on the door behind me. When I yanked open the door, I froze when I realized it was not Beckett on the other side.

"Declan." I blinked up at him, too stunned to speak.

He leaned against the doorframe as I squeezed the handle to stay upright. "You look gorgeous as ever."

I peered around his large shoulders. "Where is Beckett?"

He smirked. "Making a scene, I'm sure. He's always been good at that."

My heart hammered against my ribs as I shouldered past Declan. "I have to go."

"Kate . . ." His hand caught my upper arm, skimming the exposed skin and sending an uncomfortable chill through me.

I gently pulled my arm from his grip. I closed my eyes, calling forth every shred of composure I had left. "Declan, I just had a meltdown in front of your entire family. In front of cameras. You destroyed me. You let me believe that we were in a committed relationship for *years*. When I came to surprise you, your friends had no idea who I even was." Seething rage dripped from my voice as I recalled how utterly humiliated I had been when I had shown up in Chicago, with hope in my heart, to surprise him.

"It was a misunderstanding." He clasped his hands. "I can make it up to you."

"You're here with a date."

He scoffed. "A placeholder." My stomach went oily at the way his eyes moved over me. "I can't believe I ever let you slip away."

I turned, blinded by buried hurt and embarrassed anger. "Nothing you could ever do would make up for how small and insignificant you made me feel. Fuck you, Declan."

Through furious tears I stomped down the hallway.

Before I hit the bottom step, Beckett was turning the corner, searching for me. I crashed into him, pulling him closer. His arms banded around my back and squeezed me tighter.

I looked up at him. "I'm sorry."

A smirk lifted his cheek. "I'm not." His finger toyed with a strand of hair framing my face. "That fire is one of my favorite parts of you."

I buried my head into his chest again, melting into his strong embrace.

"Get your things, Kate. We're leaving."

It was late by the time we pulled into the driveway to his beach house. We'd both agreed heading back to Outta-towner was better than staying another second in Chicago, and I was surprised at the wave of relief that washed over me as we pulled up. The car ride was spent in strained silence, both of us lost in thought, figuring out what the hell happened at the world's most uncomfortable family dinner.

In his bed, I stared at the ceiling, listening to Beckett's slow, even breathing.

When I rolled, I saw he was awake too. I studied his profile. "How did you know I don't like mashed potatoes?" I whispered.

He glanced at me and shifted to his side, the ever-present serious line across his lips. "Uh, I'm not sure."

When I only stared at him, he rolled his eyes and

continued: "I noticed once that you mostly push them around your plate. It's just one of those things I . . . I don't know . . . noticed. Then I couldn't *not* notice it."

A slow smile spread across my face as his words sank in. "You're a stalker," I teased.

His long fingers reached for me and laced together with mine. "Nah. I just couldn't help but pay attention when it came to you. You were a mystery." He scoffed. "Still are, really."

"Me?" I laughed. "Says the broody contractor who builds literal walls for a living. I'm not a mystery. I'm the most boring girl on the planet." I ran my hand up his muscular thigh, and he shifted in the bed to drape his heavy leg over me. "I like when you let me peek over all those walls you build."

My hand reached across to run my fingers through his hair. His low groan was intoxicating. Tingles danced up my spine.

"I'm sorry my family ruined Thanksgiving."

My smile was weak. "That wasn't Thanksgiving."

The entire ride home I couldn't help but wonder how the day had gone for my own family. It was my first holiday back in Outtatowner, and once again I'd chosen the Millers over my aunt, father, and brothers.

Shame washed over me, and my heart squeezed tightly.

"It's okay." I pinched my eyes closed.

He scooted closer. "Hey. Look at me. What's going on in that pretty head of yours?"

I buried my face in his chest, too ashamed of myself to admit what I was feeling. "I don't know."

"Try," he pressed.

I sighed. "Just wondering what everyone here was up to. I haven't been to a Sullivan Thanksgiving in years. Declan always wanted us . . ." His brother's name was vile on my tongue.

"I'm sorry." Surprising, hot tears clogged my voice.

"About what, Katie-girl?" He held me closer, somehow knowing it was easier to open myself to him if I wasn't looking at him.

"I hate that I can't not think about him right now."

Beckett ran a soothing hand down my back. "It's fine. You can think about whatever you need to think about."

I pulled back to look at him. "It's strange, though, right? That I was with your brother?"

"It's different." His eyes roamed over my face. "Not ideal, sure. I don't love that he's seen you naked, and I fucking hate that he hurt you."

Feeling safe and brave, I whispered in the darkness. "Did you know?"

His long pause stretched and filled the darkness.

"Beckett, did you know that he was using me?" I hated how small I sounded. How small I *felt*.

"I didn't know the specifics, but it tracks for Declan. He's always been selfish. We don't have a healthy relationship, so I never knew much about his romantic partners. When you kept showing up for holidays, I had assumed you were together."

I nodded. "He made promises every time he came into town. I thought we were in a committed long-distance relationship. I was shocked when he suggested I take the scholarship in Montana, but somehow convinced myself that it was because he was so selfless. That he wanted what was best for me." I scoffed at how epically naive I had been. "We were coming up on an anniversary, and it had been months of nothing but random texts and a few video calls. I had made this elaborate plan to surprise him at his apartment in

Chicago. When I showed up, he was hanging out with friends." I squeezed my eyes tight, remembering the confused faces as my excitement faded like a sad balloon leaking air.

"They had no clue who I was, let alone that I considered myself his girlfriend of six years. He recovered quickly and introduced me as his *friend* Kate. I didn't even make a scene, just quietly excused myself and cried my eyes out in the car. Later, he begged and pleaded and said it was a silly misunderstanding—that I had just surprised him, and he was truly happy to see me. The lies were everything I wanted to hear."

I let the silence settle over me before fully opening myself to him.

"I almost took him back. That was the worst part—that even after how humiliated I was, a part of me was willing to overlook it and forgive him. Again." I let out a watery laugh to ease the tension in my chest. "Thank god for my best friends, Gemma and Sophie, who helped me heal and urged me to see that I deserved so much more than being someone's fallback or secret."

I deserve so much more than a life on the back burner could ever give me.

Tension radiated off Beckett as his breaths sawed in and out of him. "Declan's a fucking idiot."

An irrational burst of laughter pushed out of me, relieving the tension that hung in the air. "Well"—I laughed —"I'm not going to argue with you on that. But when I thought back, I always pushed for us to be more. That was on me."

Beckett rolled, pinning me beneath him.

"Kate." He shifted his hips and I opened for him. His body settled over me.

"Yes?"

I wrapped my legs around him, and his arms caged me in.

I was protected.

Safe.

"I know what it's like."

I looked at his serious face and my heart pinched. "What *what* is like?"

"To be the one that's passed over. To always be the stepping stone to the next *better* thing."

I shook my head in disbelief. "Beckett, you're not—"

"It's the ultimate joke," he cut in. "You know the saying, the *heir and the spare*? I'm technically the heir but such an utter disappointment that my parents pinned all their hopes on the spare from almost the moment he was born."

My chest ached for him. "How can you say that? You're at the top of your field. I've seen the magazine articles, the framed accolades in your office. I figured your parents would be proud of you."

He scoffed. "You figured wrong. I could win a thousand awards, and it would never be enough, because when I was twenty, my father wanted me to follow in his footsteps, and instead I chose my own path. To my father, not wanting to be like him was the ultimate slap in the face. No matter what I do, he will always see me as the bastard son."

Fresh, unshed tears burned, emotions hot in my throat.

"The real kicker," Beckett continued, "is one night I got drunk with Duke, and we passed out on the front porch of the farmhouse. Red found us and hauled our hungover asses up the next morning. When he heard we were celebrating my acceptance into MIT's engineering program, he didn't even hesitate. Just pulled me into a hug and told me he was proud of me."

"I'm sure your father was proud, in his own way."

A muscle moved in Beckett's jaw. "My father told me to move out."

"Why do it then? Why keep going back there if they can't accept you?"

My hand raked up his exposed back. A bone-deep sigh whooshed out of him as I accepted his full body weight.

"Hell if I know. Maybe it's the same reason you came back to Michigan. Deep down we're all just the scared little kid we've always been. She's not perfect, but for a long while, Mom was the best thing I had."

"And now?"

He looked down at me, shifting his arms to hold me closer. "Now it's different."

"What's different?"

"I've found other things to hold on to."

My heart soared and beat a wild rhythm against his. "Can you do something for me?"

He nodded.

"Make me forget."

Beckett ran his tongue up the side of my neck before a devastating grin spread across his face. "Is that all?"

THIRTY

BECKETT

FALLING for Kate was simultaneously the most natural and most terrifying thing in the world. When she stared up at me, pleading to make her forget the ugly scene with my parents, the fact another Miller had taken her away from a special family holiday, and the uncertainty of whatever was blooming between us, I was more than happy to oblige.

To forget my life and be lost in *her*.

When my hands moved lower to spread her thighs open for me, she glanced up, and her eyes nearly gutted me as she breathed my name.

Beckett.

It would never sound sweeter than coming from her lips as I filled her.

A dominating, protective need washed over me—to claim her, fill her, and let the outside world fall away. Somehow with her my life had stopped feeling like never-ending attempts to look for whatever comes next.

With her I could stop and settle. *Feel.*

She shifted beneath me as I gazed down at her. Her

body rolled beneath my appreciative gaze, unknotting all the control I had clung to.

"Christ, woman. I'm trying to have a moment here, but I can't concentrate with you moving like that."

Kate reached up, and her hand tangled in the hair at the back of my neck. "Stop thinking and get lost with me."

Her breathy pants were my undoing.

She tightened her grip on the sheet beneath her as I shifted lower, letting my hot breath move over her.

"I've been waiting for this all damn day." I kneeled above her, soaking in the sight of my woman splayed open for me.

"Waiting for what?" she probed.

My fingertips dragged over the seam of her already soaking-wet pussy. Her legs trembled, and I pushed them open wider with firm hands.

I spit on her glistening pussy and stuffed her full with two fingers. Her wicked grin widened and turned to shock as I pumped my fingers in and out. When I pulled them out again, she groaned, lamenting the loss of my fingers inside her.

"So wet for me. Aren't you, Princess?"

"Oh god . . ."

I smiled down at her, loving how easily she unraveled—her desire totally in sync with mine.

"Yes!"

Her hips arched upward, seeking, and I knew exactly what she needed.

"Kate." Her name had a bite to it and rolled off my tongue like an obscenity as I spread her legs and buried myself to the hilt. Without waiting for her to adjust, I moved inside her, needing her as desperate and aching as she made me. Her nails clawed at my back as I drove her into the mattress with my weight.

Her strangled cry was throaty and desperate.

My hand found the base of her neck, my favorite spot to feel her heartbeat hammer against my palm.

"We forgot a condom, Princess."

She swallowed hard. "I can feel every inch of you. Don't you dare take this away from me."

A wolf's smile spread across my face as I pushed deep into her. As her body moved in rhythm with mine, something shifted.

Changed in my DNA.

I didn't want to dominate or control her, but rather I was scraping up every last bit of her to savor and keep it safe. To tuck it away so I could pull it out in quiet, lonely moments and be reminded of how someone had finally awakened something deeper inside of me.

I will never be the same after her.

I had meant it when I had said Kate wouldn't end up with a man like me. She couldn't. It would go against the very nature of the goodness inside her.

I poured every ounce of myself into making her feel good.

I didn't stop until I filled her with my cum—didn't stop until we were both shaking and used up.

Kate melted with exhausted satisfaction, and I bundled her against me, not bothering to remove myself from her warmth.

When her breathing steadied, I gently slipped my cock out. Evidence of just how used up Kate was seeped from her pretty, swollen pussy. I dragged two fingers through it, smearing it around and pushing it back inside so she could walk around remembering what we did.

With care, I cleaned us both up while she cuddled into the bedsheets.

As we settled in to sleep, I watched the cold autumn wind whip against the windows and willed time to stop.

≈

"Are you ready for this?" I stood behind Kate with my hands braced on her slim shoulders.

Excitement danced off her, and my own excitement simmered beneath my skin. The back door of the farmhouse had been stained a beautiful rich color, aptly named Early American. The matte-black door handle and kickplate added a modern touch that contrasted with the fresh white paint of the exterior.

Kate turned her head and grinned at me. "I'm ready."

We stepped toward the farmhouse, and I ran my hand up her neck to give a gentle, reassuring squeeze.

"Is this a Dutch door?"

I shrugged. "Tootie wanted it."

A warm smile spread across her face, and I was reminded that at times like this, it felt like making Kate happy was the easiest thing in the world.

I reached forward and swung the door open. What was once an oddly sized mudroom was now open, airy, and functional.

Just as I had planned, the Chicago brick added an earthy, rustic touch to an otherwise fully modernized space. Just inside the door was a painted bench that Tootie could sit on to remove her rubber boots after working in her gardens or tending to the chickens.

Tucked under cabinets that hid the cleaning supplies

were a brand-new washer and dryer. Kate had picked out glass containers with labels on them to keep things organized, but in wanting to show her the final space, I hadn't let her back there to stage it properly. She ran her hand across the smooth glass of the laundry cleaning supplies, each organized in the tall glass containers.

I smiled sheepishly. "I did my best. I figured you could rearrange this however you think looks nice."

She grinned at me. "It's great."

Using old boards from the flooring project and some wrought iron hooks I had found at the local antique store, I had also created a row of hooks to hang jackets and other items Tootie would want to have organized in the space.

Ivy and other small plants were potted to decorate the otherwise bare, open shelves. I had arranged them haphazardly until the women who were far more adept at decorating than me could fix them.

"I love how everything is bright and open but not too big." Kate sighed. "This is just perfect."

I dragged a hand across the back of my neck and looked up at her with a grin. "I hate to admit it, but you were right about the walk-in pantry and making better use of this area. It makes a huge difference."

Her mouth dropped open into an O. She stepped up into my space and wound her arms around my neck. "Beckett Miller. Can you say that again?"

I looked down at her, dragging my nose along the side of hers. "Say what?"

She kissed the corner of my mouth, and I felt the warmth of her embrace spread through my chest. "You know."

I playfully rolled my eyes and pulled her closer, gently

brushing my lips against the shell of her ear. "You were right, Princess."

She leaned back to hold me at arm's length and gave me a dazzling smile. "Mr. Miller, this is the best day ever!"

I shrugged off her arms and grabbed her hand in mine. "Come on. Let me show you the rest of it."

I bent to open the enlarged trapdoor that revealed the newly renovated entrance to the speakeasy.

Still holding her hand, I carefully guided her down the freshly painted and reinforced stairs. After the electrical had been brought up to code, the crew had also installed new lighting to illuminate the once dark and dingy space. Sly also fashioned unique 1930s-era sconces to illuminate the bar area.

When we hit the bottom stair, Kate sucked in a shocked breath. "Beckett . . ."

I stood behind her and kissed her shoulder. "Yes, Princess?"

I watched as my girl walked into the space—a space that had once been hidden, tucked away, but then brought to light in the twenty-first century.

The original oak bar was sanded, stained, and polished. I would bet damn good money it looked better than it had even when it was new. The mirror glass had been replaced, but I had managed to salvage the ornate antique frame that surrounded it.

Through the mirror, I watched Kate move around the space, and I was overwhelmed at how perfect she looked—how at home in this farmhouse she truly was.

Despite how hard I had fallen for her, I knew in my bones I could never take her away from here. From this place. From her family or the history of this town.

So many questions still swirled about the speakeasy—

the ties it had to the Kings, and the items we had discovered in the small metal lockbox. I had no doubt that with time and attention Kate would pull on those threads and uncover the generations-long mystery between the Sullivans and the Kings.

Something she couldn't do if I stole her away and hid her in my glass tower penthouse in Chicago.

Fuck.

That just wouldn't do.

Kate ran a delicate hand across the table I had constructed to fit in the space. I tucked my hands into my front pockets. "There's one more thing I need to show you."

Her eyebrows lifted. I tipped my head toward the stairwell. "Come on, Katie-girl. Let's go."

As we climbed the stairs, and my hands gripped her perfect ass, I heard the now familiar sound of the Sullivan-family double-knock-and-enter.

My grin widened.

"Hey, we're here," Duke called out.

I gave Kate's butt a playful swat and winked at her. "Perfect timing."

Through the front door Tootie, all three of Kate's brothers, and Red filed in.

"Well, this is a surprise!" Kate exclaimed, wrapping Tootie in a hug.

Duke nodded. "Beckett said he had something to show all of us."

Kate pulled Wyatt into a hug. "No work today?"

Wyatt let his arm drape over her shoulders. "Beckett said it was important. Lark and Pickle are terrorizing Bartleby out back."

I pointed at Wyatt. "Good. That fucker deserves it." I

immediately pulled back my finger and looked at Tootie sheepishly. "Sorry, Miss Tootie."

She winked and patted my cheek, and she strolled past. "It's okay, honey. Just don't let him hear you talk like that. That rooster holds a grudge."

"The place looks great," Lee commented, looking around the fully renovated first floor.

Smells of fresh paint and polish hung in the air, and I sucked the comforting smells into my lungs. "Thanks for taking the time. I found something during the renovation that I wanted to share with you. Kate has seen it, but I didn't quite let her in on my plans for it."

Her sweet green eyes whipped to me, and a puzzled frown crept over her face.

From behind the kitchen island, I pulled out a long, flat board about five feet tall.

Katie sucked in a breath. "Beckett, you didn't . . ."

Emotion clogged in her voice, and I swallowed down the knot that formed in my throat.

After I had uncovered June Sullivan's handwriting, ticking off the heights of the Sullivan children through the years, a long-buried sentimental part of my soul couldn't bear to throw it away.

"It took me a minute to figure out what to do with it. But it didn't seem right to throw it in the dumpster."

Kate grabbed the long board from me, holding it out to look at it. I had added a shiny layer of protective lacquer to cover the surface so nothing could ever destroy Mrs. Sullivan's delicate handwriting. I had also constructed a small black frame around it to make it look like more of a piece of artwork than random construction debris.

Kate turned the board to show her brothers. "It's

Mama's handwriting. She had measured our heights against the wall that was taken down."

The boys stepped forward as a unit, staring down at the soft loops of their mother's forgotten handwriting.

"It was underneath two layers of wallpaper," Kate continued. "She was there all this time."

"Holy shit," Lee breathed out, barely audible.

Wyatt raked a finger across his name.

Duke stood silently staring down at his mother's writing. Without a word, he turned and wrapped me into a hug, squeezing me tight and beating his hand against my back.

"You did this?" We all turned to look at Red, who was staring down at the board.

"Yes, sir." I lifted my chin and tried to read his stern expression.

Red grabbed the board and stared down at his children's names along with the tick marks that documented their growth.

"Juney always was sentimental about how quickly those kids grew. I even had to hold Katie up as a baby so she could be on there too."

A wistful smile spread over his face as though he was remembering with striking clarity the life he'd shared with the woman he loved. It was a painful reminder that, even though his memory could be cloudy, those precious moments were still tucked away there.

Red looked at me. "You did a damn fine job. Juney would have loved to live in a house like this."

Tootie stepped forward to put an arm around her brother. "She's here today," Tootie said softly. "Her love is wrapped up in these walls, and no amount of renovation could ever take that away."

Being surrounded by the love that family shared despite

the trials they had been put through was heart wrenching. Instead of jagged edges, the broken pieces of the Sullivans had been smoothed over with time, affection, and a deeply rooted love that tied them together.

It was an honor to stand on the fringes and witness it.

This is what a family feels like.

STEAM ROSE and swirled above my coffee mug as I sat at the expansive kitchen island of Tootie's new kitchen, the old metal lockbox in front of me. Moving Tootie back into the farmhouse had been simple, and the delicate touches of her ceramic chickens and dainty hand towels made it feel more like her home than ever.

My aunt's hand found my back, and I sighed, leaning into her and resting my head against her arm. "Can you believe it's really done?"

Tootie looked around. "I didn't need all this fuss, but it sure is pretty." She grinned.

"You deserve it," I answered back. "You took care of us. Took care of Dad. You're the glue."

"Ahh," she said, attempting to dismiss my comments. "I'm just old and stubborn. And I never gave up on any of you, even if there were times you wanted to give up on yourselves."

Aunt Tootie pulled the lockbox toward her and gently opened the latch. The smell of old paper wafted up. She carefully moved her fingers through the items left behind.

"So what's next?" she asked.

I shrugged. "I'm not sure." I sighed. "I would like to figure out what some of this means and why there are old liquor bottles with the Kings' name on them and records of an illegal bootlegging operation in our basement."

Tootie gently closed the lid. "I wasn't talking about the speakeasy. I was talking about that man of yours." Her assessing eyes looked me over. "Do you think you'll go back to Chicago with him?"

I shook my head. "I don't think I can," I whispered. "I can't keep running from my past. This is my home." I swallowed hard. "But I'm also afraid to let him go. I love him."

Her kind eyes smiled down at me. "It makes sense that you would be wary to trust after what you've been through. But if you're willing to take advice from an old woman . . ." She squeezed my shoulder.

"You're not old."

She laughed. "I most certainly am. I'm old and I have my secrets too. I bet you didn't know that I also dated a set of brothers." She lifted an eyebrow.

"Tootie. You did not!"

"It's true. And trust me, back then, it was even more scandalous."

I stared in disbelief.

"Your uncle Soapy's brother Buster was the oldest. He courted me and painted promises of a life of travel and romance and adventure." She sighed and shook her head. "'Course he didn't have a pot to piss in, but I overlooked that at the time. I was wrapped up in the fantasy and promises of young love. Turns out the man was good with words, and that was about it. He had been telling those same big lies to Bug King behind my back."

My mouth dropped open, and Tootie nodded. "Over time we bonded over our mutual hatred for that man.

"It wasn't long after Buster was gone that Soapy swooped in to ease the ache in my heart. I didn't want to trust him, and I didn't want to believe anything he told me, but that man was persistent. After a whole year of flowers and walks in the park, my heart was healed enough to listen."

She laughed and pressed a hand to her chest. "I bet you that man proposed to me a hundred times." With a soft smile, she pointed a finger at me. "Now that's patience."

Tootie patted the back of my hand. "Trust me, when you've got a man's heart wrapped up, he will move heaven and earth. And Katie, you deserve nothing less than that."

I swallowed hard. "Beckett and I haven't really talked about what's next, now that the house is done."

"Don't worry, dear. I've seen the way that man looks at you. His heart hasn't been his for a while now. Maybe you need to tell him how you feel. Give that boy a nudge."

Tootie pulled an old faded photograph from the lock-box, and her brows pinched together as she pulled it closer for a better look.

"Do you know them?" I asked, focusing my attention on the photograph.

Tootie turned the photograph over to look at the faded cursive handwriting on the back of the snapshot—*James, Helen, and Philo.*

"I can't say for certain that I do," she said as she again flipped the black-and-white photograph over.

Three happy faces smiled back at us. The two men wore pressed pants and dress shoes. One had on a dark tie, loosened at the neck, while the other wore a light collared knit shirt with the top two buttons undone. The woman, in a dainty floral print dress and heels, had her hands on her hips and was captured mid laugh.

Tootie tipped the picture toward me. "But if I was a betting woman, I think there's more to the story than we realize. You might want to make a visit to the library and see if Bug can't help you rustle up some information about who these three might be."

She pointed to the woman. "Because there's no mistaking that Sullivan smile." Her finger slid over to one of the men, who stood proudly next to her. "And no one in town has shoulders like that but a King."

～

BLUEBIRD BOOK CLUB was buzzing with excitement as pictures of the newly renovated farmhouse circulated. Everyone wanted to know details about the speakeasy we'd uncovered and when Tootie might throw a party so people could see it in person.

"It seems like your followers are excited about the house. How do your brothers feel about the renovations?" MJ's sweet, genuine curiosity made me smile.

"Very impressed. It's so much more homey and open, but we also managed to keep some of the charm that reminds me of our childhood. Wyatt was trying to talk Beckett into doing something with that apartment over the barn at Highfield House next."

"Start by getting rid of that disgusting green recliner," Annie added, and we shared a laugh, recalling Lee's treasured *lucky chair* he refused to get rid of.

It was disgusting.

"Duke mostly just grumbled and shrugged," I continued. "Which is very on brand for him." I laughed and took a sip of the spiked lemonade in my hand. "Who knows, maybe he needs to get laid."

As the words came out of my mouth, Sylvie coughed, and her drink nearly pushed out of her nose. She sputtered as MJ laughed and tossed her a napkin and sat up. "Red has had a tough few days. It's probably just stress from that." She grabbed her sister's hand. "Hey, Sylvie. Come with me to the bathroom?" She smiled back at us as she dragged Sylvie with her. "We'll be right back."

Annie looked between the King sisters as MJ dragged a coughing Sylvie up and toward the back of the book shop. Annie turned to me with a pinch in her brows and lifted her shoulders. She shook her head, shooting a look that communicated a silent *What the hell was that about?*

Holding up both hands, her eyes went wide. "Whatever." Annie shifted to face me. "So have you decided? Are you going to make *Home Again* a long-term thing?"

Last book club I'd had one too many glasses of Charles Attwater-gifted wine and had blabbed to Annie and Lark my idea of working with Beckett to document historic home renovations in Outtatowner and the surrounding areas. Really it was just a fantasy, but once I'd given voice to it, I couldn't *stop* thinking about it.

Mr. Miller had also gotten my wheels turning when he'd asked about monetizing *Home Again*'s social media pages, and the more I looked into it, the more I realized that we could actually make good money through advertisements, sponsorships, and affiliate links.

Just the thought of working side by side with Beckett on a new renovation lit me up inside.

Only I hadn't had the guts to even talk to him about it. His business was thriving without me, and he kept no secrets about his mild annoyance for being ogled by strangers as the Brutish Builder.

The only glimmer of hope I clung to was how much Beckett seemed to love the moments when I pointed the camera at him and he explained the minute details of trim and molding, building structure, or historic paint palettes. He had a wealth of specific expertise that our followers ate up.

I looked at Annie. "I don't know. The idea is silly, really."

"Are you kidding me? The idea is a freaking *gold mine*. Outtatowner is only one of the historic towns along Lake Michigan. There are *hundreds* of houses and properties you could get your hands on. Just think about what else you might find. One day you could have a TV show like on HGTV!"

Annie's untethered excitement only furthered the fantasy. In my head, it made total sense. Beckett could still have his business, but together we'd market on social media and document the renovation of historic homes, starting in my very own hometown.

In my heart, I worried.

I shook my head. "I haven't had the guts to talk to him about it yet."

Annie lifted an eyebrow and sipped her wine. "Did you grow the balls to talk to him about wanting to get married and have all his babies?"

"Shut up!" I hissed before playfully sending her a bland look and balling up a napkin in my fist. "Have you talked to Lee?" I tossed the rumpled napkin at her, and she playfully swatted it away.

"Shh!" she scolded. "It took *years* for people to stop asking us when we were getting married despite the millions of times we assured everyone we were just friends. I don't need that old rumor rising from the ashes to bite me on the ass again. Charles and I went on our fifth date, and that's about the time men get all weird about my friendship with your brother."

I sighed in defeat. "I know. It's fine. A sister can hope is all. The last thing I want is a sister-in-law that I don't like."

"Trust me, I don't think you have anything to worry about. Your brother will never settle down."

"What about Charles?" I teased. "Is he the marrying type?"

She shrugged. "I don't know about that yet, but he is the make-out-in-the-backroom type." She slyly sipped her drink as her words sank in.

"You did not!"

Her smile widened, and I leaned in to get every girly detail about her latest date with our town's newest resident.

Affection for my hometown poured through me. I missed the friendships. My family. The sense of belonging that was all a part of living in Outtatowner.

I looked over at my aunt and smiled.

Tootie preened and basked in all the attention the Blue-birds were giving her.

Bug was shooting daggers from the corner. Her pursed lips and crossed arms were frosty enough to scare even a King away, but I was determined.

Once Annie left early to meet Charles for a sponta-neous walk on the beach, I plopped down next to Bug with a sigh. "Hey there, Ms. Bug. Can I get you a refill on that sweet tea?"

She peered down her slim nose at me. "I take it unsweet."

Of course you do.

"I'm fine," she continued.

I cleared my throat, hoping the general camaraderie of the book club would allow her to open up a bit and offer some help in identifying the three people from the photograph.

I observed Bug as she watched the women circle Tootie, asking questions and fussing over her.

"Pretty wild that something like a secret room was tucked away all that time, isn't it?"

She gently lifted a shoulder. "Lots of things get hidden over time. Some things are best kept that way."

Her dark eyes looked over me, and a tiny shiver ran down my spine.

She looked me over. "You know the Remington County historical society is having a field day with this."

I nodded. "They've called Aunt Tootie several times, asking to photograph and document the space. I also think they're hoping she might donate a few items to the town museum."

So far, as a family, we had kept to our pact to not reveal any information about the connection to the Kings we had uncovered in the speakeasy. Having the county historical society poking around would splash something like that all over town, and the busybodies would have a field day with any scrap of information about our families and the feud.

Half the time I wondered if the feud hadn't been kept alive for so long simply because the residents of Outta-towner loved to gossip about it.

"I could be salty about the fact Tootie is reveling in all her newfound attention." She lifted her chin. "But jealousy isn't my color."

"Of course not," I assured her. I swallowed back the nerves as I pulled the photograph from my purse. I needed

Bug on my side, and buttering up the prideful woman seemed like my only option. "With your experience as the record keeper at the library, I was hoping you might be able to help me with something I found."

I held the photo out for her and she took it, looking over the faces smiling back at us.

Her eyes narrowed as she whispered, "Where did you get this?"

My eyes went wide, and my heart thunked beneath my ribs. *Does she know something?* "I found it in the speakeasy. It was in a little locked box we found hidden beneath the bar."

Her soft wrinkled hand gripped mine tightly. "What else did you find?"

My brows pinched together. "Not much else. Some papers and other things I can't make much sense out of without context. This photograph is the best lead I've got about the history of the speakeasy."

Releasing my hand, she took a slow, steadying breath before gently clearing her throat. "Bring what you have to the library, and I might be able to help you go through the archives." She paused. "Come tomorrow after closing. We'll have more privacy then and can go through it together."

A tiny ripple of unease rolled through my belly at her startling reaction to the photograph. I tamped it down and smiled. "Thank you."

Despite tiny warning bells telling me not to trust a King, I needed to know the secrets my family and that house were keeping.

∽

"Do you really think she recognized someone?" Beckett looked over the plate of Thai noodles we shared, his chopsticks resting gently in his fingers. My eyes appreciated the cut lines of his bare shoulders and torso as he sprawled across the rug in front of his fireplace.

I tilted my head back and wove a noodle into my mouth. I thought, chewing, and shrugged. "She was acting weird. Surprised, maybe?"

"If she knows more, maybe it has something to do with both families." His eyes narrowed, considering. "Business deal gone bad?"

"Boring," I offered with a sly smile. "Love triangle?"

"Betrayal and backstabbing. That's fun," he teased. "Maybe the woman was a witch and they were her henchmen." His eyes danced with humor as we came up with more stories for the three friends in the photograph.

"Neighbors who bonded over a love of blueberries and bourbon."

"Nudists who took one annual clothed photo."

"Maybe," I said, giggling. "Or maybe one guy was desperately in love with Helen but never said anything. He enlisted in the army, and when he came back, she was with the other guy."

He rolled his eyes. "So a love triangle, like you said."

I pushed a piece of steamed broccoli toward him, and he pinched it between his chopsticks before popping it into his mouth.

"Sure, a love triangle, but a *heartbreaking* one." I placed my hand over my heart for dramatic emphasis.

He shrugged. "Maybe they were just friends . . . before their families got in the way and started whatever bullshit feud has lasted all this time."

I stared down at the picture, knowing the simplest

answer was probably right. "Yeah, maybe. I just can't help the nagging feeling that it *means* something, though. Someone cared enough about the photograph to keep it."

Staring back at me from the photo was a woman who was free. You could almost hear the lightness of her laughter. She was *happy*.

I wanted that too.

I gathered up my courage and pushed my plate aside so I could settle in next to Beckett.

"So I've been kicking around an idea . . ." I swallowed hard as my nerves threatened to get the best of me.

Beckett kissed my shoulder and pulled me closer. "Oh . . . does it involve you getting naked again?" he teased.

"Not exactly. It's a business idea. Well . . ." I let out a gentle, nervous laugh. "Business and personal, I guess."

He sat up, letting his forearms drape over his bent knees. Seriousness settled over his features as he positioned himself to listen. "Okay."

I smoothed back my hair and pulled the blanket tighter around my shoulders.

Shit. I really should have put on more clothes before having this conversation.

"People have been asking for weeks what our next *Home Again* project is. What if we, ya know . . . did one?"

My heart tumbled as a frown pulled at his lips. "Another reno project? Together?"

I blinked, trying to recover from his less-than-enthusiastic tone and remain upbeat. "Yes. You run the crew. I document on social media. We could monetize like your dad—"

"I've got jobs in Chicago lined up." The way his curt tone cut off my words sliced into me.

"Oh." My nervous laughter gave me away, and I felt

more naked than ever. "Of course you do. It was silly." I swatted the air between us and fought back a wave of embarrassed tears.

"It's not silly." He shook his head, and a tiny ember of hope sparked to life in my chest.

"It's not?"

He scooted closer, his warmth seeping into me as his arms pulled me to his chest. "No. It's not. But I have questions—things like what properties, timelines, buy-in costs, a hundred other things. A business partnership is a significant undertaking."

Of course it was. Beckett is a successful businessman, and I'm a girl with an Instagram page and a hopeful heart.

"Of course. I know that. I just—I don't know. I thought it would give us more time to figure out what this is between us."

I pinched my eyes closed as the words escaped my lips.

His voice was rumbly and low. "You'd want that? To work with me on building projects and document it all for your page?"

Tension in my shoulders eased as his embrace comforted my worried heart. "Well, *someone* has to put up with your salty attitude every day."

We laughed, but I didn't miss it when he shifted the conversation, and that very worried heart of mine still hung in the air without an answer.

THIRTY-TWO
BECKETT

IRRITATION STORMED through me as I stared out the window into the whipping wind and snow that danced across the raging waves.

I couldn't shake the hope in Kate's voice when she'd pitched her idea for expanding the *Home Again* page to an actual business and taking on another project together. I wanted to scoop her up. Laugh and shout at the ceiling that it was the best fucking idea I'd ever heard.

In fact, I had already been thinking of alternatives—selfish ways to keep her in my life. For the past few years, I had made a habit of visiting Outtatowner nearly monthly to catch up with Duke and soak up the simplicity of quiet small-town living. There had to be a way I could transfer some of my business to Michigan or work remotely out of Chicago. Half of the time the jobs could run themselves, and with Gloria at the office, there had to be a way to make it work.

I didn't give a shit if I never saw a dime from *Home Again.* Just the thought of working with Kate every day was enough to send sparks of excitement dancing through my veins.

It was hope.

Happiness.

Unease.

Kate didn't seem to realize it, but her star was about to skyrocket, and a grouchy builder with a piss-poor attitude and shitty self-esteem would only drag her down.

But I couldn't bring myself to face that. Not yet.

My eyes scanned the familiar beachfront as the glass protected me from the howling wind and snow. My heart was heavy, knowing that I would be holding Kate back.

She had awoken a part of myself I didn't even know existed, and yet it wouldn't be enough.

I wouldn't be enough.

My business already demanded nearly all my time and attention, and I couldn't risk losing everything I had worked for, only for Kate to realize she'd mistakenly hung her hopes on a man like me.

A man who would always be a placeholder for the real deal. Only with Kate I wasn't sure I'd ever recover when our relationship inevitably came to an end.

But I would do it.

For her.

I could see myself, years down the road, running into her in town and forcing myself to smile. Seeing some other man's arm around her shoulders and willing my heart to stop pounding against my ribs and force myself to be happy for her.

Fucking schmuck.

I huffed out an exasperated breath. *Great. I'm already jealous of a fictional man.*

Fresh memories of Kate flooded my mind—the way her

laugh buried itself into my bones, the way her eyes sparkled when she looked at me. I didn't want to let her go, but I couldn't ask her to give up her family and life in Michigan to follow me back to Chicago. I had nothing to offer her but late nights waiting up for me in a fancy penthouse when she deserved to blossom in her coastal hometown.

I closed my eyes and tried to calm my racing thoughts. I couldn't stay in my cold, heartless house on the dune and stew all night. I pulled my phone from my pocket and dialed my best friend.

Duke answered on the third ring. "What's up?"

"You up for a drink?"

"Out of little sisters to prey on?" Duke's voice was stern, but laced with the subtle humor I had missed.

"Very funny," I shot back. "Ms. Bug agreed to help Kate with some after-hours research at the library."

"The Grudge in thirty?"

"Meet you there." I slipped the phone back into my pocket and bundled up against the dipping December temperatures.

A beer with Duke would be just the easy, familiar way to pass the time that I needed to dislodge the spike that had wedged between my ribs.

As expected, the Grudge was nearly empty. I scanned the room, looking for Duke. I spotted him at the far end of the bar, accepting two beers from the server. I made my way over and took a seat beside him.

"Hey, man. How's it going?" Duke asked, turning to face me.

"Fine. Good," I replied, then took a sip of my drink. "Just needed to get out of the house for a bit."

Duke nodded. "I hear you. Sometimes you just need a change of scenery."

We sat in comfortable silence, sipping our drinks and watching the other patrons.

I sat straighter when I spotted Kate across the room, talking to JP King.

My heart skipped a beat as I watched them, trying to discern the nature of their conversation. I couldn't hear what they were saying, but I saw him make a comment that made Kate's face contort in disgust as she stood.

Before I could even think, I was on my feet, storming over to them.

"What did you say to her?" I demanded, my fists clenched at my sides.

JP King sneered at me, sizing me up. "Who are you?"

Prick.

He knew damn well who I was, and a hit of jealousy and possessiveness burned through me. "I'm her boyfriend, asshole," I growled, standing tall and proud.

"The fuck is this?" Duke stood next to me, simmering with anger. "Katie? What are you doing here with him?"

"It's nothing," Kate huffed as she corrected the strap of her purse on her shoulder. "I was just leaving."

JP stood tall, smoothing a hand over his pressed shirt. An air of arrogance and confidence radiated off him. "Think about what I said. That money would pay a lot of bills at Haven Pines."

Duke took a step forward. "What did you say?"

JP raised his hands. "We were talking business."

"Any business you have with her, you have with me." Duke crossed his arms as Kate rolled her eyes at her overprotective older brother.

"Duke, it's fine." Kate dusted off her palms and looked bored as she raked her eyes over JP. "This idiot thought he could use Dad to get us to convince Tootie to sell them the farmhouse."

JP's nostrils flared at her calling him an idiot. "Come on, I thought you were the smart one, Catfish. Guess I should have known." He glanced my way, and rage bubbled beneath my skin when he smirked. "What? Did you think you'd try this guy on for size when his brother was done with you?"

She'd wounded JP's pride, and he'd lashed out.

Big fucking mistake.

Her shocked gasp was all it took for me to lose control. My arm wound in front of her, pulling her out of the way as I stepped into his space.

Gripping JP's collar with one hand, I pulled my right fist back and plowed it into his face. Blood spurted from his nose, and the bar erupted in a flurry around me. I took a punch to the face, followed by a jab to the side, which forced me to release my grip on JP.

Duke was locked up with another man as they fought. Others I didn't even recognize picked a side and started brawling.

It was total chaos inside the Grudge Holder.

In the scuffle, Kate stepped between her brother and whoever he was beating on. In a blur, she stumbled and fell, her butt smacking against the gritty surface of the bar floor. Bending at the waist to catch my breath, I took in a shocked Kate as she scooted backward to get out of the fray. A screaming buzz filled my ears when I saw her wide eyes and stunned expression.

Immediately I scooped her up, setting her on her feet and checking her over for injuries.

The owner of the bar stepped in, holding a baseball bat

and separating the fighters. "Enough!" he bellowed. "Cops are on the way. Get the hell out of my bar."

I was breathing heavily, blood dripping from my nose, and my eyebrow stung. I looked over at Kate, who was staring at me with a mix of shock and anger.

"Oh my god! You're bleeding." Kate ran her fingers over my eyebrow, and a fresh sting settled over my throbbing eye. "What the hell were you thinking?"

"No one speaks to you that way." I'd never be sorry for putting that asshole in his place when it came to her.

"I swear the men in this town don't think!" Kate shot her brother and me a look that made us both shrink back.

In true Outtatowner fashion, once the fight was broken up, most people went back to their tables and drinks as though the scuffle had never happened. JP dusted himself off and shot a look of disgust our way before striding toward the exit with a few stragglers in tow.

Duke pinched the bridge of his nose. "Goddamn it, my face hurts."

Kate looked at her brother in horror. "Someone hit you in the face?"

There was a long-standing unspoken rule of no hits to the face. At one time it had allowed Kings and Sullivans to hash things out with their fists without bringing home evidence of their fighting to their parents.

Duke gestured to me. "Hotshot over here threw out the rulebook when he clocked JP in his smug fucking mouth."

I winced. "Sorry, man."

Duke shook his hand, flexing it and turning it over. He sighed. "I'm going home."

I looked over at the bar owner, who pointed his bat toward the exit. "Yeah, me too. Come on, Princess."

I looped my arm over Kate's shoulder as we moved

toward the exit. She pulled me into her car and headed toward the beach house. Once inside, she dumped her purse and keys on the kitchen island and pulled a bottle of water from the fridge. She took one sip and slid the rest toward me.

My heart hiccuped at the sight of her moving so comfortably in my kitchen.

"You gonna tell me about that meeting with JP?"

Kate let loose a frustrated sigh as she planted her hands on the island. "Don't get me started." She raked a hand through her long brown hair. "It was a setup."

I stepped forward. "A setup? What happened? Are you okay?"

She sighed. "I'm fine. Just annoyed. Turns out Bug was less interested in helping me and more interested in having JP try to get me to convince Aunt Tootie to sell the farmhouse."

"Sell it?"

She nodded. "They cornered me in the library after everyone had left. And do you know what the worst part is? He offered to pay for my father's cost of living at Haven Pines if I convinced her to sell the house at a reasonable price."

I blinked at her. "Kate, that's—"

"Completely out of the question," she cut in. Anger flared in her green eyes, and I didn't continue.

"It's just been a long day." Kate's head hung as she leaned on the island for strength. I wanted to soothe things, make them better.

"How's your ass?" I asked, trying to lighten the tension between us.

She turned her head and looked at me, smiling.

I moved to her, caging her in with my arms as I came up

behind her and planted my hands on the island. "I'm sorry I lost my cool. I didn't like how he was talking to you." I nuzzled my nose into her hair and let the floral smell of her shampoo soothe me. "I swear, when I saw you fall, my heart stopped."

Kate was quiet for a moment, but when she spoke, my heart stopped beating. "Beckett, what are we doing here?"

Her voice was strong, and my heart thundered against my ribs. Kate turned around to face me, still locked between my arms.

I studied her face, trying to find the right words.

When I didn't speak, her eyes searched mine. "The farmhouse is done, and I need to know. Are you going back to Chicago?"

"Kate, I—"

The words lodged in my throat. Every part of me needed her love, but fear held me back. The fear of *knowing*.

There was a finite amount of love she could give me. If I used it all up too quickly, when she spent enough time to see the mess I was inside, she'd be gone that much sooner.

She exhaled and closed her eyes. "Beckett, somehow you've managed to have all of me. How many pieces of you do I get? I just need to know."

I stood to meet her eyes. "I have to go back, but I care about you. I'd like to see you again. Of course I would."

Her brows pinched together as her eyes searched my face. "See me again? What does that mean?"

I sighed and raked a hand through my hair. "I can come here when work isn't taking up my time. Maybe even look into taking a few local jobs if there's an opening in my schedule. You're always welcome at my place in Chicago."

Her chin wobbled as she nodded. I needed her love, but all I was doing was breaking her heart.

"I need more, Beckett."

My jaw worked. "It's what I can give you."

Her green eyes bore into me, tearing my soul from my chest. "I know."

Defensive anger simmered in my veins. *Why is she doing this? Why isn't it enough?*

She swallowed hard and looked past me to see my suitcase against the wall. Seeing it only dumped gasoline on the frustration burning inside her.

She gestured to the suitcase. "That's it? You're just leaving?"

"Kate, I have a job, *a life* in Chicago. I was always going back. That doesn't mean we can't still see each other."

She shook her head. "But what does that mean? *See each other?*"

I let loose my own frustrated sigh. I didn't need her putting all the broken parts of me out for display. "Are we really having the *What are we?* talk? I'm not like my brother. I won't string you along."

Kate took a breath before pinning me with her stormy green eyes. "What you're doing to me is so much worse than what he ever did. At one time I may have imagined a lot between Declan and me, but he never once made me believe he felt it too."

The spiraling realization burrowed inside me.

She was right, but I was too fucked up to give in to the dream of having her forever.

I had always known that I had some dreams that would come true and some that wouldn't, but I slowly realized that what I could give her would only hurt her in the long run.

"I'm not the one you marry."

Her eyes flew to mine and simmered with unshed tears that were a knife to my gut. I tracked one finger along her jaw, moving the hair back so I could see her face. "But, Katie-girl, if I was the marrying kind, there wouldn't be anyone else."

She swatted my hand away as she stepped away from me in disgust, the loss of her heat already chilling my bones.

"Don't you dare," she whispered. "Don't you dare make this harder on me, just to make yourself feel better."

I braced my hands on the kitchen island and dropped my chin. Every possible scenario for how this could play out ran through my head. My mind snagged on the very likely scenario where she got smart and left me. My stomach pitched and rolled.

I stood, unable to move, despite knowing the words that could get her back. Words that screamed inside me but wouldn't come out.

Instead, I didn't say anything at all as I watched the best thing I'd ever had walk out of my front door.

THIRTY-THREE
KATE

"I'M SO EMBARRASSED. I'm an idiot." I closed my eyes and sighed into the phone. The call with Sophie and Gemma was the only thing holding me together.

"You are NOT an idiot. He's the idiot." *Sweet, fierce Sophie.*

Gemma snorted. "Amen, sister. I can't believe he didn't stop you from walking out."

"It's my own fault. I knew from the beginning this was just a hookup, and I had to go and catch feelings and imagine it was more than it was. Typical Kate."

"Stop that shit," Gemma interjected.

Frustrated, I fought the tears that burned behind my eyelids. "I'm serious. Why am I like this? At first it was sexy and so wrong that I couldn't help but find it hot. Then I had to go and fall in *love* with the guy. It's like a pathetic repeat of Declan, and it makes me sick."

"Only he's not Declan. He fell in love too. Don't forget that." Gemma was strong, and I leaned into her strength.

"I know. He's not. And I thought his feelings were

changing, but now . . . I don't know. Maybe I imagined all that too."

"His choices don't lessen your value, Kate."

"Thanks, Soph."

"Seriously. If he doesn't realize what he had, then he needs to wake the fuck up." Gemma huffed a breath through the phone. "And if he doesn't, there's only one thing to say."

Oh boy . . .

"Fuck that guy."

Fuck that guy.

I rehearsed the words in my head over and over, but despite how much I wanted to believe them, they always fell flat.

A cavern opened in my stomach as I left Beckett's beach house the night before. I hadn't allowed myself to think past the renovation, and now that it was completed, there was nothing. With him, I was lost in a bubble of deliciously rough sex and tender touches, laughter, and teasing banter. I let myself hide where it was safe and comforting.

It no longer mattered to me that he was my ex-boyfriend's brother, or that he was Duke's best friend. I had already endured a few judgmental stares and headshakes from the gossips in town, but it hadn't mattered.

Beneath his surly attitude and pigheadedness was a man who was alone. Someone who tried desperately to measure up and always felt as though he came up lacking. It hadn't mattered that the Sullivans cared for him over the years or that they'd practically adopted him while I'd been living in Montana.

He couldn't see it, and it wasn't something I could fix.

A lump lodged in my throat, and tears burned at the corners of my eyes. When I had asked Beckett to define what we were, I already knew the truth.

He loved me.

Only he was too fucking scared to admit it. Too afraid that he couldn't measure up to put himself out there.

Despite how hurt I had been, I was still so *sad* for him.

Thinking back, none of it had worked out like it was supposed to. Returning to my hometown and falling for a rugged contractor should have been easy, like it was in a romance movie.

He'd smile. I'd swoon. We'd live happily ever after. Boom. Roll credits.

Only we'd still been tangled up in our own bullshit and forgot to sort it out before we both blindly dove in headfirst. A part of me knew, deep down, that Sophie was right.

I deserve better than that. We both do.

Which was why I was freezing my ass off and trudging my way up Main Street. I'd made a plan and needed to walk it out in order to gather the shreds of courage I would need to actually execute it.

As I walked down Main Street, I bundled up my coat and scarf, taking in the sights and sounds of my hometown of Outtatowner during Christmastime. The air was crisp, and fat snowflakes gently fell from the winter sky, covering the town in a blanket of white.

Each storefront was decorated with twinkling lights, and wreaths adorned the doors. The town square was transformed into a winter wonderland, complete with an ice-skating rink and a towering Christmas tree.

Case in point: perfect Hallmark holiday movie.

I pushed thoughts of Beckett to the back of my mind as I

took in the sights and sounds of my hometown. I felt a sense of comfort that I had never experienced anywhere else. It was like the town itself was wrapping its arms around me, welcoming me home and comforting me with open arms.

I couldn't help but smile as I passed by the Sugar Bowl, where the scent of freshly baked gingerbread cookies wafted out onto the street. Through the huge glass window, I saw Huck and waved at him. He gestured for me to come in, maybe even warm up with a hot cup of coffee, but I only waved and burrowed myself more tightly into my coat and scarf as I kept walking toward the lake.

The snowflakes were beginning to stick to the ground, creating a soft crunch underfoot as I continued down the sidewalk. The town was truly transformed during the holiday season, and I couldn't help but feel grateful for this time with my family.

Everywhere I looked, there were reminders of the memories I had made in this town, with the people who had always been there for me, even when I had left. The Christmas decorations that adorned the lampposts and the storefronts were a reminder of the years of holiday seasons I had spent here with my family and friends.

As I walked, I couldn't help but feel like I was exactly where I was meant to be. Despite the heartache I was feeling over Beckett, being home in Outtatowner filled me with a sense of peace that I couldn't find anywhere else. It was a feeling of belonging that I had never experienced anywhere but here, and I knew that no matter where life took me, Outtatowner would always be my home.

I paused and looked around me, taking in the beauty of the town. Being the offseason, the only cars that passed were those of townies. The holiday lights sparkled like diamonds, and the festive music that played in the background filled me with joy.

I took a deep breath and looked around. The town was so quaint and charming, and there was something about the small-town atmosphere that made me feel comforted and at peace. I knew that I was exactly where I was meant to be.

A pang of sadness and loneliness washed over me.

As I continued my walk, I smiled at the shop owners and exchanged pleasantries with the locals. Despite fault lines drawn between Kings and Sullivans, everyone knew each other, and that sense of community was something that I had always treasured.

When my face froze in the bitter cold and my hands were ice, I trudged through the snow toward Beckett's house.

With a frozen fist, I knocked on the door and sucked in an icy breath.

THIRTY-FOUR
BECKETT

I HATE THIS HOUSE.

When a knock sounded at the door, I was pulled from my spiraling thoughts. I'd made a mess with Kate, acted like a fool, and had done nothing to stop her from walking out.

I pulled open the front door, and when I saw her, wide eyed and shivering, I pulled her inside. "What the hell are you doing?"

My arms banded around her, and I tortured myself with a hit of her floral shampoo before releasing her.

"Went for a walk and I needed to clear my head."

"It's the middle of winter."

She shivered again. "I noticed."

Annoyed, I guided her inside, helped her remove her coat, and deposited her in a chair by the fire. Tension radiated off her, and I could see her anxiety, the questions written all over her face.

You did that.

I was at fault for why Kate even questioned my feelings for her. She deserved a man who didn't choke on his words.

A man who would never have allowed her to question how deeply in love with her he had fallen.

But still, I hadn't left Outtatowner. I couldn't—not before I saw her one last time and committed every inch of her to memory. The curve of her neck, the roll of her laughter, the green and gold flecks of her eyes. I wanted to soak her in.

Those eyes shifted to me, full of sadness, as I handed her a hot cup of coffee. "Thanks."

I frowned down at her before grabbing the cup back out of her hand and setting it on the table beside the chair. Without a word, I pulled her up and shifted so I was sitting and pulled Kate onto my lap.

"Come here." I wound my arms around her.

Kate's frozen body melted into me, and I breathed her in deep. Snuggled together, I listened to her slow, even breathing.

After a moment, she finally whispered, "Are you okay?"

My voice was thick and rusty. "No."

I am so fucking far from okay.

Her breath hitched, and we fell silent, the only sounds filling the cavernous living room were the shallow ins and outs of our breathing and the soft crackle of the burning wood.

Finally, Kate sucked in a wobbly breath. "Beckett, I know you need to leave. Like you said, your whole life is in Chicago. I wanted you to know that I understand and I don't hate you."

I hated the sadness that seeped through her words. I shifted, forcing her to look at me, and the unshed tears clinging to her lashes gutted me.

"My life may be in Chicago, but my heart is right here."

One tear tumbled, and I brushed it away with my thumb. She lifted her eyes to mine. "I can't wait for you."

My chest went hollow at her words as she buried her face into my neck.

This is it. I'm actually losing her.

"I know you can't, Princess. And I know I can't ask you to."

"The thing is . . . I realized I have spent my life living for other people—my brothers, my dad, every boyfriend I've ever had. I need that to stop. I want to put down my roots and feel what it's like to thrive in a place of *my* choosing. To grow and change and truly be tethered. I *want* to be tied to a place. To this place." Her chin wobbled, and her hands gripped my shirt as I held her. "I can't do that if a piece of me is missing. I'll always be wishing I was with you in Chicago or sad you're not here with me. I don't want to catch myself waiting by the phone, wondering when you'll call."

I steeled myself despite the voice screaming in my head to protest. "I understand." I moved my fingers under her chin so she could look at me again. "Listen to me. I want so much for you. You deserve it all, and this town deserves the full Catfish Kate experience."

Her watery laugh cut through the tension, and I held her closer.

"You deserve it too," she whispered. "To be truly happy."

I swallowed hard, knowing full well the key to my unwavering happiness was bundled in my arms. "How about this?"

She looked up from my chest. The hope in her eyes nearly cut me in two.

"I'll find a way."

Kate blinked at me as my words settled over her. A long, tense silence stretched between us as I repeated my vow to her in my head.

I'll find a way to make this work, Katie-girl. I promise.

"I need you to find something in here." She pressed her hand to my thumping heart. "Find the man who's playful. Who sneaks treats to a rooster who hates him. Who hasn't given up on a family that doesn't even deserve him. The man who treats his crew with respect, as equals. I need you to love that man as much as I do."

Her words were like a dagger to my heart. It wasn't enough to say I loved her. She needed me to love myself—something that felt like an insurmountable task.

But I couldn't give up on her. On us.

"Okay." The word clawed its way out of my throat, and panic coursed through me.

Kate deserves more, and all she's asking for is time.

The thought ran itself on a loop in my head and steeled my determination to figure my shit out. I swallowed back the tears that burned my throat and threatened to escape.

If time was what Kate needed—for herself and for me—then that was what I could give her.

She shifted, looking at me. I was lost in the depths of her green eyes. My heart remained a bloody pulp on the floor.

"Promise me? Promise we'll both put in the work and this time apart isn't forever?" Her eyes were searching for comforting reassurance. I had never been more sure of anything in my entire life.

I rested my forehead against hers. "The only thing that's forever is you and me, Katie-girl. I promise."

THIRTY-FIVE
KATE

TIME WAS a strange and lonely thing. Two weeks had passed since Beckett and I had reluctantly agreed to separate in order to work out our issues, and since then nothing felt right. My clothes were itchy. Short winter days stretched out far too long. My smiles were forced. The skies were thick and heavy with gray clouds that matched my mood.

Time inched forward.

The only problem was, I had no idea how long it would take and whether a relationship built on shaky footing was strong enough for Beckett to be there on the other side of it.

Before he left, I had made him promise not to wait around for me, but the words were wooden as they left my mouth. While I hated the idea of him moving on and possibly meeting someone new, he needed this time as badly as I did.

Maybe even more so.

Aunt Tootie always said, "You can't pour from an empty cup." My cup was bone dry at the moment.

I sat alone in the Highfield House apartment and stared

into space. After Beckett left, I couldn't stand to stay in the farmhouse with my aunt. It was too painful. Every detail, from the period-appropriate color palette to the restored wood trim, reminded me of him.

Not even my own house felt safe for my heart. I sighed and let my head hang.

How did we get here?

The cold wintry air howled outside. I made a hot cup of coffee and lost myself in wrapping the small gifts I'd picked up for my family as soft music played in the background. Lately I couldn't stand the silence of my own thoughts.

It was the first Christmas in years all the Sullivans would be spending together, and I desperately needed it to be the start of new, happy memories. I needed to feed my roots if they had any hope of flourishing.

I looked out the window toward the home across the gravel driveway. Wyatt, Penny, and Lark were still living there while they planned the build of their dream home come spring.

For Christmas, Highfield House was trimmed in colored lights, and a fresh wreath with a big red bow hung on the front door. Garland wound around the handrails on either side of the porch stairs. In the far distance, across the yard, I could see rows and rows of dormant blueberry bushes shivering against the frigid Michigan winter.

My insides felt just as cold and dead, but unlike the blueberry bushes that held on to life until the spring thaw, I felt permanently numbed.

Movement on the porch caught my attention. Bundled up, my niece Penny stomped out the front door. I watched with a small smile as she stepped to the edge of the top stair and cupped her hands around her mouth.

"Aunt Katie! Are you coming or what?"

Wyatt appeared behind her and dropped a gentle hand on her shoulder, probably scolding her for shouting up to me, if the deep line in his forehead was any indication.

I laughed, and it sounded strange to my ears. I pulled open the door. The frigid air slapped at my cheeks, and I waved my hand toward her. "Just getting my coat!"

"Well, hurry up!" Penny called.

"Pickle," Wyatt scolded at the same time.

I closed the door and wrapped myself in my thick puffy coat and gloves, then pulled a knit hat over my ears. I wound a thick wool scarf around my neck and braced myself to face the bitter cold. To face my family and pretend everything was fine and I wasn't thinking about Beckett every second of the day.

I carefully made my way down the steep, rickety steps of the apartment and met Wyatt and his family by his car. He grabbed the bag of presents in my hand, and I piled into the back next to Penny and tried not to feel like a little kid as my brother drove us to the farmhouse.

Penny leaned toward me. "Aunt Katie, what are your thoughts on Santa?"

My eyes met Wyatt's in the rearview, and the subtle panic in his expression was clear.

"Well," I said, "I think he's pretty great."

"Did you ever consider that he is basically a big jolly burglar who breaks into your house and leaves presents instead of taking your stuff?"

Lark barked a laugh from the front seat as Wyatt grumbled and looked at us in the rearview mirror.

A soft laugh escaped me. "I mean, you're not wrong."

"Kind of creepy, right?" she added.

Wyatt glanced back as he drove us toward Aunt Tootie's

house. "Keep calling him creepy, Pickle, and he might skip right over our house."

My eyes went wide, and I looked toward Penny, whose cute face twisted when she realized there may have been a sliver of truth in her dad's words.

I leaned in to whisper, "Santa wouldn't do you like that. Especially not when you're the coolest kid I know."

When I winked and her smile bloomed, warmth and affection flowed through me.

Maybe I wasn't so dead after all.

The car pulled down Tootie's driveway, and a fresh stab of pain pinched under my ribs as her home came into view. The farmhouse stood proudly against the fresh white snow. The boys had come with their ladders and trimmed it out with white Christmas lights that twinkled against the dark winter sky. On each of the tall wooden columns of the wraparound porch, Tootie had hung huge festive bows. The home looked like it had been plucked right out of a holiday magazine.

We did that.

Lark turned from the front seat and looked at me with soft, kind eyes. "Ready for this?"

I swallowed hard and faked a smile. "You bet."

At dinner, I sat at one end of the large oak table, surrounded by my family, trying to focus on the delicious food in front of me. Christmas had always been my favorite holiday, but this year was different.

It had been weeks since I'd seen Beckett, and though we had exchanged a few texts, the distance between us seemed to stretch on, just as I feared it would.

My mind raced back to the night after their fight at the Grudge, when I had pushed too hard and asked if he loved me.

I didn't regret that. He needed to know how I felt, and I needed to hear it from his mouth.

Only he didn't. He couldn't. It was the exact moment I knew we each had to work on ourselves if we ever had a chance at true happiness together.

I pressed my eyes shut and sent up a silent prayer that he was putting in the work, too, and that all this would be a temporary blip.

As my family passed dinner dishes around the table, my mind wandered to Beckett's Christmas.

I wondered what he was doing, where he was, and whether he was thinking about me too.

My brother Lee tipped his chin toward Duke as he plopped a heap of sweet potatoes on his plate. "I saw the Miller place finally sold." His eyes softened when he looked toward me, as if to apologize for even bringing it up.

My heart sank.

Despite how cold and out of place it was, the Miller beach house now held more happy memories than sad, thanks to Beckett. It was where we had spent time exploring our relationship, and each other. Inside its walls held first kisses and whispered secrets and soft, satisfied moans. A place where we once laughed and talked about everything and nothing.

And now, another part of us was gone, sold to someone else.

I tried to keep the disappointment off my face and pretended to be interested in Aunt Tootie's latest story, but my thoughts kept drifting back to him.

I missed him so much my chest physically ached.

I looked back at Lee and attempted to shift the conversation to more neutral territory. "I've been thinking about ways to get back at the Kings for putting peanut butter under your door handles."

A wolfish grin spread across his face. "Excellent."

"Can I help?" Penny shouted across the table.

"No," Lark and Wyatt called out in unison.

"Crisco."

Our heads turned toward Dad, who was frowning down at his plate.

"What's that, Dad?" I asked.

"Crisco all over the car windows. Can't rinse it off. Makes one hell of a mess."

Lee grinned and pointed his fork in Dad's direction. "Yes."

I laughed and gently shook my head. It was childish, sure, but I was thankful the rivalry seemed to find its footing in playful pranks rather than breaking and entering. Since moving back home, Tootie hadn't had any suspicions about people trespassing, though we had asked the local police to make an extra round or two down her street.

I knew deep down there was more to the Sullivan–King rivalry than petty pranks, and I would continue digging. If anything, it helped keep my mind off the ache that permanently resided in my chest.

After dinner, we all gathered in the living room to exchange gifts as Elvis crooned holiday music in the background. My brothers teased me about being *Instafamous*, but I laughed it off, not wanting to reveal my heartbreak to them.

I desperately tried to focus on the joy of the moment, the warmth of the fire, the twinkling lights of the Christmas tree, and the happiness of being surrounded by my family again.

"You're awfully pretty to look so glum."

I looked up to see my dad smiling down at me. "Thanks, Dad."

I patted the seat next to me, and he settled into the plush sofa. I leaned my head against his strong shoulder. "I'm not sad."

His chest shook with a laugh. "Always were a shit liar. You remember that time you took Tootie's car for a joyride and broke an axle right before prom?"

My eyes flew to his, and my mouth popped open.

"Well, I know Wyatt took the heat for it, but I'm not as dumb as I look."

"How did you . . . ?"

Dad grinned. "Like I said, you're a shit liar." He nudged my shoulder with his. "You're also a good eight inches shorter than your brother, and I picked up the car from the impound. No way in hell he could have fit behind the wheel with the seat pushed up like that."

A slow grin spread across my face, and the tingle of laughter tickled my belly. Wyatt had covered for me after I had called him, bawling my eyes out, and sure my plans for the perfect prom would be ruined. All this time we'd thought we had actually gotten away with it.

"So tell me, darling. What ails you?"

I sighed. Moments like this with Dad felt fleeting and precious. He deserved my truth. "I'm in love, but we're trying to work out some things first. It's . . . complicated."

He let out a frustrated sigh. "Shouldn't be that complicated. Love is the simplest thing in the world. If that Miller boy has his head up his ass—"

My heart sank. In his mind, timelines often got muddy, and I was sure he assumed I was talking about Declan. "Oh, Dad, Declan and I aren't—"

"I'm not talking about that little shithead. His brother. The older one who Duke got into a tussle with."

I swallowed hard. "Beckett." His name was a thousand tiny pokers under my ribs.

"That's the one. Your mama always liked him. Said deep down he had a lost soul but a good heart."

Emotions welled inside me.

"I'm in love with him, Dad," I whispered.

Dad put his arm around me and squeezed. "Well then, sugarplum, he's the luckiest man in the world. Sometimes it feels like I don't know much, but I do know that."

As the night wore on, Dad grew more and more tired. Nighttime routines were important for him, so Lee took him back to Haven Pines to settle in. Wyatt and Lark corralled a bouncing Penny out the door, and Duke quietly made his exit right after them.

I hugged everyone goodbye and headed up to my childhood bedroom, feeling a sense of loneliness wash over me. I couldn't help but think about Beckett and what could have been if we weren't separated by distance.

My father's words flooded back to me. *Love is the simplest thing in the world.*

As I crawled into bed, I pulled out my phone and stared at it, wondering if I should text him. In the end, I decided against it. I didn't want to bother him, and I didn't want to seem desperate. We'd made a promise, and as far as I could tell, we were both sticking to it.

I breathed in the familiar, comforting smells of the farmhouse. I closed my eyes and tried to push away the ache in my heart, hoping that someday I could find what we lost.

THIRTY-SIX
BECKETT

I SAT ALONE in my Chicago penthouse, staring out the window at the bleak, gray skyline. It was Christmas, but there was no joy in my heart. The place felt cold, empty, and lonely without Kate. I missed her terribly, and it hurt to think about her spending the holiday with her family in Outtatowner.

I tried to distract myself by flipping through TV channels, but nothing seemed to hold my attention. The only thing I could think about was Kate, and how much I wished I was there with her. I knew I had made a mistake by letting her go, and now I was paying the price.

I thought about picking up the phone and calling her, but I didn't want to bother her during her time with family. She needed them as much as they needed her.

I had already texted her a few times, but the distance between us felt more significant than ever. The thought of her being so far away made my heart ache.

As I sat there looking around my sterile home, I couldn't help but think about how different my Christmas must have been from hers. I knew from years past, Outtatowner would be decorated with holiday lights and cheer, while my pent-house was cold and lifeless.

She was surrounded by loved ones, while I was alone and miserable with my thoughts.

It was nearly eleven when my phone buzzed with a text.

> **DUKE**
>
> Ring me up. I'm freezing my balls off down here.

I stared at the message as my brain tried to catch up. Sure enough, just outside the building doors, Duke's pissed-off face filled the video screen. I pushed the button to talk. "What the hell are you doing here?"

"Will you just buzz me up? It's colder than a witch's titty out here."

Laughing, I punched in the code and unlocked the door. Minutes later, the private elevator to my house dinged, and Duke was at my front door.

I opened it for him and pulled him into a hug. We embraced, clapping each other on the back. "What's this?"

He strode past me, dumping a small overnight bag on the floor before walking to the fridge and scooping out a beer.

"Lee's got Ed. I'm staying the night. Didn't seem right for you to be alone on Christmas."

Duke stretched out on my couch, his feet hanging off one end. "I figured if you looked half as miserable as Katie did, the last thing we needed was for you to be up here alone and brooding."

My heart thunked. "She was miserable?"

He shot me a blank stare. "You're an idiot."

I blew out a frustrated breath. "Yeah. I know."

Duke sat straighter and took a pull of his beer bottle.

"But for some reason, you're *her* idiot." He shook his head. "Gotta say . . . didn't really see that one coming."

I let out a soft laugh. "You and me both. But she's stubborn, that one."

He smiled. "Yeah." Because she's stubborn and strong and pulls everyone into her orbit with kindness and laughter.

She always had.

Awkward silence fell over us as we stared at each other across my living room. "Listen, I know I told you I wouldn't hurt her. That I wouldn't fuck it up. I really have no right to promise you that, but I want you to know that I'm working on it."

Duke looked at me. Really looked. "You know the wildest part of all this? I decked you for flirting with my girlfriend, but now you're tangled up with my little sister, and all I can think is how I didn't see it sooner."

"You can still punch me in the face if you want," I teased, though really I wasn't joking. If Duke wanted a free shot, he could take it.

"And unleash Katie on my ass? Fucking hard pass." He looked me over and shook his head. "Besides, you're good for her. You never tried to change her. Dim her light or whatever. You let her *be*. I'm not sure she's ever had that."

I didn't know what to say without flaying myself open, so I stayed quiet and looked at my feet. Duke drank another swallow of beer and unfolded himself from the couch with a groan. "Great. Now that I fulfilled my older-brother responsibilities . . ." He moved to the bag he had deposited on the floor and unzipped it. Inside he pulled out a small square box wrapped in Christmas paper. "Now I can be in best friend mode." He flipped the box toward me. "Merry Christmas, asshole."

I stared down at the small gift in my hands. I swallowed hard. I looked up at my best friend. The man who was the closest thing I had to a brother.

I took a deep breath and gathered my courage to speak. "I want you to know that I'm going to marry her, but I need to handle my shit."

He settled back down on the couch and smiled at me. "Good. Just don't make her wait too long."

THIRTY-SEVEN
KATE

I LINED UP THE SHOT, crouching low to frame Bartleby Beakface perfectly with the sunny, yellow chicken coop behind him. His bright iridescent feathers stood out against the harsh white snow, and the expression on his face was defiant, as if the mere act of weather pissed him off.

Somewhere along the way, the followers of *Home Again* had become invested in the battle of Bartleby and the Brutish Builder. Even the hashtag #TeamBeakface was trending.

In truth, the rooster was a little depressed now that he was no longer receiving daily treats and attention from Beckett.

Dude, same.

Even without a new renovation project, followers continued to roll in. People seemed to love giving their input on home decor, and I had found that styling the interior of the farmhouse was nearly as much fun as renovating it in the first place.

After speaking with an accountant, and scouring the internet for tips, I forged ahead on my own with the idea to turn *Home Again* into a business. I had even made an appointment at the bank to discuss securing a loan for the next project I was going to undertake.

All that was left to do was find the perfect property.

I felt accomplished. I was proud of myself. I was not only doing something to help revitalize my community, but I had found something that I loved.

Something for me.

Trouble was, I didn't actually have a clue what I was doing . . . but I was doing the damn thing, and that felt pretty fantastic.

I had the added bonus of burying myself in direct messages, sponsorship requests, and administrative tasks for getting the business off the ground, which meant I reserved very little time to think about Beckett and how much I missed him.

Word had gotten out around town that I was looking for a new renovation project, and there were a few properties I was set to look at. While it seemed like one was more dilapidated than the next, the more I dug into the histories of each property at the library, the more excited I got about the potential of each of the homes.

In a photo editing app, I finalized the picture of Bartleby and typed out a caption:

Home Again *I'm not angry, I just have resting Beakface*

Then I checked my notifications.
Holy. Shit.

Brutish Builder started following you.

Whooshing hammered between my ears as my heart

thrummed against my ribs. I immediately clicked on the profile.

There, with a slightly annoyed look and cocky half grin, Beckett's broody gray eyes stared back at me.

I pressed a hand to the sharp pain in my chest.

Duke had checked in on me and let it slip that he had been to Chicago a few times to look in on his friend. He even mentioned that Beckett was seeing a therapist, and I was convinced that little admission was intentional.

After hearing that, I had gone home that night and cried my eyes out. I missed him but was so proud that he was doing the work we had both set out to do. Work on getting ourselves to a place where we could give to each other freely. For Beckett, that meant battling a lot of the demons he carried around inside himself.

It was important to me that he saw the man I saw when I looked at him. Someone strong and kind and worthy. Someone who wasn't a placeholder, but the prize itself.

I stared down at the profile picture and accompanying bio in disbelief.

Brutish Builder *Cleaning up my act one renovation at a time for the woman who stole my heart.*

I could practically feel the heat of his touch on the back of my neck and the warmth of his breath, as if he'd whispered in my ear, *We are going to get through this.*

I looked at the sparse Instagram grid and clicked on the only posted picture—Beckett standing in front of a massive pile of interior construction rubble.

Brutish Builder *Strong buildings are built on strong foundations. Whether it's a home or a skyscraper, the key to*

long-lasting structures is a solid base. As a builder, I know
the importance of starting with a strong foundation and
building up from there. It's not just about the materials we
use, but the craftsmanship and attention to detail that go into
every step of the process. Let's build something that will
stand the test of time. #constructionlife #buildingthings
#strengthinconstruction #thinkingofher

I stared at his face, my jaw clenched tight, as I willed myself not to cry all over the phone.

~

LATE JANUARY WINDS rolled over the icy Lake Michigan waters. My hair was a tangled mess as the strands fought the cold air, but I was tucked inside the warmth and safety of my car. Until then I hadn't had the guts to drive past the Miller beach house, since it had been sold. In a moment of weakness, I decided to torture myself, just a little.

It had been sold and completely gutted, like several others on that particular stretch of beachfront. The large vacation homes all along the private section of beach dune were being overhauled or even torn down, and newer, larger vacation homes to be rented out were being put up in their place.

My emotions were at war. For so long, the house was a sad reminder of how I'd let Declan use me, how naive I had been about the status of our relationship. Slowly Beckett had replaced those sad memories with better ones. Memories of passion and laughter and lazy days on the beach.

Heartache.

I tapped on the Instagram app, my heart doing the same

excited thunk-thunk every time I pulled up his profile. Instead of his typical project updates, I stared back at a picture of me, silhouetted by the light streaming in from the expansive beach house windows. I had no idea he'd ever taken the picture.

Brutish Builder *Sometimes even a brutish builder can't help but be taken aback by a beautiful view. She was looking at the lake, but I was always looking at her.*
The right windows can make all the difference, not just in terms of aesthetics but in bringing in natural light and allowing us to enjoy the beauty of the outdoors from the comfort of our homes. What do you think @HomeAgain—do you prefer an open view or the classic look of a paneled window?

My breath hitched. His posts often asked the opinions of his growing following but had never before tagged me or outright called me out.

Brutish Builder *She was looking at the lake, but I was always looking at her.*

A thrill of excitement and affection sparked in my belly as I typed out my reply:

Home Again *@BrutishBuilder, for a lakefront house? An open view. No question.*

"Have you talked to him?" I sat across from Annie at the Sugar Bowl as we enjoyed a quiet Saturday morning together.

Annie frowned when I shook my head. "We agreed to work things out for ourselves first. It's so freaking hard, but honestly? It's been . . . *good*. I don't have to stress or worry about whether or not he's going to call. I know he isn't, and that's actually okay. He's buried in work, and I am making headway on turning *Home Again* into something that fills my bucket *and* makes me money. Right now, I think I'm where I need to be."

"What about Beckett?"

I looked up at the concerned eyes of my friend, who had known me since childhood. "Duke said he's in therapy."

She nodded thoughtfully. "That's great." She reached over and squeezed my hand. "We're all rooting for you."

I looked up from my coffee to sneak a peek at her. "Have you seen the Instagram posts?"

Annie laughed. "Girl. *Everyone* has seen them. It's so obvious he's calling you out." She let out a wistful sigh. "It's so romantic."

"At first I thought I was imagining things, but then he started tagging the *Home Again* page constantly. It's definitely creating a buzz for both pages, and the one about the windows? It went viral. It's weird to have people publicly speculating about our relationship, but the mystery of it all is also kind of fun." I shook my head and then let out a frustrated sigh to the universe. "Ugh. I can't wait until this is all over."

Annie let her soft eyes soak me in as she sipped her latte. "Did you hear about the beach house?"

I shrugged. "I know it sold and the new owners wasted

no time turning it into an Airbnb. At least, that's what people are saying."

"JP King sold it, so it's no wonder we haven't heard much about it. I'm sure it'll be another vacation monstrosity that will be full of tourists come summer."

At least it wasn't a King living in Beckett's house.

Annie's attention dropped to her phone. "Speak of the devil. Looks like you got another tag." She spun her phone toward me. The snapshot was of an interior room, walls gutted down to the studs. As I always did, I scoured the picture for any hints or clues, any scrap of detail that could make me feel closer to him. It was a closely cropped picture of him in front of the two-by-fours, his sexy scowl on full display.

Brutish Builder *Collaboration is key—in relationships and in any successful construction project. As a builder, I know that it takes a team effort to create something truly special. My client asked for a quiet reading and office space. @HomeAgain—which would you choose? Rolling ladder or reading nook? Maybe both?*

EVERY SPRING in the Midwest there were a handful of days that were so warm, everyone was irrationally hopeful that winter was finally over.

My face turned up to the warm sun, and I prayed this was not one of those days, but a true sign of spring. The waters of Lake Michigan were still brutally cold, but the snow had thawed, and the crocus and hyacinth blooming in Tootie's garden beds were the ray of hope I needed.

The cold, dark winter was finally coming to an end, and

I couldn't help but feel like something had blossomed inside of me as well.

I was thriving.

Since putting down my roots and settling into my hometown, they had embraced me. People no longer questioned how long I was in town for, but called to make plans, and I could see a bright future unfolding. I was finally settling into my small coastal town.

But it was a future that I couldn't imagine without Beckett.

The first weeks were brutal. I knew we were torturing ourselves by sticking with our promise to limit communication and work on ourselves. Most people, including my beloved aunt, thought I was a fool for being so stubborn about it, especially when she could see through my brave facade to how heartsick I was.

When we separated, I knew there was a risk that he would get tired. Move on and take the easy route. But, with every Instagram post that was not so subtly directed to me, I knew he was holding on to the same sparks of hope I was.

But it didn't stop the prickles of nervousness. *What if I asked too much? What if being apart only proves he doesn't need this? Need us?*

I tamped down the nagging thought. Everything unfolding in my life proved to me that being here, investing in my hometown, was the right choice. My relationships were stronger than ever.

I laughed—freely and often.

I was home, and that was only possible because I had made the choice to be present. To give myself to my friends and family in a way that was never possible before, because I'd always chosen to wrap myself up in a relationship.

For the past few weeks, I'd also begun to realize I

couldn't stay in the barn apartment of Highfield House forever. The newly improved life of Kate Sullivan also meant branching out on my own. Last week I had mentioned to Lee that I was looking for a place to call my own, and he promised to keep an eye out. He could barely contain his excitement that I was looking for something permanent in Outtatowner. Of course, once Duke heard, he called to offer one of his many spare bedrooms.

Absolutely fucking not.

Taking advantage of the warmer weather, the real estate agent I was working with asked whether I wanted to see a few rental properties around town. With nothing better to do, I had agreed. So, with a light jacket and a tender heart full of hope, I climbed into my car to head to the first property and tried not to wonder what Beckett was up to.

THIRTY-EIGHT
KATE

"IT'S SO . . . MAUVE." My stomach lurched as my wide eyes took in the cramped bathroom. It looked as though Barbie's dream house had vomited all over the tiny space. Pink toilet, pink sink, pink shower and tile. The rest of the apartment had shaggy brown carpeting, and the wallpaper in the living room was peeling.

"A touch of nostalgia." The agent smiled.

"Um . . . what's the policy on renters making some changes?"

She frowned. "Oh, I'm sorry, dear. The rental agreement specifically states that there are to be no permanent changes to the apartment."

Awesome.

I tried not to make eye contact with Ms. Bunny—an Outtatowner real estate agent whose unfortunate nickname came about due to her oversize front teeth.

A strange noise came from the far end of the bathroom. I cautiously entered, wondering what could be making such a racket. And then, to my horror, the pink toilet started to shake and vibrate, like it was about to take off.

I jumped back, startled, and the agent rushed over, looking concerned. "Oh, don't worry about that," she said, as if it was a normal occurrence. "The plumbing is just a little old. It'll settle down in a minute."

As I stared at the quivering toilet, I couldn't help but wonder if I was in the middle of some kind of horror movie.

But no, it was just an outdated apartment with a pink bathroom and a very lively toilet. Thanks to my newfound business loan, I had only the tiniest sliver of wiggle room in my personal finances, and the budget for an apartment was proving difficult.

I thanked Ms. Bunny for her time, politely declined the apartment, and made a hasty retreat. As we walked back to our cars, I couldn't help but laugh at the absurdity of it all —*Home Again* had just landed on a list of the top twenty up-and-coming renovation and decor accounts, and I would be living in an apartment straight out of a 1970s porno.

"There's nothing else?" I pleaded as I opened my car door.

Her eyes softened. The pink bathroom monstrosity was the third property we'd visited and, by far, the nicest.

"I have one other."

Hope bloomed in my chest. "Perfect! Thank you. I'd love to see something else."

She instructed me to follow her to the outskirts of town to the last remaining rental space on her list.

As we drove, my heart sank when I realized wherever she was taking me would be a stone's throw away from what was once the Miller beach house. Since the day I'd cried my eyes out in front of it, I hadn't been back. It was too painful of a reminder.

When her car rolled to a stop in front of it, I froze.

Putting my car in park, I opened the door and stood.

"Ms. Bunny, I think there's been a mistake . . ." The words faded to a whisper as I stared up at the newly renovated home.

My breath caught in my throat.

It was a modern masterpiece, with floor-to-ceiling windows and clean lines that spoke to my aesthetic soul, but instead of the cold and harsh house that had once stood there, the outside elevation had been completely updated. Now the house blended seamlessly with the coastal landscape.

The harsh exterior had been painted a soft neutral, and dormers had been built to create a quaint, cozy feel, despite the home's massive size.

"Do you want to take a look inside?" she asked.

Sick curiosity got the best of me as I closed the car door and moved forward—as if the house itself was pulling me inside.

The interior was completely unrecognizable. New, floor-to-ceiling windows offered breathtaking views of the ocean, and the interior design was light and airy, evoking a sense of peace and serenity.

The decor was a perfect blend of modern and coastal, with a color scheme of soft blues and greens that reminded me of the water just out of reach. The furniture was sleek and stylish, yet still looked comfortable and inviting.

The living room was open and spacious, with high ceilings and an abundance of natural light flooding in from the large windows. The plush couches were upholstered in a soft, cream-colored fabric, with accent pillows in shades of blue and green. A large, modern rug tied the room together, with a subtle wave pattern that added to the coastal vibe.

The kitchen was a chef's dream, with stainless steel appliances, sleek cabinetry, and a massive island perfect for entertaining. The countertops were made of a beautiful marble, with subtle veins of blue and green running through them.

The bedrooms were equally stunning, with comfortable king-size beds and luxurious linens. The primary bedroom had maintained the stunning view of the ocean, with an added balcony that was perfect for enjoying a cup of coffee in the morning. The en suite bathroom was a spa-like retreat, with a large walk-in shower and a deep soaking tub that Beckett would have adored.

Every cozy touch made the house feel like a home, not just a showpiece. The shelves were adorned with books and trinkets, and there were plenty of cozy blankets and throw pillows scattered throughout. The overall effect was a space that felt both inviting and luxurious, like a place where you could truly relax and unwind.

Breathe.

As we made our way through the house, I couldn't help but feel a sense of envy at whoever was lucky enough to call this place home. It was the perfect blend of style and comfort, with a sense of peace and serenity that I had never experienced before.

Hygge—the Danish word for comfort and a hot trend for creating home spaces that evoked a sense of coziness and calm, was the only word that came to mind.

"I think this is the best room in the house." Ms. Bunny pushed open the double doors to a small room that had been transformed into a cozy library. It was the perfect escape from the rest of the house.

The room was bathed in soft light, with a comfortable high-back armchair nestled in the corner and a large book-shelf that stretched from floor to ceiling. A rolling ladder, exactly like the one I had wanted Beckett to build at

Tootie's house, was attached to the shelves, adding a whimsical touch to the space. The shelves were packed with books.

In the center of the room was a plush armchair, upholstered in a rich blue fabric that complemented the coastal color scheme of the house. A matching ottoman was positioned nearby, perfect for propping up my feet while I read. A small table sat beside the chair, holding a stack of books and a lamp with a warm, inviting glow.

As I ran my hand across the soft fabric of the back of the chair, I noticed a stunning chandelier hanging from the ceiling. The delicate capiz shell design was exactly like the one I'd gushed over with Beckett's designer friend, Sly.

And I knew.

My heart swelled with emotion, and tears pricked at the corners of my eyes.

"I think you should see the deck off the back." Ms. Bunny smiled at me with kind, knowing eyes as I fought away tears.

Please. Please let it be him.

Ms. Bunny opened the sliding doors that led to the back deck but didn't join me outside. "You let me know what you decide, dear."

With a smile, she closed the door behind me.

THIRTY-NINE
BECKETT

I sensed her before I heard the hitch in her breath. I had used the small-town phone tree to my advantage, and Ms. Bunny was more than happy to send Kate on a wild-goose chase, showing off Outtatowner's most horrific rentals, before bringing her here.

Home.

Duke had been a lifeline in the months Kate and I had been apart. He knew my coming back to Outtatowner while Kate and I worked on ourselves would be too difficult, so despite grumbling about it, he had made the trip to Chicago. I'd seen Duke more times in the last three months than I had in three years.

He listened as I talked through the childhood issues that came up in therapy. Nodded in understanding when I needed to vent my frustrations. Got downright pissed off whenever negative thoughts about myself reared their ugly heads. I owed my sanity to him, because without Duke, I would have gone crazy in my time away from Kate.

I was still a work in progress, but my mind was clear.

I knew what I wanted.

What I deserved.

When the back door opened, my stomach flipped. My heart thundered so loudly I couldn't hear what Ms. Bunny said to Kate as she left.

I could see only her.

Her hair had gotten a little longer—something I hadn't noticed when I stalked her social media pages for any kind of update on her life. She was a little thinner, too, but I loved to cook for her, and I would.

Now that I was here.

Now that she was mine.

Against the backdrop of the home I had purchased from my parents, she was breathtaking.

She looked around, still getting her bearings. "Beckett, I—"

In two steps I pulled her to me, crashing my mouth to hers. On a moan, I dove deeper, claiming every molecule of her being as mine. The last, most precious part of me clicked into place with Kate in my arms.

When we finally broke apart, her lips were pink and swollen. "Beckett, the house . . ."

"It's yours, if you want it."

She blinked up at me, and I brushed my thumb across her swollen bottom lip. "Mine?"

I stepped back so she could take in the sweeping view of Lake Michigan. "You gave your input. From the windows to the porch swing . . ." I gestured to the two swings hanging from the ceiling of the porch.

Her eyes went wide. "You didn't!"

Kate moved toward the swing and sat. "I was only half joking when I commented that traditional porch swings were old fashioned."

I shrugged. "You weren't wrong. These are more whimsical. A lot more fun."

She beamed up at me as I stepped behind her to gently push her on the swing. "I never felt like this place lived up to its potential." I chuckled at the irony. "Kind of like me. Working on it was a part of my therapy. Doing something for myself. A project that truly meant something to me."

Kate stayed silent and panic sliced through me. "Unless you don't want it. Say the word and I'll bulldoze it to the ground. We can start fresh if—"

"No. No, it's perfect. But how did you do all this?"

I slowed the swing and stepped in front of her. "Gloria helped me close out the remaining projects in Chicago. I'm done. Officially dissolving Miller Custom Homes in an effort to find something else."

Kate swallowed hard and looked at me. "Something else?"

I scrubbed a hand across the back of my neck. "I was kind of hoping you might need a contractor for your next *Home Again* project." I peeked up at her and shrugged. "If you'll hire me."

Kate's delicate hand moved to her mouth as she stifled a sob. I knew it was now or never—if I didn't get it all out there, lay it all on the line, I would never be able to say what I needed to.

"Kate, I never realized how small I was living. How much my negative self-image was seeping into every part of my life. But the day you casually touched my arm when you were taking a picture, I knew. That's all it took. One touch."

Kate wrapped her arms around my neck, and I sighed into her, relief flooding my system. Her embrace rooted me to the ground. I pulled her closer, reveling in the fact that she was standing in my arms with her heady perfume mixing with the coastal spring air.

Her voice was small when she finally spoke. "I didn't wait for you."

A buzz vibrated my skull as my stomach plummeted. I pulled her back to search her eyes for answers.

Tears glistened on her lashes as she continued: "I didn't wait. I missed you so badly, but I didn't wait. I lived my life. I laughed and danced and made new friends and *lived*. I stopped compromising and prioritized myself for the first time. But you know what I realized?"

My throat was thick. "What is it, Katie-girl?"

"I don't need someone to choose me, because I chose myself. I know I can be happy and centered and loved *right here*. I needed that breathing room to really discover that part of myself. But through it all, I never stopped loving you."

My hand found the side of her face as I tipped her head back. "I choose you, Princess. I've *always* chosen you. I have loved you since before I thought I was worthy of that love. Just let me prove it to you."

My mouth moved over hers. I savored the press of her body against mine as my hands moved over her back.

Months. Months without the woman I love in my arms.
Never again.

The crisp spring air cut through my shirt, and I bundled Kate closer to give her my warmth.

She smiled up at me. "I can't believe you did all this, right here, without me realizing it. Were you in town the whole time?"

"While the Brutish Builder is good, he's not *that* good." I grinned at my woman. "You asked for space, so I respected that. I handled a lot of the project remotely while I tied up loose ends in Chicago. Duke sent pictures if I needed to make decisions. Your input from the Instagram posts made things a hell of a lot easier."

Humor danced in her eyes. "You are sneaky, Beckett Miller."

I bent at the knees to lift her from the swing and toss her over my shoulder. Kate yelped in surprise as I smacked her ass and gave it a playful squeeze while I walked us inside. "You've got no idea, Princess."

Her laughter floated on the coastal air and filled my soul.

We never should have worked.

I was her ex-boyfriend's jaded older brother.

She was my best friend's little sister.

But all along she was the only woman who could force me to face my own demons and have the strength to choose her own happiness along with it. Kate was never the demure pushover I thought she was. She was a powerhouse and the greatest woman to ever walk into my life.

I was determined to show her what it meant to be possessed by a man completely consumed by her, right there in the home we'd build together.

EPILOGUE: KATE

I looked around the beautiful coastal Victorian house, and a sense of pride washed over me. It was hard to believe that just a few months ago, this place had been run-down and nearly forgotten. But with our passion for historic preservation and our skills as contractors, Beckett and I had managed to bring this beautiful home back to life.

The Queen Anne house had been built in the late eighteen hundreds and had fallen into disrepair over the years. But with careful planning and attention to detail, we had managed to restore it to its former glory, documenting every step for *Home Again*. We had replaced the crumbling foundation, rebuilt the porch, and repaired the ornate woodwork that adorned the exterior of the house.

She was the gorgeous Painted Lady she was meant to be.

Inside we had gutted the entire house and started from scratch. We had worked tirelessly to restore the original hardwood floors, patching and sanding them until they shone like new. We had also restored the original crown molding and baseboards, making sure to match the original profiles as closely as possible.

The home had new plumbing and electrical systems, and Beckett had even managed to salvage the original fireplace, which had been hidden behind a layer of plaster for years. We had also worked hard to source antique fixtures and hardware, giving the house an authentic feel. What we couldn't salvage, Sly created, and it was spectacular.

As we stood in front of the house, admiring our handiwork, I felt a sense of satisfaction wash over me. This was what we were meant to do. To take old, forgotten houses along coastal Michigan and turn them into something beautiful again.

Beckett put his arm around my shoulder, drawing me close to him. "This is our best work yet, Princess. I can't believe how amazing she looks."

I leaned into him, feeling a sense of contentment wash over me. "I know it." I glanced at my watch. "But we better get going. Tootie and the gang will be waiting for us."

With a stern nod, the grumpy love of my life started packing up his tools. A cleaning crew would be in early tomorrow morning before I staged the last of the furniture and took the final photographs.

"Hey, grab the pad of paper from my toolbox, will you? I want to leave a note that the paint in the back room is still tacky."

I smiled and moved toward the toolbox Beckett brought with him to every job. After I flipped open the top, I stared.

A small ring box sat on top of his tools.

I was taken aback, my heart skipping a beat. I turned to look at Beckett, who was behind me, down on one knee, a smile on his face.

"I have something to ask you, Katie-girl."

The world shifted beneath my feet as my mind raced to catch up to what was happening.

"I want to dance with you in every kitchen we design together. After any long day to come, I want to soak with you in the tub and let our troubles melt away. You calm me. Soothe me in a way I never knew I needed. Will you be my wife, Princess?"

I pressed my tongue to the roof of my mouth to keep from crying. "Yes," I managed on a sob as I threw myself at him.

Nearly tackling him, I straddled his lap and rained kisses over his face as his arms wound around my back.

"You are my sun, my moon, and all of my stars."

I traced my fingertips over his features. "Did you write that?"

He shook his head. "E. E. Cummings, but it couldn't be more true. I am so hopelessly in love with you."

Choking back a fresh round of sobs, I leaned in for another kiss.

Beckett reached behind him and pulled out his phone to take a selfie of us wrapped in each other's arms on the front porch of our Painted Lady.

Beneath the photo showing my wild grin and tearstained face, Beckett typed out a caption and shared it with the world:

Brutish Builder *Wherever we go and whatever we do, I know that I will always be home again as long as I am with you. #shesaidyes #homeagainwithher*

"Mmm, that feels good." I sank deeper into the bath as Beckett pressed his thumbs into the arch of my foot and I melted into the hot water.

"You feel good." His mouth lowered, and he pressed a kiss to the tender skin on the inside of my foot.

I giggled at his touch, but heat spread through me.

His mouth made a slow path up my ankle, and his hands massaged higher on my calves.

"You feel *really* good, Kate Miller." Beckett grinned.

I fluttered my lashes at him. "I'm not Kate Miller yet."

"I don't care what your last name is," he said. "As long as I can call you mine."

The engagement ring on my left hand glittered as I sat up and wound my arms around his neck.

"Everyone seemed happy about the news."

I tossed my head back and laughed. "Happy? Lee *cried*."

Affection for my older brothers flowed through me. When we had gathered for a family dinner and had told them the news of Beckett's proposal, they were all thrilled for us.

Lark and Annie immediately had a thousand questions and wanted to see the ring. Beckett had chosen the perfect emerald-cut, soft-blue diamond, with each side holding three oval white diamonds that looked like they bloomed from the center. It was a gorgeous art deco-inspired ring. The blue diamond itself was one of the rarest—a diamond made from stardust itself.

You are my sun, my moon, and all of my stars.

Beckett's words still made me feel as though I could cry. Apart we were whole, but together we were perfect.

Penny also demanded that she be a junior bridesmaid and not a flower girl, because she *wasn't a baby*. She had nearly fallen out of her chair when I told her I would much prefer her to be one of my bridesmaids and not relegated to the title of *junior* bridesmaid.

Everyone at our family dinner was overjoyed.

Even Bartleby took a break from his typical passive-aggressive assaults on Beckett. With only a few low bawks, he circled the yard once, staring Beckett down, but after Beckett flipped him the middle finger, Bartleby ignored him the rest of the night.

When my phone dinged with an incoming message, excited nerves tickled my belly, and I immediately sat up from the tub.

"Uh-uh." Beckett shook his head. "We said no working after hours."

"I know." I sighed. "But I can't get that email from the producer out of my head. What do you think he wanted?"

I chewed my bottom lip as the thousand possibilities ran through my head.

Beckett shrugged—calm and collected as always. "Could be another sponsorship proposal," he offered.

I nodded, considering that was a likely possibility. Our sponsorships had been lucrative, but this was the first time a television producer had been the one to personally reach out. Something about the message felt . . . *bigger*.

"Please," I pleaded to Beckett and gave him my best doe-eyed look.

He rolled his eyes and grumbled. "Fine. But I'm only agreeing to shut you up." He leaned in closer. "And then I get to have my way with you."

He sat up and pulled me closer, my legs resting on top of his as we sat in the hot bath.

I leaned over to grab my phone off the ledge. With wet

hands, I fumbled to open my phone and look at the email waiting for me.

"Holy shit." My eyes scanned the words as disbelief flooded my brain.

"What is it?" Beckett leaned in to read over my shoulder.

As I read through the email, my heart raced. The production company was offering us our own TV show, focused on our renovation business and showcasing our passion for historic preservation of homes right here in our area. They had already lined up a network to air the show and were eager to get started on filming.

Recently, Beckett and I had talked about the possibility of sharing our love for renovating old homes with a wider audience, and this was our chance to do just that. We had built up a significant following on social media, expanding from Instagram to YouTube, but a TV show would take our business to the next level. It would mean more exposure, more clients, and more opportunities to save historic homes from demolition.

"They even want to keep our name, *Home Again*." Tears flooded my eyes.

As I laughed, Beckett pulled me closer and ran his calloused hands up my back.

"Of course they do. Get ready, Princess. You're about to take over the world."

Smiling down at him, I lowered my mouth to his, sinking into his touch.

Need more of Kate & Beckett? Check out this exclusive BONUS SCENE here!

SNEAK PEEK OF ONE CHANCE

Fake dating my best friend? Total disaster.

With his cocky grin and devilish charm, firefighter Lee Sullivan makes every woman in our small town swoon. Every woman except for me.

Which is why I'm shocked when he steps in at the town's Matchmaker's Gala and outbids my crush during the charity auction, committing us to six prearranged dates.

Six dates where we, *very publicly,* pretend to be falling in love.

Despite my objections and our efforts to set each other up with other people, Lee is convinced *pretending to date each other* is the perfect opportunity to get the women in town off his back (and out of his bed), while also helping to nudge my non-committal crush in the jealousy department.

Stupidly, I agree.

After the disastrous blind dates he set me up on, what's a few months of letting Lee worship the ground I walk on? He owes me.

Trouble is—every fake kiss, every lingering

touch, **every filthy word he whispers when no one is around—is starting to feel very, very real.**

We know everything about each other—from my orphaned past to his irrational hatred of dolls. The only secret I have ever kept from Lee spans all the way back to his time in the Army and it's the one thing that could ruin our friendship forever.

Because where Lee is concerned, I have learned to guard my heart. Suddenly, he's asking for the opportunity to feel something real. **He's asking for the one thing he wouldn't want if he ever knew the truth:** *one chance*.

Check out One Chance at https://geni.us/ onechance

ACKNOWLEDGMENTS

There may have been a time or two I wondered about an ex-boyfriends moody, older brother. Unfortunately for me, none of those brothers ever wondered about me. However, I did absolutely love exploring the idea of two people who knew a relationship was so wrong, but couldn't help but be drawn to one another. Toss in the complication of him being your brother's best friend and it's my catnip.

I am also a sucker for a good home renovation. My toxic trait is watching hours and hours of TikTok's or YouTube home renovation videos and convincing myself I could tear up my bathroom or kitchen all before lunch.

To my readers, I will forever be in awe that you love my stories and keep asking for more! Your enthusiasm and love for my books is fuel to my fire. I am so grateful for each and every person who picks up my books!

To my husband who holds space for me, no matter how I show up. Your unwavering love is far beyond book boyfriend status. Thank you for loving me in all my forms.

To my assistant Stephanie, your enthusiasm and creative ideas are fuel for my fire. It's so refreshing to have someone who just "gets you." You are my people.

To the Spicy Sprint Sluts, y'all are my first text of the morning and I wouldn't have it any other way. Thank you for motivating, encouraging, and lighting me up. Your friendship means so much to me.

To Kat, thank you for pushing me to explore PR boxes

and answering my many (many) questions! You have lit a fire in me and helped me see marketing in a whole new way. You're an amazing gal to have in my corner (even if you do take seventy-two days to answer a text!).

To my alpha reader and dear friend Nicole. You have such a way about you that helps me see stories in a unique way. I know there's an editor hiding in you somewhere!

To my sweet friend Jenn, how is it possible to be so connected to someone you've never met in person? The way I am energized by our conversations is everything!

To my beta readers Anna and Trinity, thank you for the many laughs and honest opinions. Your feedback helps make my story the best it can be. I hope you're ready for the rest of the series, because you're stuck with me now!

To Becca, James, and Julia, I still don't know how to use a comma and you don't hate me for it. For that, I will be forever grateful. Thank you for challenging me to put my characters through the wringer and for asking the hard questions. I promise I love you for it.

To my cover designers Echo and Sarah, WOW. I continue to be blown away by your creativity and eye for design. You take the jumbled ideas in my head and make them so pretty! Thank you!

Finally, thank you to my ARC readers and Content Creator team members, THANK YOU! Your excitement for my books is infectious and I know I wouldn't be here if it weren't for you. Thank you for taking time to make flat lays, TikToks, Reels, and posts to share my stories with your friends and followers. It makes a huge impact on indie authors like me and I know the time and effort that goes into each post. Thank you for always being there for me!

HENDRIX HEARTTHROBS

Want to connect? Come hang out with the Hendrix Heartthrobs on Facebook to laugh & chat with Lena! Special sneak peeks, announcements, exclusive content, & general shenanigans all happen there.

Come join us!

ALSO BY LENA HENDRIX

Chikalu Falls

Finding You

Keeping You

Protecting You

Choosing You (origin novella)

Redemption Ranch

The Badge

The Alias

The Rebel

The Target

The Sullivans

One Look

One Touch

One Chance (coming fall 2023)

One Night (coming winter 2023/2024)

One Taste (charity novella)

ABOUT THE AUTHOR

Lena Hendrix is an Amazon Top 20 bestselling contemporary romance author living in the Midwest. Her love for romance stared with sneaking racy Harlequin paperbacks and now she writes her own hot-as-sin small town romance novels. Lena has a soft spot for strong alphas with marshmallow insides, heroines who clap back, and sizzling tension. Her novels pack in small town heart with a whole lotta heat.

Manufactured by Amazon.ca
Bolton, ON